Scarlet studie

"And you plan on doing that by keeping me prisoner in these rooms?"

Liall looked pained. "It is not what I want. You may move about the palace freely, but only with Jochi. He is not merely a translator and teacher: he is also a bodyguard. There are those who will seek to harm me here, and the easiest way to do that is through you. There are not even any laws in Rshan to protect your life, Scarlet."

"Because I'm lenilyn."

"Do you know what that word means? Not just outlander. *Non-person.* Many Rshani do not even believe you have a soul. They think you little more than a pretty animal."

Scarlet was shocked. He had known they disliked Hilurin, but the extent had escaped him.

"Do you see now?" Liall went on. He drew Scarlet close and spoke with his lips pressed against Scarlet's forehead. "If any evil should befall you, it would be entirely my fault. The only reason you are here is because of me. I brought you here, Scarlet, but I do not think I can survive burying you here."

Scarlet wanted to remind Liall that it was he who had had insisted on following, but he felt the slight tremble in Liall's hands. "Is all this worry for me?" he asked, considerably moved.

"I love you."

This is a work of fiction. Names, characters, places, and incidents either are the product of the author's imagination or are used fictitiously. Any resemblance to actual events, locales, organizations, or persons, living or dead, is entirely coincidental and beyond the intent of either the author or the publisher.

Scarlet and the White Wolf Book Three: Land of Night
TOP SHELF
An imprint of Torquere Press Publishers
PO Box 2545
Round Rock, TX 78680
Copyright © 2007 by Kirby Crow
Cover illustration by Analise Dubner
Published with permission
ISBN: 978-1-60370-493-9, 1-60370-493-0

www.torquerepress.com

First Torquere Press Printing: September 2008
Printed in the USA

**If you enjoyed Land of Night,
you might enjoy these Torquere Press titles:**

Scarlet and the White Wolf Book 1: The Pedlar and the Bandit King by Kirby Crow

Scarlet and the White Wolf Book 2: Mariner's Luck by Kirby Crow

Windbrothers by Sean Michael

Land of Night

Scarlet and the White Wolf Book Three:
Land of Night
by Kirby Crow

www.torquerepress.com

for J.

Land of Night

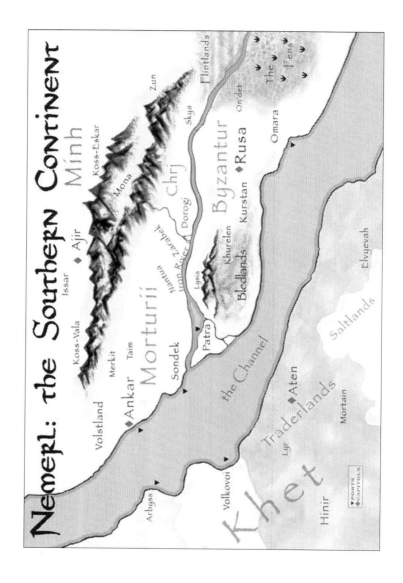

Nemerl: the Southern Continent

Land of Night

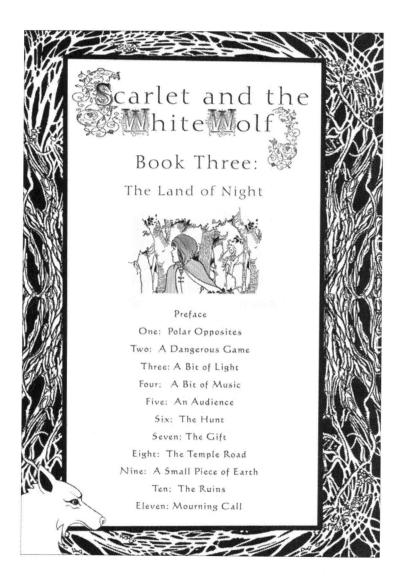

Scarlet and the White Wolf

Book Three:

The Land of Night

Land of Night

Preface

This is the conclusion of SCARLET AND THE WHITE WOLF.

Book One, *The Pedlar and the Bandit King*, told the story of Scarlet of Lysia, a young and honorable Hilurin pedlar, who by chance met a Kasiri bandit on a toll road through the mountains. The Kasiri was Liall the Wolf, a feared and famous giant of a man from the far northern lands of Rshan na Ostre, and a famous atya, or chieftain, among the tribal Kasiri kraits.

Their first meeting was less than polite. Liall demanded a kiss in toll for Scarlet's crossing of the bandit road. Scarlet angrily refused and insulted the atya, and Liall sent Scarlet packing back to his village.

In Lysia, a stranger named Cadan –an Aralyrin soldier in the Flower Prince's Army– began asking questions about the Kasiri blocking the mountain road. Cadan seemed to focus much of his attention on Scarlet, and questioned the young man repeatedly about Liall. The Aralyrin and Hilurin peoples, though sharing a common ancestry, had been waging a sporadic, unofficial war against each other for years, and did not trust each other. The Hilurin have long guarded the secret of The Gift: an ancestral Hilurin ability to use magic, and to suddenly have an Aralyrin taking up residence in a Hilurin village, watching the doings of bandits, roused Scarlet's suspicions. Scarlet refused to speak to Cadan any further, and angrily ordered the soldier to leave him alone.

For the next several days, as Cadan watched closely, an inventive battle of wills ensued between Scarlet and Liall.

Scarlet tried to sneak by the road in the dead of night, then hid inside a cart of crockery, and finally dressed in his mother's clothing with his black hair powdered to crone-gray. Liall was fooled by none of it, but highly amused, until Scarlet took the game further and accused Liall of being a brigand and probable murderer.

Enraged, Liall cut the dress from Scarlet and humiliated him in front of the Kasiri. Peysho –Liall's Morturii enforcer– put a stop to it before it went too far, but the damage was done. Scarlet fled down the mountain road, and a regretful Liall followed him.

While escaping the Kasiri camp, Scarlet ran straight into Cadan, who was lying in wait for the pedlar. Cadan attacked Scarlet, meaning to leave his dead body for the village to find and lay the blame on the bandits, but Liall arrived in time to save Scarlet, wounding Cadan and driving him off.

Liall returned Scarlet to his people to recover, and explained to Scarlet that Cadan was a former Kasiri in Liall's krait. Cadan had proved to be more of a brutal outlaw than a Kasiri, and Liall had marked and banished Cadan from his krait three years earlier. Cadan's attack on Scarlet was motivated purely by revenge against Liall.

Deeply ashamed of his actions that put Scarlet in such danger, Liall refused to see Scarlet when he recovered his health and chanced up the mountain road, but granted the traveling pedlar full and free passage through any road that the Longspur krait controlled, forever.

Two months passed. A messenger arrived for Liall from his northern homeland of Rshan na Ostre, summoning the northman on a mysterious quest to return to his family. Scarlet traveled to Ankar, a Morturii city, to work in the souk. There, he made plans to move away from Lysia and join a trade in Ankar, but decided to make one more trip to his village to see his parents and inform them of his decision.

Approaching Lysia, Scarlet could see tall columns of smoke on the horizon. He raced into the village, only to find everyone dead, the homes burning, and the village full of Kasiri. Scarlet assumed that the Kasiri had attacked the village, and drew a knife to attack Liall. Liall protested that that the attack was an Aralyrin raid, bent on murdering the Hilurin, and refused to fight Scarlet. Liall's men disarmed the grieving pedlar, and Liall gently informed Scarlet that his sister, Annaya, survived the raid. She was safe in the Kasiri camp.

Two days passed while Annaya recovered in the krait, tended by her brother, until another survivor straggled into camp: Shansi, the blacksmith's apprentice and Annaya's betrothed. Shansi confirmed that it was the Aralyrin who destroyed Lysia. Liall has his men sifted the ashes of Scarlet's home to find the bones of Scarlet's parents, and Liall helped Scarlet bury them in a peaceful field.

With the seasons turning and Lysia destroyed, the krait prepared to break camp and move back to their base in Chrj. Liall tried to find a way to be alone with Scarlet so that he could investigate Scarlet's willingness to stay with the krait, but Scarlet resisted all of Liall's invitations and the offer was never made. Liall prepared to return to Rshan alone, turning over the leadership of the krait to Peysho, and said goodbye to Scarlet on the mountain road where they first met. Scarlet gave Liall two copper coins –a fair toll for a pedlar crossing a bandit road– and departed with Shansi and Annaya.

A week later, Shansi, Annaya, and Scarlet were settled in Nantua with Shansi's parents. Shansi planned to be a blacksmith there and marry Annaya, and Scarlet was torn between his desire to stay with what was left of his family or to take to the road again as a pedlar. Annaya chided her brother for being a coward and not going after what he really wanted –which was Liall– but Scarlet decided to go with his original plan and return to Ankar.

On the road to Ankar, Scarlet was attacked by a band of Aralyrin soldiers under the command of Cadan. Cadan escaped from Liall with only a broken leg, and was searching the roads for him. A bounty had been placed on Liall's head in every port and garrison in Byzantur by a mysterious Northman, and Cadan believed Scarlet knew where Liall was. Cadan and his men prepared to torture the information out of Scarlet, but Scarlet called on his Gift to escape them, killing Cadan. Scarlet immediately set out for Volkovoi to warn Liall, and also to thwart the vengeance of Cadan's soldiers. In escaping with his life, Scarlet had made also himself a wanted man in Byzantur.

In the meantime, Liall had crossed the Channel and reached the rough harbor port of Volkovoi. There he awaited the arrival of a Rshani ship that would make the long and hazardous crossing through frozen seas, back to Rshan. While walking the docks one rainy night, Liall was attacked and beaten by a pair of club-wielding bravos (hired guards), but saved by the arrival of Scarlet. Two long-knives against two wooden clubs, and the bravos were defeated.

Scarlet helped Liall back to his inn. There, he told Liall about the attack by Cadan and that there was a bounty on Liall's head, withholding the facts of Cadan's death and his own fugitive state. Scarlet asked to accompany Liall to Rshan, but Liall sadly refused, fearing the pedlar would not survive such a long, harsh journey. Too, the Rshani do not tolerate foreigners, and Liall knew that his countrymen would be hostile to Scarlet.

A Rshani brigantine, the Ostre Sul, arrived with the dawn, and Liall met with the ship's captain, Qixa, to book passage. When it came time for the ship to depart, the harbor was guarded by many more bravos on the lookout for Liall. Scarlet distracted the bravos while Liall boarded the ship, and the ship began to leave. At the last moment, Scarlet made a daring leap from the docks with the bravos in close pursuit, dropping to the deck of the Ostre Sul.

The Rshani mariners did not want Scarlet on the ship and were prepared to throw him overboard, but Liall forestalled any violence by promising to put Scarlet ashore to the north, in Ankar. Being no less stubborn than any Hilurin, Scarlet had his own plans about the voyage and was determined to stay with Liall.

Book Two, *Mariner's Luck*, chronicled the journey of Scarlet and Liall across the vast stretch of ocean between the Southern Continent and Rshan na Ostre. At the beginning of the voyage, Scarlet fell gravely ill from water-fever, contracted at the port of Volkovoi, and nearly perished. Liall nursed Scarlet through his illness and realized that he was falling in love with the young man. As Scarlet regained his health, the pedlar ventured outside the cabin more and more, coming into closer contact with the resentful Rshani mariners, one of whom propositioned him. Scarlet refused and a fight ensued. To reduce the tension, Liall ordered Scarlet to stay close to the cabin for the remainder of the voyage, a command that did not sit well with the fiercely independent Hilurin. Liall was invited to dine with Captain Qixa, and heard from Qixa what he already knew: that the old king-consort of Rshan had died, and that the Crown Prince, Cestimir, was too young to inherit and could not hold the support of the barons.

As the Ostre Sul ventured into colder waters, they were pursued by a swift schooner flying an Arbyssian flag, but neither Liall nor the captain were deceived. The schooner was filled with Minh and Morturii pirates who overtook the Ostre Sul and attacked. A pitched battle followed, ending only when the first wave of fighters were beaten back by the mariners and Scarlet used his Gift to set fire to the sails of the schooner. The enemy ship veered away from the Ostre Sul and burned at sea.

A few weeks later, despite acquitting himself well in battle, Scarlet was attacked by a gang of the mariners. Liall saved him, but the incident proved to Liall that the Rshani hatred of Hilurin was still very much alive in his people. The mariners were duly punished and Scarlet avoided their company thereafter, growing closer to Liall in his isolation.

Shortly thereafter, the Ostre Sul sighted land and they arrived in Rshan na Ostre, the Land of Night, where the sun had set for the winter and there would be no daylight until spring, only an endless blue twilight.

There were many surprises for Scarlet in Rshan. They were greeted at the snowy port and given a sleigh, which took them out of the city and into the white lands and hills further inland. At last they approached a magnificent castle fortress where many Rshani men and women clad in furs and jewels waited to greet them. Scarlet was introduced to Queen Nadiushka, and Liall informed Scarlet that the queen was his mother. In shock, Scarlet stumbled through the greeting and followed Liall into the palace. There was little time for the pedlar to grow accustomed to the notion of being in love with a prince: Liall –now Prince Nazheradei– left Scarlet in the Rshani servant's care to meet with the queen.

At the meeting, Queen Nadiushka informed Liall why he had been sent for: She was gravely ill and Cestimir, her youngest son, had been named Crown Prince and her heir, but her stepson, Vladei, an older man of much power and malice, disagreed with her choice and vied to be king himself. Nadiushka intended to appoint Liall as regent over Cestimir's minority.

Liall could not refuse his mother, though he wished to, and he reluctantly agreed. Mother and son avoided speaking very much of Liall's own exile many years ago, and Liall made his way back to Scarlet, his heart aching, where the pair made love until morning.

The next day, Liall was drawn away for a meeting with the Barons of Rshan, and encountered Khatai Jarek, Nadiushka's military commander. Liall and Jarek had been lovers long ago, and Jarek confronted Liall about the truth he was hiding from Scarlet and the reason Liall was exiled from Rshan na Ostre. Liall was angry and answered that he dared not tell such an honorable Hilurin the truth about himself: that he had murdered his own brother. Liall feared that Scarlet would leave him if he knew the truth. Jarek left Liall to gather her troops, which Nadiushka had ordered northward to quell an uprising in Vladei's province of Magur, and Liall sadly took up his new duties.

Scarlet and the White Wolf: Book One
The Pedlar and the Bandit King
    And
    Scarlet and the White Wolf: Book Two
Mariner's Luck
    can be purchased directly from the publisher at http://www.torquerebooks.com

Land of Night

1.

Polar Opposites

Scarlet was dreaming.

Sounds entered his sleep: the slow crackling of the fire in the hearth, the tiny clink of glass from the kitchen, the sibilant voices of the servants nearby. They twined in and out of his unchained mind, weaving visions of their own in passing. The clink of glass was the sound of a diamond tumbling from Queen Nadiushka's crown. The voices became the whispers of the Rshani courtiers and their women as they stared, their pale blue eyes filled with curiosity and malice. The crackle of the fire became less random, more measured, the tramp of boots, a march, an army...

Scarlet awoke in a bed of silk, surrounded by veils of gauzy material draped over the bed's massive wooden frame. The heavy velvet bed-curtains had been drawn back, leaving only the inner veils. A crystal lamp like a large, hollowed sapphire burned low in the room beyond, casting deep blue shadows in the corners. Scarlet sat up, pushing the covers away as he tilted his head, listening.

He was a slight young man, a Hilurin by birth, and bearing the beauty of that race, with his silken black hair, his jet-black eyes, and his pale skin. His mouth was a dusky rose, pursed sleepily, and his eyes were heavy and drowsy. Another mark Scarlet bore that set him apart from the race of giants he now found himself surrounded by: he was marked for luck, born with only four fingers on his left hand, a sign of Deva's favor.

Scarlet slid naked from the bed. His feet sank into soft carpeting as he padded soundlessly to the casement and pushed aside the heavy woolen draperies to look down at the ward far below. Unlike the common room of this suite, the bedroom afforded a view of the inner ward of the Nauhinir Palace, and he could see a double column of many soldiers marching from an arch to the north, crossing the ward as they made for the outer gate that Scarlet had glimpsed last night. It was snowing lightly over the icy landscape, and all was shrouded in that blue twilight that Scarlet still mistook for evening. He was in Rshan na Ostre, the Land of Night.

Look at them all, he thought. Where can they be going in this weather? Surely not to war?

At the head of the column, riding a black horse and carrying a long blue banner that glittered with silver, was a magnificent woman. The Rshani warrior wore heavy armor beneath a blue cloak, and her pale hair was unbound and trailed behind her like a flag. She wheeled her horse around and looked up at the castle, seeming to stare right at him. Scarlet gasped and watched, spellbound, as the woman looked long and searchingly at the casement, and then finally, seeming not to find what she sought, turned and spurred her horse to the head of the column.

Scarlet found he could breathe again, and he exhaled slowly as the stream of horses and soldiers continued to flow out of the palace. A sound behind him made him jump and scamper back for the bed. Just in time, too, for Nenos, Liall's aged and kindly servant, was in the doorway: competent, polite, and oblivious to nudity. Scarlet's face burned with embarrassment. Of course, Nenos had heard them last night. Liall, in particular, was not shy at all about making noise during loveplay.

Or showing off his body, Scarlet thought resentfully, remembering how Liall had climbed naked from the bath in front of all those handsome servants. Now Nenos stood gazing at Scarlet with a knowing expression, smiling slightly and bowing before he departed, probably to bring che, which was custom here as well as in Scarlet's own country of Byzantur.

Scarlet flopped back on the bed and stretched, remembering last night and Liall's hands on him and his mouth and gods, where was a word for it? He had heard stories, but who could have told him that Liall would make him feel so lost inside his own skin? In bed with Liall, Scarlet had felt himself becoming transparent, and he had finally reasoned out why some called it *taking*. Even with the bed empty and his eyes open, Scarlet could still feel Liall with him. The man had settled inside him like a seed, and for a mad moment, Scarlet wondered seriously if there was room enough in his spirit for someone like Liall: a man who had so much presence that people moved out of his way even when they believed him a pauper. When Liall spoke, lesser men went silent. When he entered a room, he took it over.

Scarlet feared what that meant for him. He valued his freedom. Could he share so much of himself with anyone? Would Liall feel confined in the space Scarlet could allow him, or, like the conqueror the man was born to be, would Liall forever be taking more of Scarlet than he knew how to give? As close as they had become, Scarlet was not one of Liall's people. He was not royal like Liall's family, nor clever like the silken ladies and men of the court, nor educated, nor even very big.

Will I be enough for him?

Nenos would not leave Scarlet alone to dress after the che, but laid out a set of clothing on the silken bed. Scarlet balked at the colors, blue and gold velvet, with so many rows of shiny buttons that they dazzled the eye.

"Where do you expect me to wear this, a bhoros

house?" Of course, the old man couldn't have understood the words. Perhaps there weren't even bhoros houses here! But Scarlet reasoned that Nenos could read the disgust on his face, at least.

Nenos sighed and urged Scarlet in low, incomprehensible tones to accept the clothing, but Scarlet continued to refuse. Eventually Nenos handed Scarlet a robe and called Chos in. Chos's round, placid face reflected concern and his voice rose, but Nenos silenced the servant with a look and gave curt orders that Scarlet did not understand.

Chos vanished and soon returned with a sulky expression and a gray, knee-length woolen jacket that Nenos indicated was called a hapcoat. Scarlet had glimpsed other men in the palace and in the city wear these, and it did not disturb him as it might have if they had brought him a version of the virca – a sort of tunic joined with a full skirt – which Liall had worn on their first night in this palace. He may be a stranger to Rshan, but he'd be damned if they were going to dress him up like a girl!

As far as Scarlet could tell, only men wore the hapcoat. They were long, somewhat slender coats with tailored sleeves that came past the wrist almost to the knuckles. This coat, somber gray with silver stitches, was held closed by discreet ties down the side that ran from under the arm to the gathered waist, and from there the coat fell in folds and pleats to the knee and was left halfway open in front and in back. For ease of movement, Scarlet presumed. They also brought him breeches of some kind of soft, ash-colored material. There were new boots, too, brushed leather, surely to be worn only inside. The hapcoat was made of wool that was soft as velvet, but there was little embroidery on it and none of the rows of glittery buttons Scarlet was beginning to dislike. He signaled to Nenos his acceptance of the garment, but he could not manage the laces up the sides, so he had to submit to more of their attentions. The shirt they wanted him to wear beneath the coat was dark gray silk which felt oddly cool on his skin, but at least he felt comfortably clothed when they were finished.

Properly plumed and trussed, Scarlet stood in front of the tall mirror and made a face.

"Well, I don't look as bad as I feared," he said to Nenos, who did not speak Bizye and would not understand, "and nowhere near as frilly and primped as some of the men I've seen in this palace, but I don't look like myself either." He flexed his left hand. At home, he usually hid the mark with a special glove, but here, where everyone had already seen his too-slender hand with its missing fifth finger, there was no need.

Uncomprehending, Nenos stood a little behind him with Chos, smiling and nodding, and Scarlet could not help but make comparisons between his reflection and theirs. Nenos was as tall as Liall, if not taller, with wide shoulders and long legs. The top of Scarlet's head barely reached Nenos's chin, and Scarlet was slender and compact beside them. Their hair was pale gold or white and their skins amber. Scarlet had hair black as jet and skin like a white rose. Their eyes were blue, his were black. Hilurin and Rshani. Opposites.

Scarlet brushed a nervous hand down the front of his hapcoat. Nenos smiled again and stepped forward. The old man made a gesture as if to cover his face with both hands, then extended his palms outward, and Scarlet got the gist of what the old man was trying to tell him: that he was beautiful.

"Want-wit," Scarlet growled at him, and then was ashamed at his lack of respect for an old man. At least Nenos could not understand him. Scarlet was embarrassed but also grateful for the reassurance.

Nenos chuckled, but there was one last thing before the old man was satisfied with Scarlet's appearance. Nenos opened the drawer of an elaborate wooden wardrobe with fittings of silver and withdrew a little green ceramic pot with a tight-fitting lid. He handed it to Scarlet, who stared at it.

"What's this, then?" he asked, trying the lid. There was a type of waxy salve within, yellow and sharp-smelling. Nenos took pity on his confusion and swiped his fingertip over the top of the ointment, and then gently brushed it across the healing scar under Scarlet's right eye.

"Oh, too late for that," Scarlet shrugged. The cut that the mariner, Oleksei, had given him aboard the Ostre Sul had already mended into a pale red line just above his cheekbone. He surveyed it critically in the mirror, turning his head. "I'm afraid it's there to stay."

Nenos shrugged as well, as if to say *it can't hurt to try*, and took the pot from Scarlet. He signaled for Scarlet to follow, and the servant led him into the more formal common room where Chos was at the stone and glass casement, pulling the curtains open. Outside, the everlasting Rshani night glittered sapphire blue with bands of dark silver and twinkles of pale stars. Though logically Scarlet knew it was morning, the twilight disoriented him. He began to wonder if he would ever see the sun again.

Nenos patted Scarlet's shoulder and turned him toward the table, where dishes were laid out. Scarlet recognized fried eggs, porridge, and the small brown cakes with red fruits. There were also huge slabs of bread spread with yellow butter, although the butter was a deeper color than he was used to back home. Che was noticeably absent, but Nenos excused himself and returned a moment later with a brown earthenware che pot wrapped in a thick towel.

"*Orna,*" Nenos said warningly, tapping his finger on

the pot and jerking it back.

"Hot?" Scarlet said.

Nenos smiled, like Scarlet was inviting him to a game, and pointed at the eggs.

"*Terg.*"

"Eggs."

Nenos chuckled and poured the che for him, which was not green, but dark and savory amber. He tasted it and nodded his thanks. Nenos's attention was not unlike a genial innkeeper Scarlet had known in Morturii, and even with the language barrier, he could sense the old man's kindness. He was just trying to make the guest comfortable. Scarlet repeated one of the stock phrases for *thank you* that Liall had taught him, and Nenos sketched a short bow before leaving him to enjoy his meal in silence.

The food was plain but good, and Scarlet had been eating salted fish and waybread for so long that almost anything would have tasted like heaven. He devoured all the cakes and the oat porridge, but the eggs had a musky taste that he could not get used to. He was finishing up the che when Nenos entered with a man he did not recognize.

The stranger was carrying a small case and bowed to Scarlet. He had a thin but not unpleasant face, and he was tall, which for Rshani was like saying he breathed air, but his honey-gold hair was done up in a strange braided style that Scarlet had not seen before.

Nenos indicated the man and spoke several sentences in Sinha. Scarlet let him get into it a bit before he shook his head.

"*Sun man'an neth tueth degal,*" he said. I do not understand.

"Ah." Nenos hesitated. He made a motion for Scarlet to wait and left quickly, returning a moment later with a maid, presumably from one of the neighboring apartments.

Nenos made an expansive gesture to the maid. She cleared her throat, clearly nervous. "Excuse me, ser," she said in halting Bizye, "but this man that Nenos has... bringing... he is a man of cloth."

"What?"

"Cloth. Cloths." She fingered the collar of her blouse. "For wear."

"Oh! Clothes."

"*San ma suenma.* Yes, clothes. He will make you clothes."

"What's wrong with the clothes I have on now?"

She seemed momentarily distressed. "But of course, ser, you must have new clothes. All new. All your own."

I must, must I? It didn't seem worth it to argue. He nodded at the tailor and the man took it for assent and laid his case on the brocaded couch, opening it and taking out tools that any pedlar would recognize: measuring tape, a pack of iron pins, small pieces of charcoal-stick for marking. Nenos signaled that the maid should stay and the next three hours were one long, very polite quarrel between Scarlet and the servants of the Nauhinir. First, once the tailor was finally done with measuring him, Scarlet expected him to go. Instead, Nenos went to the foyer and rang a little bell, and the room began to fill with servants carrying bolts of bright cloth and silk and boxes of colored spools of thread.

"What's all this?" Scarlet exclaimed in alarm, looking to Nenos.

Nenos only smiled and nodded, pushing forward one maid who carried a bolt of red wool shot with deeper red embroidery and little silver knots like flowers. She bowed and extended the bolt to him, signaling that he should feel its softness.

"What? No, it looks like something my sister would wear."

"*Edsite' hnn?*"

"Flow-ers" he said emphatically, like she was deaf. "No flowers or frilly laces or bows. Not so many buttons. Not so pretty. Understand? *Degala sr esu?*"

The first maid, the one who spoke broken Bizye, piped up, and there were strained but polite smiles and some of the more outrageous fabrics were taken away. Plainer materials were offered, fine wools and cotton weaves instead of silks and satins, some in lilac and mauve hues, some in varying shades of black and dark gray, and some in deep, vibrant blues that were truly astonishing and which Scarlet felt drawn to. He chose some of the gray wool and approved the sturdy black cottons, and even one of the best blues, but then two of the maids came lugging a heavy, folded length of tanned hide. They laid it on the floor and spread it out, and at Nenos's urging, Scarlet felt its smooth, buttery softness. It was very fine.

"This would make a coat good enough for a prince," he mused.

"What color for this, ser?" The maid asked.

He knew at once. Rising, he went to the closet where his traveling clothes had been stored, digging through the grimy packs. He turned and held up his old, battered pedlar's jacket proudly. The shoulder was torn a little and the hem ragged and both elbows were showing lighter patches in the red dye.

"Can you make this for me?"

The tailor took it from him gingerly and examined it. It was none too clean. He spoke to the maid, who shrugged.

"Everything, ser? The color, the cut?"

"Yes. Everything. Exactly. What is the word for exactly?"

"Jesut'srr."

"Jesut'srr," he decided. "Yes."

The tailor shrugged, not happy with Scarlet's choice, but he bowed and the maids began to pack up. Obviously, they were done. When Nenos had seen everyone out, including the Bizye-speaking maid whom Scarlet thanked very politely, the servant brought another pot of che into the common room. The che was green this time, and Nenos set the table with a huge plate of the dumplings, the kind Scarlet had enjoyed the night before.

"Thank you," Scarlet breathed, glad that they were all gone. "I feel like a plucked chicken."

Nenos nodded, getting the gist if not the exact words. Chos came in a few moments later and asked, through motions and signs, if Scarlet wanted another bath.

"Later," he said. *"Shey."* Which meant, *some other time*, or *when I'm ready*, but there was one thing he did want. Scarlet ate another dumpling and wiped his fingers on the napkin before he gripped a lock of his black hair and made scissoring motions next to it, miming a haircut. The men were shocked.

Nenos rattled off a spate of Sinha and Scarlet didn't catch a word of it, though the meaning was clear enough.

"What do you mean, I can't cut my hair? It's my hair. Why not?"

Nenos answered him patiently, bowing, and Scarlet heard the name *Nazheradei* several times. Chos just looked frightened.

So, he was not to cut his hair for fear of angering Liall? What was he, a doll? Scarlet folded his hands on the table and regarded Nenos with a steady eye. "I just want a pair of scissors," he said. "Surely you can do that."

But Nenos shook his head, the matter patently settled in his mind. Scarlet stared him down for a moment, and then shrugged. "Fine." He reached down and slid a sharp little dagger out of his boot, testing its edge with his thumb. "I've made do with worse than this."

From their mutual expressions, Scarlet realized that it never occurred to them that he might be armed. Nenos muttered an order aside to Chos, and the young servant exited quickly. The old man held his hand out.

"Edas," he said. Please.

"I don't think so."

Nenos sighed heavily, sat down beside Scarlet at the table and began to speak at length, slowly and with great patience. Scarlet only caught a stray word here and there, completely meaningless, but Nenos was obviously saying, plainly; "I need you to give me that dagger" and hinting at consequences if Scarlet did not comply.

Bugger that.

"I'll make you a trade." Scarlet again made cutting motions with his fingers. "The dagger for scissors."

Nenos shook his head tiredly. There was a noise at the door, and Liall –tall and white-haired and imposing– entered the room, followed closely by a fretting Chos. Liall gave Scarlet a flat smile. Nenos rose and bowed to Liall.

"You're awake. And dressed," Liall said, ignoring Nenos.

Liall wore a dark gray virca with his white hair neatly brushed, all of his clothing new and the leather of his boots polished. We're both looking rather fancy lately. Scarlet thought, and could not help making comparison in his mind between the prince before him and the bandit Kasiri atya who had stopped him on a mountain road and demanded a kiss.

"And eating." Scarlet toed one of the chairs away from the table with his boot. Liall hesitated and then sank down.

"Chos says you waved a dagger around."

Scarlet laughed. "I did not!"

"I said Chos said that. I do not believe it happened precisely that way. You have a temper, but you would not pull a weapon just because you did not get your wants satisfied." Liall waved the servants off imperiously and they went without a backward look.

"You have to show me how to do that," Scarlet said, miming the wave. He slid the dagger back into his boot. "I just wanted a pair of scissors, for Deva's sake. I don't know why you were disturbed for that."

"It is complicated." Liall eyed Scarlet's plate, distracted. "You like the dumplings?"

Scarlet wanted to ask if Liall had made any progress in his mission, but if Liall was not volunteering, he was not asking. "Very much."

Nenos came and set a pottery cup of green che in front of Liall before vanishing again. The scent of roses wafted up. Liall lifted the cup, cradling it in his hands for the warmth, and suppressed a yawn.

"One would think you hadn't slept at all," Scarlet said meaningfully. He only meant to tease Liall, but Liall set the cup down quickly, his spine stiff.

"I know..." Liall began. He seemed to think better of what he was about to say, and started over. "Last night... if only ..."

Scarlet nearly laughed again. "What are you on about?"

Liall raked his fingers through his white hair. "I am not doing this correctly, am I? Very well, I want you to know something. If you were one of my people and what happened last night... if it were our first time..."

"It was our first time."

"I am well aware of that," Liall snapped. He lapsed into brooding silence and stared at the fireplace, his jaw tight.

Scarlet stared for a moment, and then reasoned that it must have been a trying day already for Liall. "I'm listening."

"In another time, I would have woken you with gifts befitting a prince. Now... I have nothing to give you that comes from myself alone, and so I have nothing. I just wanted you to know that I meant you no dishonor, that I would never willingly deceive you or slight you."

"Are you done?" Scarlet waited as Liall sat with his face closed and set. "I don't need gifts, Liall, and I'm more than a little grateful you feel you can't give me any."

Liall seemed puzzled, but not terribly. "Oh?"

"I'm not a prize that you've won, or a thing that crawled to you because you were a prince and could give me jewels and pretties. You're not Prince Nazheradei to me; you're Liall, the bastard bandit Kasiri. I expect no more than *he* can give." *And I hope you expect no more of me than plain Scarlet of Lysia could give,* he prayed silently.

Liall was quiet for a moment, and Scarlet thought he was angered again.

"You shame me."

"Oh, enough of your foreign nonsense," Scarlet said in disgust. He shoved the plate of dumplings in front of Liall. "Have something to eat, you look awful."

Scarlet half-expected Liall to explode, but he took up a fork and picked at the dumplings. "You are the foreign one here, you know."

"Doesn't feel that way to me. No matter how far I go, I'm still myself."

Liall snorted, but his heavy mood lifted and he began to eat a little.

"Bad morning?"

Liall nodded around a mouthful. "No worse than I

expected, but bad enough. They have not forgotten me, which is not altogether good for my purpose here. I do not have many happy memories of Rshan."

"Are you making progress in... whatever it is you came for?"

The fey look in his pale eyes boded ill for someone. "Not yet." Liall finally seemed to notice that Scarlet was not wearing his usual clothing. "Why, you are done up like a proper princeling! Is this Nenos's doing?" His fingers plucked the bright row of stitching near Scarlet's collar and he whistled lowly. "The color suits you," he judged. "But gray is too serious. I like red better."

"I noticed that not many of your people wear it."

He shrugged. "The color red has fallen out of favor since Ramung's time. It is the color of his House."

"Who was Ramung?"

"A very ruthless Baron who created a great deal of strife inside Rshan. Now it has become almost tradition to reserve that color for his House, except for things like hats and scarves and gloves. I pay no attention to such customs, and now red reminds me only of you. But if you wish, you are entitled to wear the royal blue and silver of my House."

Scarlet was certain there was more to that than Liall was telling him. He made an indifferent motion with his hand. "I don't think so."

Liall did not press the point, perhaps because they were very good at misunderstanding one another. "One day," Liall said, noncommittal. He ate the last of the dumplings and wiped his mouth with a starched linen napkin so white it hurt the eyes. "And now, I must abandon you again." Liall stood up.

That amused Scarlet. "Is that how you see me: a lost little waif in your giant country with your giant folk?"

"Well... I am a little concerned for you."

Obviously, since he came running when Chos called. "Liall, I'm a journeyer. Meeting new people is what I do. I'm not going to pine away like a caged bird just because you're not in my line of sight. Besides, if you ignore me too much, I have my own ways of making you regret it."

Liall laughed. A little too loudly, Scarlet thought, but Liall's hand on the back of his neck was warm, as were the lips pressed to the spot under his ear.

"I will heed your warning, and not ignore you too much when I return," Liall murmured.

Liall made to leave, and then Scarlet remembered. "Liall... why don't they want me to cut my hair?"

"Oh, that." He seemed embarrassed. "Pay it no mind. I will straighten it out. Nenos believed my permission was needed first."

"Per..." Scarlet was speechless. So they did think he was Liall's property. "And the dagger?"

"Unless you are a bodyguard, it is not usual for anyone, even a lover, to be armed in the presence of a prince when they are closeted alone together. I will explain your status to the servants and you will not be bothered again about it."

"What exactly is my status?"

Liall grinned suddenly and the years fell away from him. He didn't look much older than Shansi then, with the firelight from the hearth and the blue glow from the lamps. "You are my t'aishka. And why not let your hair grow longer? It would please me."

When he had gone, Scarlet wondered again what t'aishka actually meant, and resolved to ask Liall about it later. He did, however, decide not to cut his hair.

2.

A Dangerous Game

Liall left early the next morning, gone before Scarlet had woken. Several hours into the day –telling time here was an impossibility– Scarlet was seated in the smaller room adjoining the common room. Liall called the room a *den*, like it was a warren for some animal. The term amused Scarlet and he used it now when he referred to the smaller, cozier room with its big couch and shelves of books and the huge, stone casement with the tinted panes of glass. He was seated on the couch once more, watching the people come and go in the torchlight on the snowy walkway far below. A book was open on his lap, though he couldn't read it at all. The book was interesting enough that he didn't mind, with colored pictures of beasts and strange buildings, and script that looked like branching vines across the pages, curiously beautiful, but foreign. Everything here was foreign.

He had other books strewn about the table. These were ones without words, just pictures of men and women, but drawn with an eye so delicate to detail that it made him flush with pleasure just to look at them. Scarlet glanced at the window again, looking down, and saw what he thought was a bare, snow-trimmed tree suddenly bend and move out of the way of a lady in a sapphire robe trimmed with white fur. Scarlet gaped and rose up to his knees on the couch, his book sliding to the floor. Clumps of snow slid off the tree and its trunk suddenly parted to reveal thick, dark-skinned legs that carried it swiftly away from the walkway. Scarlet's heart began to beat faster. That was no tree, but a man, yet a man far larger even than the Rshani, with a round, bald head and arms that swung like saplings at his sides. He was about to call out for Nenos when he realized yet again that he had no way to tell the old man what he had seen, or ask him for an explanation.

Scarlet sank back onto the couch slowly, his heartbeat gradually returning to normal. What was that thing? Was it a real man, or something else? No one on the walkway had paid the creature any attention, and there was no way they could have missed him. The dark giant must be something new, something he had not seen before.

He realized with a start that he *had* seen something like it before: the wooden statue of the Shining One in the Fate Dealer's tent in Ankar. The statue had frightened him then, and he was no less shaken now. It was impossible, wasn't it? The Shining Ones had been dead for thousands of years. What, then, had he just seen?

A few hours passed and Scarlet was finishing up one of the thicker volumes when a soft knock echoed in the quiet room. Nenos answered it, and a young man with a most gentle expression stood there, his thin hands folded in front of him. He wore a plain, ankle-length virca of blue wool and his hair was long and straight like an icefall or a fold of white silk. His eyes were not pale blue, like Liall's, but a deep gold, most unusual. He bowed his head to Scarlet and smiled, and then spoke to Nenos, who bowed in turn.

"I am Jochi," the man said in accented but perfect Bizye, still smiling, and finally Scarlet recognized him.

"You were at the port."

Jochi smiled, as if happy to be recalled. "I was, yes.

I had been waiting for many weeks. It is kind of you to remember." Jochi was handsome without being pretty, and his manners were fine as a king's but somehow comforting, as if his whole purpose was to make Scarlet feel at ease. "The queen has asked me to bring you to the hall to join us for dinner."

Scarlet felt a flash of relief at understanding and being able to make himself understood, right before it vanished and he realized what Jochi had said. "Dinner? You mean with the queen?"

"And several hundred courtiers and servants. Have no fear, ser, this is very normal." His voice was uncommonly gentle.

"Now?"

"Of course, now, ser."

Scarlet rose. "Thank you," he said, casting a nervous glance aside to Nenos, who nodded. He put the book down and started toward Jochi, but stopped suddenly and looked down at his clothing.

"You look very well," Jochi assured. "Fear not on that account."

"Thank you. I haven't spent much time in castles."

"It is only larger than most places," Jochi said, smiling a little. "Come, ser."

As Jochi guided him through the corridors, he explained in his soft voice the shape of the palace and pointed out things to remember as guiding landmarks. He was dressed in plain wool but his manner was too studied for him to be a commoner, yet Scarlet was not sure he was a courtier or nobleman, either.

"There are one thousand and twenty-two rooms in the Nauhinir, ser," he said, pretending not to notice Scarlet's shock. "One thousand, eight hundred and four windows, one thousand seven hundred and six doors and ninety-four staircases."

A courtier may not have been so diligent of pointing out the many landmarks inside the palace. Jochi reminded Scarlet of a teacher, and he said so.

Jochi was pleased. "That is precisely what I am, ser. A teacher."

"Will you tell me something else, teacher?"

"If I can."

"I saw something odd, today." Scarlet began to relate the story of the man he had mistaken for a tree.

"Ah, yes. That is Melev, one of our most honored residents at the Nauhinir."

"Melev. Is he a Shining One?" Scarlet asked with some dread.

Jochi laughed. "Indeed not. Melev is an Ancient, but that will take more explanation than we have time for at the moment. See? The great hall is just there."

The hall, when they arrived, was enormous and noisy. "This is the dining hall, ser, what we call the great hall. It is the largest one, and we use it for both dining and meeting and many other purposes."

It was plainer than any room Scarlet had seen so far, with bricked fireplaces roaring at either end of the place. There was a huge window on the other side of the room, the heavy draperies thrown open to reveal the ceaseless blue twilight, and he could make out the shape of a frozen river in the landscape beyond, quite near the palace.

"That is called the Neb," Jochi explained as he led Scarlet into the room. "The sacred river."

Scarlet had thought this room plain, but when he chanced to look up at the vaulted ceiling, he saw that it was made up entirely of small mosaic tiles in many colors. The design sprawled across the entire expanse of the ceiling, a rendering of many birds of all kinds in flight across a sunlit sky.

A row of wide tables extended down, four abreast,

and Scarlet could see Liall at the high table, beside the queen. Just seeing her put a knot in his belly again, but Jochi put his fingertip on Scarlet's arm to guide him to an empty seat just below Liall and the queen at the end of the third table, next to a woman as lovely and distant as the moon who stared pointedly at Scarlet.

"Lady Shikhoza speaks your language," Jochi informed him. "I will rejoin you later, ser Scarlet." He touched Scarlet's shoulder briefly. "Enjoy your meal."

I'd rather be eating stones, he thought. He glanced up and saw Liall's mouth curve slightly, saw him lift his cup in his direction. Resigned, Scarlet sat carefully next to the woman. *Lady Shikhoza,* he reminded himself.

"Good evening, Lady," he said, remembering his manners.

She gave him a wintry smile. "Ser Keriss," she said and lifted her cup to drink.

Whatever that means, he thought. Maybe it was a pleasantry. A servant leaned over his shoulder and poured him a drink. Wine as red as rubies spilled into his cup. He tasted it. It was probably a good vintage, but he would have rather had bitterbeer. Still, he sipped to avoid giving offense.

The meal was endless. The man across from him was –to say it plainly– fat. Folds of flesh spilled out from the top of his hapcoat, and his heavy jowls reminded Scarlet of a sow that Rufa the alewife had owned once. The fat man ignored Scarlet, and Lady Shikhoza glanced at him often, but said little. Scarlet stole many looks at Liall and his mother, who conferred almost constantly during the meal.

Hats, it seemed, were not worn in the palace, and while the men were all clothed in either vircas and breeches or hapcoats and breeches and were bare-headed, most women wore arrangements on their piled hair that seemed to be wide, starched lengths of colored linen in the shape of large crescent moons, set with wire and beads and jewels into a fringed crown. He would be sure to ask Liall what they were called later. The most starting thing were the women's eyes. They ladies of the court painted their eyelids above and below with a deep blue cosmetic that made them appear quite large and startled, like wild deer, or else like satisfied cats.

Despite what he had told Liall, Scarlet was suddenly taken by a wave of longing to see his own people again. All this wealth of strangeness made his head hurt. Even though Liall had taken pains to warn him, Scarlet realized that he had not fully grasped how difficult it would be to be surrounded by dislike for a long stretch of time. He already knew the Rshani did not tolerate foreigners well or graciously, but he realized now that he had been hoping that the court men and women would be better behaved than the mariners. Scarlet glanced around the hall, getting only cold stares in return, until he gave up and stared into his cup. This foreigner was beginning to think he didn't care much for them either, except for one of them in particular. He had never really felt homesickness, but now, for the first time in his career of wandering, Scarlet was lonely.

A loud voice interrupted Scarlet's reverie and he jerked his head up to stare in dismay at the man across from him. The fat man was obviously speaking to him, but he had no idea what the fellow was saying. He glanced at the Lady in appeal, and she smiled, still like ice.

"He asks how long you have known Prince Nazheradei."

"A bit more than a year."

One corner of her mouth lifted. "You must address the Baron."

"I don't speak Sinha."

"No, of course you don't." She patted Scarlet's hand, smiling more fully. "Say this, then." She leaned close to his ear and said something that, for once, made Sinha sound liquid instead of guttural to Scarlet.

He repeated it nearly soundlessly and she nodded approval.

Feeling a little more confident, Scarlet looked at the Baron and repeated it again.

The fat man proved to be unexpectedly light on his feet as, with a roar, he drew a broad, short sword and shoved his chair backwards. Scarlet scrambled back out of his chair and to his feet as the fat man leapt to the table, kicking wine cups out of the way, and leveled the tip of his blade at Scarlet's throat.

Scarlet glanced at the Lady, whose expression was carefully blank, and he understood. She had tricked him into insulting the fat Baron, and insulting him quite badly. Or well, depending on how one saw the matter.

Liall was suddenly there. He shouted something at the Baron that made the Lady frown slightly. The Baron's expression shifted to one less furious and he said something back to Liall in a tone of grudging respect.

Liall spoke again, at length, and rested his hand on Scarlet's shoulder. The gesture felt odd and fraught with a hidden meaning Scarlet did not understand. Scarlet bowed politely, trying to look apologetic when he couldn't decide whether he was scared or furious.

The Baron softened further and sheathed his blade, then leapt down from the table with that astonishing grace again. Liall spoke again to the room at large and nodded satisfaction when everyone again sat down. His hand on Scarlet's shoulder was heavy as he turned Scarlet toward the doors. "I told you to engage in no quarrels," Liall hissed.

"I didn't!" Scarlet muttered hotly. "At least, I didn't

intend to."

Golden-eyed Jochi met them halfway down the aisle, looking extremely distressed. Liall's fingers gripped tight enough to bruise before he released Scarlet. Scarlet winced.

"Take him back to our apartments, Jochi, and for the sake of us all, keep him out of trouble!"

Scarlet's shoulder ached. He looked at Liall's set face. Liall would not meet Scarlet's eyes, and suddenly Scarlet remembered the ship, and how Liall had hurried him off the deck and into the cabin after the mariner had offered the coin to buy Scarlet's body. Liall had thought him in the wrong, then. Was it the same now?

Without another word, Liall went back to reclaim his seat at the high table, and Scarlet walked stiffly with Jochi to the doors. As they drew near the exit, passing tables with glittering men and women seated at their meals, he heard a man's voice mutter something that included Nazheradei and t'aishka in the same breath. Scarlet looked that way and then at Jochi.

"What did they say?"

"Ser Scarlet, you must not heed it," Jochi said uncomfortably. "When it comes to gossip, some people are no better than commoners." Jochi took Scarlet's arm to lead him away.

Scarlet's face stung with embarrassment. He supposed that Jochi had no way of knowing that he was one of those same commoners, but it still pricked him.

Why did he come here with Liall? A matter of necessity, he had supposed. It was either run or be hanged, and after that there was the honor he owed to his ancestors to repay the blood debt to Liall. But Hilurin honor seemed to mean little to Liall, and Scarlet suddenly wondered if Liall thought him ridiculous, especially after tonight's performance.

"Jochi, will you translate something for me?"

Jochi glanced at him worriedly. "I'd be happy to, ser."

He repeated the phrase Shikhoza had taught him.

Jochi blinked, arched an eyebrow. "It, ah, is a very crude invitation. I do not think it is language you would wish to use."

Scarlet had known it, but to confirm the thing made matters worse. He was silent the rest of the long walk back to Liall's apartments.

Nenos seemed angry after Jochi spoke with him, though Scarlet could not tell if the anger was directed at him or the situation in general. More food was brought, more of the dumplings Scarlet liked, some che, hot and steaming and familiar from Morturii. It was the che that comforted, oddly, that and Jochi's presence. Jochi sat with him politely and tried to be his dinner company, reciting stories of Rshan. Scarlet listened with half an ear, still stinging over the unfairness of his abrupt dismissal at dinner.

"Have you always served here?" he asked Jochi offhand, and then, "I'm sorry if that's rude, I just—"

Jochi smiled reassurance. "Not rude at all. Surely two strangers may question one another in order to become less foreign. Have you been asked many questions since you arrived?"

"Some. Why?"

Jochi's smile was knowing. "As you've already guessed, some subjects are more perilous than others. May I offer you some advice?"

"Please."

Jochi leaned forward a little. "Feel free to answer any inquiries the courtiers and ladies may pose to you, but beware of offering too much. In Rshan, sometimes a wrong word or a phrase spoken in a certain tone will give rise to rumors." He shrugged. "Most of the time, rumors are harmless. They entertain us and they give the court something to do, but matters are... difficult at present." His eyes pinned Scarlet. "Questions about Prince Nazheradei are to be avoided, if possible. Among us, there are polite ways to avoid answering a direct question. I will teach you, if you wish."

"You're very helpful," Scarlet answered, carefully neutral.

Jochi laughed. "Perhaps you have no need of my instruction, ser. I may have misjudged you. And now, it is only fair I tell you about myself; I am from a land east of Nauhinir. Tebet is its name." He sketched a shape in the air with his fingers at eye level. "Here we are now, in the capitol," he said, pointing to an imaginary spot that was somewhere level with his chin, and then his hand rose higher, near his eyes. "And here is where I was born. I lived there with my parents and brothers until I came to serve the queen. And you?"

"I was born in Byzantur, in Lysia: a village on the other side of the border from the Bled, south of Morturii."

Jochi nodded and poured more che. "Tell me of Lysia, if you don't mind."

Scarlet laughed bitterly. "No, I don't mind. It was ... it *is* near the Iron River that stems off the Channel, and to get to the rest of Byzantur you must either take the ferry downriver or cross over the Nerit, or take the Salt Road further south. Lysia is isolated because we have the river on one side and the mountains on the other. The storytellers say that's why Lysia is the oldest village in Byzantur, because our ancestors retreated beyond the mountains to escape from the Shining Ones, and the mountains held a magic iron ore that repelled them." He belatedly remembered the story Liall had told, and he hesitated, hoping he hadn't insulted Jochi.

Jochi smiled, untroubled. "We have stories like that, too," he said. "But you said *was*. Is your village—"

A loud knock at the door interrupted Jochi's words. Nenos, silent and attentive, entered the common room immediately from a side door and stood waiting with that patient air he had. Jochi motioned to Nenos to open the door.

A tall man who looked to be a little older than Jochi stood there. The man had a lean, almost sly face with grooves of self-indulgence deeply etched around his mouth, slightly narrow eyes, and long, braided hair of that snowy white color that Liall had said was associated with royalty. This man was more richly dressed than Jochi and pushed past Nenos like he was invisible. Scarlet went stiff with unease at this insult to an elder, and Jochi stood up immediately, which confirmed to Scarlet that he should be wary. Jochi and the man spoke to each other. Their tones were courteous, but also oddly strained, and Scarlet sensed tension.

Jochi turned to Scarlet and bowed. "Prince Eleferi has dismissed me," he said, his tone peculiarly tight. "So I shall attend you in the morning, if that is agreeable, ser."

Scarlet rose. Another damned prince! "I don't want you to be dismissed. How am I supposed to talk to him?"

"It's quite all right," said Eleferi, stepping forward. His manner was oily and Scarlet instinctively disliked him. "I speak your language as fluently as Jochi."

Scarlet was not reassured. So had the Lady.

"Welcome to our land, ser Keriss," Eleferi smiled brilliantly.

Scarlet eyed the newcomer with distrust. "Thank you."

Eleferi looked at Jochi and spoke again. Scarlet could not understand a word of it, but Eleferi's tone was edged.

Jochi bowed to Eleferi and answered, then smiled stiffly at Scarlet. "The Prince Eleferi is Prince Nazheradei's step-brother, and half-brother also to the Crown Prince Cestimir." He bowed again politely, though his eyes bored into Scarlet's. "I bid you good evening, ser."

Scarlet watched Jochi leave. Nenos moved into the room, scowling, and took the che pot. He offered Eleferi a dark look and a bow.

Eleferi ignored him and seated himself in the chair that had been Jochi's. The prince fussily rearranged his silks –gold with a border of red– before speaking. "I apologize on behalf of all Rshan for what happened in the great hall," he said airily. "These misunderstandings... and the eastern nobles are always short of temper."

A misunderstanding. Scarlet nodded stiffly and sat down. "I meant no offense," he said, which was honest enough.

"No, no. No offense," Eleferi gushed, too heartily, his voice high and lilting, like a girl's.

Scarlet disliked this Eleferi and he was certain he did not trust him, but at least he was pleasant, even if his manners were overdone. Like a house with too many colors of paint and none of it matching. Nenos returned with another steaming pot and a fresh cup for Eleferi. He poured while Dvi, the young cook, brought a tray of white pastries with flowers dusted on them in colored sugar. Eleferi took two on a small plate.

"So tell me, where did you meet my brother?"

Scarlet's nerves prickled. *Questions about Prince Nazheradei are to be avoided, if possible.* He chose to interpret Eleferi's question narrowly. "In Volkovoi. On a trade ship."

"A trade ship! How exhilarating and romantic! Tell me more."

He began to embroider vaguely, wondering when Liall would return and hoping it was soon. To Scarlet's great relief, Nenos never left the room.

Prince Eleferi was teaching Scarlet to play a board game when Liall returned. The game was a complex system of carved pieces that moved in leaps and jumps on the board's squares, and Scarlet had nearly gotten the trick of thinking five moves ahead when the door opened.

Eleferi fairly leapt from his chair to greet Liall, rattling off a fluid stream of Sinha. Nenos bowed and went into the kitchen,

"He is not a guest," Liall interrupted in Bizye, his voice cold. "It is not proper for you to be here."

Scarlet wondered at Liall's temper, and Eleferi's face went tight in offense.

"Forgive my impropriety," Eleferi said, giving Liall an overly apologetic glance. "I thought to show ser Keriss a more hospitable face than he witnessed tonight, brother. I've been teaching him to play harts."

"So I see." Liall's expression was hard to decipher. "And where is Jochi?"

Eleferi glanced at Scarlet briefly. "I dismissed him."

"Did you?" Liall's tone was dangerous.

Eleferi cleared his throat. "Well, I had best be going," He bowed shortly to Scarlet. "Ser Keriss," he said, and then bowed more deeply to Liall before leaving.

Liall watched the door close, his lips flattened into a thin line. "Lascivious jackal," he muttered and turned to Scarlet. "I tell you to stay out of trouble and here I return to find one of the *essima* at my own hearth?"

Scarlet stifled his first answer, which would have been to tell Liall to go stuff himself, and coolly began moving the pieces back to their original squares. "He wouldn't have left, even if I'd asked. Should I have left instead? And what in Deva's hell is an essima?" He thought it sounded like their word for viper.

"A serpent the color of snow," Liall growled. "It is native to these lands, our only venomous animal."

"What is ser Keriss? They keep calling me that."

"I will tell you later. Now heed me: *never* allow Jochi to be dismissed, especially by the likes of that." Liall stalked away to speak with Nenos in the kitchen.

Scarlet gave up on rearranging the harts board and got up to stand in front of the fire. After several minutes, Liall joined him.

"I crave your pardon, Scarlet," Liall said at last. He put a warm hand on Scarlet's shoulder. "I have no right to take out my ill temper on you."

"No, you don't." Scarlet kept his voice low, his mind busy turning over the puzzle of Jochi and Eleferi and the glittering lady in the hall. So many puzzles here, so much he did not grasp. Scarlet had always been quick to take command of a situation, always so confident with strangers. Now, for the first time in his life, he had to admit he was in waters deeper than he could swim.

"You were right," Scarlet said dispiritedly. "Perhaps I was wrong to follow you so far when you warned me against it. Perhaps I don't belong here."

Liall took Scarlet's shoulders and turned him around. "Ah, Scarlet, it's far too late for doubt. Whatever you might have chosen before, now it is done and there is no road back. Life is complicated here, much more complicated than in Ankar, or even the palace of your Flower Prince. It takes many years to be able to navigate a royal court with safety, and you should not be either too eager to do so or very disappointed when it turns out badly. Do you understand?"

"No."

Liall sighed. "And that is my fault, I know, but... I have no remedy."

Scarlet's fingers dug into the fabric of Liall's sleeves. "Yes, you do. Teach me."

"I cannot."

"Can't or won't?"

Liall slid his hand under Scarlet's chin and lifted it. "Listen to me, please. None of this was supposed to happen to you. We were to part on the Nerit, remember? This is an accident, your being here. A long set of circumstances that I tried to avoid, but somehow we kept getting thrown back together, as if we were *meant* to be together. Now you are here, and to me that is a very frightening thing." Liall's hand dropped. "Rshan is an ancient civilization, and as such it is often wicked and stagnant, and devours innocence wherever it finds it. I will not allow you to be corrupted so much that going back to Scarlet of Lysia becomes impossible for you."

Scarlet studied his face for a long moment. "And you plan on doing that by keeping me prisoner in these rooms?"

Liall looked pained. "It is not what I want. You may move about the palace freely, but only with Jochi. He is not merely a translator and teacher: he is also a bodyguard. There are those who will seek to harm me here, and the easiest way to do that is through you. There are not even any laws in Rshan to protect your life, Scarlet."

"Because I'm lenilyn."

"Do you know what that word means? Not just outlander. *Non-person.* Many Rshani do not even believe you have a soul. They think you little more than a pretty animal."

Scarlet was shocked. He had known they disliked Hilurin, but the extent had escaped him.

"Do you see now?" Liall went on. He drew Scarlet close and spoke with his lips pressed against Scarlet's forehead. "If any evil should befall you, it would be entirely my fault. The only reason you are here is because of me. I brought you here, Scarlet, but I do not think I can survive burying you here."

Scarlet wanted to remind Liall that it was he who had had insisted on following, but he felt the slight tremble in Liall's hands. "Is all this worry for me?" he asked, considerably moved.

"I love you."

"I can defend myself," Scarlet reminded him, but was warmed by his declaration.

"You are untainted by the habit of intrigue," Liall said. "Perhaps you can defend yourself against bravos on a city street, or a brigand chief, but there are things in the shadows here that you would never think to guard against."

Scarlet gripped the front of Liall's hapcoat. "If I knew who I was supposed to avoid, I would. You didn't tell me to be wary at dinner and then you were furious!"

Liall's hand cupped the back of Scarlet's neck and worked at the tight knots of muscle there. "Please," he pleaded softly. "Please say you agree."

Scarlet sighed. "I promise not to wander and to fly from my cage only when Jochi is with me."

Scarlet could feel the tension melting out of Liall's body. He pushed Liall away a little to stare up into his lover's pale eyes intently. "Why won't you tell me what's going on here? What are you afraid of?"

"Come sit with me." Liall took his hand and drew him to the couch. "I crave your pardon for snapping at you. The fault is mine."

Scarlet sighed again. "It's not fair that you keep secrets from me."

"No, it is not. And if I had thought... I have left orders that Eleferi is not to be admitted in my absence. Neither is Vladei."

"Who's Vladei?"

"Just remember the name and keep Eleferi decently out of our apartments when I'm not here."

It sounded like an accusation. "He's your brother."

"Never be alone with him!" Liall growled, and then gentled his tone. "In fact, he is my step-brother. And royal houses are not like your decent home with Scaja and Linhona: the poison of power and intrigue is everywhere in an imperial house. Here, even a brother may kill a brother."

Scarlet was appalled. "What?"

Liall must have seen how his words affected Scarlet. "Have you never heard of these things?" he asked sadly. "I assure you, such horrors do exist."

Scarlet studied this man to whom he had tied his life. The lines of sorrow and bitterness had returned and settled in all around Liall's eyes and mouth. Scarlet suddenly forgot his temper and trailed his fingers down the curve of Liall's face.

Liall closed his eyes, seeming almost in pain. "I am too old for you, too bitter and cynical."

"You are not."

"I am, but that does not mean I will let you go." He pulled Scarlet into his arms and tightened his embrace as if to keep Scarlet prisoner, and Scarlet laughed and loosened the ties on the silken shirt Liall wore under his virca. He pressed a kiss to the warm skin beneath. Liall tasted very faintly of salt, and Scarlet licked the hollow of his throat, feeling Liall's fingers tangle in his hair.

Liall pulled back and kissed him, his tongue slipping

between Scarlet's lips. Oh Deva, he had been afraid of this before, but what he knew now...

Scarlet shivered, remembering what it had felt like to float in the darkness with only Liall's voice and touch. Scarlet pressed his hand between Liall's legs, and the prince drew back quickly, looking at once startled and amused.

"I have created a wanton."

"Then you must deal with your creation," Scarlet smiled, his hand roaming.

"I intend to." Liall pulled Scarlet closer to his chest. "But I am tired and worried, t'aishka. Later, perhaps?"

Scarlet nodded, disappointed but not very much. "Liall... at dinner? That woman told me how to address the Baron."

Liall went very still. "That woman?" Very softly: "Lady Shikhoza?"

Scarlet nodded. "Yes. She told me what to say and how to say it. What did I say, anyway?"

Liall stroked Scarlet's dark hair. "Let us merely say that it was very rude, but pronunciation can be difficult."

"I repeated her words exactly," Scarlet said resentfully, for he felt suddenly that Liall might have been defending her. "She said I'd gotten it right."

"The Baron understands that it was an error."

Scarlet wondered about that. Perhaps it would be good to have Jochi with him to navigate the court's undercurrents. "All right, but I don't think that lady likes me very much, for some reason. They way she looked at me gave me the shivers, like she was walking over my grave."

Liall drew slowly away. "And now, it grows late and there is one more matter I must to attend before I sleep. But first, I want a bath."

Hot water sounded good. "Do Rshani bathe *every*

night?"

"Usually. Why do you ask? On the ship, you washed every day. I remember you were insistent on it."

"Well, it was a filthy ship, and I was only washing in a bucket, not filling a great tub with hot water and sitting in it twice a day."

Liall nodded in that preoccupied way he had when thinking of other things. "Well, here we bathe once a day at least. Twice, if you're picky."

It sounded like an awful lot of trouble to get the same result as a basin of water and a cake of soap could. But there were some things you could do in baths that were very pleasant. "Want some company?"

The smile Liall gave him was distracted and –Scarlet fancied– a little false. "Not tonight, but I will return later this evening." Liall hesitated. "Thank you for agreeing."

"How late will...?" But Liall had already turned and walked out the door, calling for Nenos. Scarlet slumped back against the pillows. Well, fine: no one to talk to, nothing to see, not even a friendly taberna to pass the hours in. He could understand that Liall felt the need to shield him and that he was a liability to the prince, but if Liall thought his fears were going to pen Scarlet up in this big castle the way they had penned him in that tiny ship's cabin, Liall had another thought coming.

3.

A Bit of Light

Lady Shikhoza was playing cards in one of the many salons adjoining the main hall that led to the queen's tier when Liall found her.

"I would speak with you," he said lowly.

The fire popped and crackled and the noblewomen seated with Shikhoza tittered and hid their smiles behind fans of lacquered playing cards, their blue-painted eyes merry. A silent servant drew the heavy velvet draperies away from the casement panes, revealing a landscape of perpetual twilight and snow. Liall was still unused to seeing such a sight again, and glanced twice at the casement, as if he expected to see the brass orb of a Byzan sun hovering over an arid land.

He had left Scarlet abruptly, perhaps too much so, and he was already feeling guilty over it. He knew Scarlet was not satisfied with his answers regarding his purposes here, a point certain not to escape the discerning pedlar, and it would not be long before Scarlet began to insist on knowing what was happening. Liall knew Scarlet well enough by now to realize his silences were either irritation or mere tolerance for Liall's "foreign strangeness", and that it would not be long before his beloved red-coat's fiercely inquisitive nature began to demand answers.

There are so many undercurrents here, Liall worried. How well I remember. I can feel them in every glittering hall I pass through. So many plans and treacheries brewing. I cannot allow Scarlet to be involved in any way. He would be lost in the webs they spin here, food for the fat, ruthless spiders of a bored royal court.

Shikhoza neatly laid a gilt-edged Prince card over her companion's Page card, drawing a round of sighs.

"I win again," Shikhoza smiled, laying down her playing hand on the embroidered cloth. She gazed pointedly at Liall's hand and would not rise until he gave it. Liall led her out of the salon gruffly, not liking the idea that there would be gossip now, and that it might reach Scarlet's ears.

"There was no cause for that display," he growled once they were in the wide hall and strolling towards the queen's tier, Shikhoza's hand still upon his.

"What, helping me out of my chair?"

"You know what I mean."

"Ah. Perhaps I do," she smiled. Shikhoza's long tarica —deep ruby-red and intricately sewn with blood-red garnets— flashed little sparks of crimson in the lamp light, and her skin was like poured honey. Shikhoza's pale golden hair, which would come down to her ankles when unpinned, was piled high on her head in an intricate pattern of braids, and her carved features were as perfect and composed as ever.

Only Liall, who had known her as a girl, could see the changes in her: the small lines around her eyes, the firmness to her lips. They were both much older.

"You must allow me my games, Nazheradei," she was saying. "There is little else to occupy a discarded Lady in this court."

"You were not discarded," Liall answered snappishly, being drawn into her moods despite his vows not to be. "I was exiled. You were not. It is as simple as that. You could have married another."

"Who would have me?" she answered lightly,

bestowing a stunning smile on a courtier as they passed by a knot of brightly-garbed young men idling under an arch. The young man turned all the way around to stare at her, even after they passed. "After betrothal to a crown prince, I was either too high or too low for any man at court. As wife, at any rate. I had many offers of becoming a mistress."

"I was not the crown prince," Liall muttered. "That was Nadei."

"That is not the way they remember it."

They, of course, were Liall's people, the subjects of Queen Nadiushka, his mother. "So, whose mistress are you now?" he asked sharply, wanting to wound her.

"My own."

That, at least, was truth, and something he could believe. "I wish to talk to you about Vladei," he said abruptly, naming his eldest step-brother.

"Talk, then. What is there to say?" She turned her head, her chin lifted proudly, and smiled at him as they passed open door after open door, enjoying the attention they were drawing. "Vladei wants to be king. He has some claim, after all. Your mother wants Cestimir to be king. That is only natural, since Cestimir is her son and Vladei merely a step-son. But Cestimir is only fourteen. Vladei is a man of your years and already rules a large barony. He is tested and tried, and the barons know him, even if they do not like him. Cestimir is only a child."

"So you put the queen's choice down to mere sentimentality?" Liall snorted. "You know her better than that."

"Everyone knows her better than that," she quipped. "And yet, Nadiushka felt the need to send for you. She feels her case is weak."

"Little wonder, with enemies like you working against her."

"I am not her enemy, Nazheradei. Or yours. I am simply more on my side than anyone else's."

Though it was growing late, the Nauhinir was filled with sounds and light and movement. Liall was very aware of the many eyes on them. He pitched his voice low. "Tell me what Vladei plans."

Her sudden laugh was so bright that it made heads turn. "My dear prince," she answered in that same low tone "even if I knew, why in the world would I tell you?"

"Profit," Liall answered easily. "One thing you can always be counted on to do, lady, is act in your own self-interest. Aid Cestimir, and you will prosper."

"Cestimir called me a poisonous bitch last winter," she said, nodding and smiling to an admirer.

"As you say, he is a child."

"If that excuses him for his tongue then it should excuse him from the throne!" she shot back, with her first touch of venom.

"Ah," Liall smiled. "There is the loving tone I know." He began to lead her past yet another salon, when Vladei and Eleferi stepped out of the door.

The brothers were a matched pair, both with the pure white hair of the Lukaska line, both tall and lean with long, elegant hands and rugged, aquiline features so like Liall's own, but there were differences. Vladei, the elder, had a larger nose and his eyes were misty gray, not blue. Eleferi was smaller than either of them, and his face was leaner with a sly cast, almost like a fox. Eleferi's hair was longer and pulled back from his face with a gold ribbon.

"Lady Shikhoza," Vladei said loudly, again calling attention to them. His humorless mouth smiled. "What a lovely gown."

Shikhoza bowed a little, giving Vladei an inviting look.

Yes, Liall thought. She is still beautiful, and yet, I would cut my hand off before touching her again.

"I chose it in honor of our returned prince," Shikhoza said to Vladei. Her manicured hands with their painted nails smoothed the folds of her red tarica. "It is his favorite color."

Not on you, Liall yearned to say. Her skin was gold, not purest cream, and her eyes had no love for him, only spite and a desire to harm. He knew she was not above her pettiness, either, and that these jibes would continue.

"You show me too much favor, dear Shikhoza," Liall said, and saw the barb sink into Vladei. His step-brother had never forgiven him for taking Shikhoza away, though the betrothal had not been Liall's idea. Nadiushka had thought the match with the female heir to the barony of Jadizek wise, and Liall had been too young to see beyond Shikhoza's most obvious attributes and his own youthful lust for them. Later, he came to regret his lack of discernment, but by then it was far too late.

"We have arranged a prince's greeting for you, brother," Eleferi announced with a smile on his sly, fox-like face. "A snow bear hunt."

At first, Liall was not sure he had heard aright. It seemed the height of bad taste: a snow bear hunt, at this crucial time, knowing his family's long and unlucky history with that creature? Then Liall saw that Vladei and Eleferi and probably Shikhoza had meant to throw him with this news. He suddenly felt befouled, as if he fallen into a pit of filth. Nothing had changed here. They were still the same poisonous, vapid little meddlers they had always been, like a pack of cruel children let run loose, except children did not kill their playmates when they tired of them or when they were crossed. Truly, Liall was not enjoying his return to Rshan.

Liall made his mouth into something resembling a

smile. "A bear hunt. How considerate of you. I will be sure to attend."

Liall saw their preening and slyness and allowed himself to hate them. Yes, it was a trap. How not? But knowing that it was a snare did not mean he could refuse to go. There were other means of trammeling up an inconvenient prince, but at least this way, Scarlet would not be involved. A bear hunt was for skilled and seasoned trackers, and Liall knew that Scarlet had never killed any beast that large.

Shikhoza sketched Liall a little curtsy, and Liall pretended to admire her dress. "It is a most fetching gown," Liall said. "And how fearless of you to wear such a bright shade. I've heard it washes the color from a mature woman's face."

The implication of encroaching age hit her like a slap. Liall gave her a sunny smile and regretted having to excuse himself when he saw the baron of Tebet waiting for him further down the hall. Shikhoza looked like she had been served a plate of rotten meat.

Liall greeted the baron and led him into the queen's tier for the scheduled meeting, but he could still see Shikhoza's outraged and affronted expression, and he savored the sense of satisfaction he had derived from sticking her back a good one. After a time, though, his gloating turned to depression, and he was sad he had said it and angry with himself for losing his temper. He needed the woman's favor, damn it! Why had he risked it just for the pleasure of insulting her? Rshan seemed to bring out the worst in him.

I do not like myself here, he admitted. I could do nothing else but obey the summons to come, but I do not like it here. I want to leave. I should tell Scarlet that we are not staying, as soon as I see him again.

Hours later, when he returned to the apartments he

had occupied as a young man, Scarlet was fast asleep, and he looked so peaceful that Liall had not the heart to wake him. The next morning, Liall thought better of giving his promise not to stay, for he did not know what the future would bring, and so he said nothing at all.

The next several days passed in a blur of activity. Liall saw little of Scarlet except for late evenings when Liall crawled into bed beside him, and often Scarlet roused enough to bid him a sleepy goodnight or, rarely, to invite him to loveplay. One morning about a week later, Scarlet woke with a headache that persisted for days. So engrossed was Liall in negotiating with the Barons and winning them over to Cestimir that he missed all early signs of what was happening.

A hunting virca wrapped in dove-gray silk arrived with breakfast, a gift from Cestimir. No doubt he had gotten word of the hunt and wished to see his half-brother fitted out well. Or perhaps it was a safety measure. The art of poisoning fabrics was well known in Rshan. Liall thanked Nenos for the package and closed the door, asking Scarlet to pour him another cup of che before he had to be off.

"What's that?"

"It's a hunting virca. See the emblems here? Snow bears."

Scarlet straddled the couch backwards, putting his knees on the cushions and crossing his arms over the headrest, and looked at the odd virca with interest. It was longer and heavier than most garments and also carried the badges of the House of Camira-Druz. Outside, the snow was falling in that slow, sullen way that told Liall it would last for days.

Scarlet watched Liall closely. After the ugly scene at dinner with Shikhoza, Liall had not thought it wise for Scarlet to leave the apartments again. So far, Scarlet had not complained much, but only because Liall had not been there to hear it.

"Are we going hunting?"

"We? Not at all." Liall shook his head. "I am going on a bear hunt," he explained patiently, moving about the apartment.

Scarlet considered this. "With who?"

"Many enemies who wish me dead."

That alarmed him. "Can't you say no?"

"It is not possible for me to refuse," Liall evaded carefully.

"Why?"

"There are some things only a Rshani would understand."

Even Scarlet knew this was true by now, but he gave Liall a look that said he was annoyed. "I don't like it. Something bothers me about it, like a voice in my head warning me to—"

"Hush," Liall begged. "Do not say such things." He opened the wardrobe –an enormous thing of dark, polished wood with red fittings– to put the virca away. "In any case, I will not have you to worry over. You are staying where it's safe."

"No."

Liall did not take his meaning right away. "No?" he asked idly, inspecting the virca. He was only half-listening: one mistake of many.

"I'm going with you."

Liall uttered a short bark of laughter and folded the virca into the wardrobe. He closed it and walked past Scarlet. "That you are not. A bear hunt is no place for a

Hilurin."

"Rshan is no place for a Hilurin, but I'm here," Scarlet said hotly.

Too hotly. Liall thought his irritation out of proportion. He turned to Scarlet with a dark frown beginning. "Calm down. I do not wish to quarrel today. Please cease behaving like a child and accept sense for once."

Scarlet closed his eyes and took a breath before responding. "I'm not a child, a servant, or your property, Liall. Is it still Liall?" He climbed off the couch and took a step towards the tall man. "Or should I call you Prince Nazheradei now?"

Liall's voice was subdued. "I will always be Liall to you."

Scarlet ignored that and crossed his arms over his chest. "I feel like your pet dog locked up in here. I'm sure that's how your new friends see me."

Liall regarded him coldly, and inwardly he was angered that Scarlet should start this again, this petty concern for how others might see him. What did it matter here? He was a Blood Prince and Scarlet his t'aishka and the people must be polite whether it pleased them or not! When was he going to realize they were no longer in Byzantur? Scarlet seemed to cringe a little under Liall's scrutiny, and Liall disliked that. Had he become such a brute to Scarlet?

"They are not new friends, but old ones I am becoming reacquainted with, and I have never locked you in," Liall said, but his calm was slipping.

"No?" Scarlet stalked to the antechamber door and opened it. Nenos was standing there, hands folded and democratically blind. Scarlet slammed the door. "What do you call that?"

"Nenos is there to care for you, to keep you—"

"A prisoner!"

Liall sighed and held his temper in check, but Scarlet

was exasperating him. Liall would never curse the fates that put Scarlet on the ship with him in Volkovoi, but sometimes he was tempted to remind the boy that he had never asked him to come to Rshan. "You are not a prisoner."

"Can I go outside? Can I go to the harbor, on a sleigh ride? Can I even walk beyond these rooms without your permission?"

Liall glanced away uncomfortably, knowing that Scarlet had won a little. Still, as Scarlet claimed, he was not a child, so he must understand that there was only so much freedom one so close to the royal family could have. Liall felt unfairly accused to have to defend this point so often, and he began to tell Scarlet so, but suddenly Scarlet pressed his fingertips to his temples and screwed his eyes shut.

"I just... I want... you can't hold me penned up in here. I have to get out sometimes!" It came out plaintively, and Scarlet's fingers massaged his temples. Liall noted his hands were shaking. "I can't live in a box, I can't. My parents, Deva keep them, tried to pen me in at home, and I couldn't stay, not even for them. I had to be free, and now you... and I can't..."

Liall strode across the room and put his arms around Scarlet. "Enough," he said, greatly ashamed. "You can go. You hear me, Scarlet? You can go on the bear hunt."

Gods, he thought, is this the best I can do? All these years without love, has it changed me into this? This clipped, growling man who snaps when he should be comforting, who answers in anger when he should be thankful?

So much to be thankful for lately, and he was so out of the habit that it was Scarlet's heart that bore the brunt of his stupidity. He would have to learn how to be a lover again.

Scarlet kept his eyes closed and pressed his cheek to the breast of Liall's coat. "It's always so dark here," he mumbled. Then; "My head hurts so."

"I know, love."

After a long moment, Scarlet pulled away and walked a few paces to the window, where he stood staring out at the landscape. "I do not like this place, I think," he sighed out. "And I'm not sure it will ever like me."

Liall tried to ignore what that meant, though it set his heart to beating faster. "Your headache is my fault," he said, turning Scarlet to look at him. "Your people are acclimated to the sun, and you are used to spending all your time outdoors and traveling. You have been deprived of light for weeks now and I have not given one thought that it might affect you badly."

"There are lamps," Scarlet said.

"It is not the same." Scarlet's look was blank and Liall saw that he did not understand. "The Southern Continent is a temperate one and your seasons are mild," he explained. "You have never had to stay inside a great deal of the time because of weather, have you?" Scarlet shook his head. "Here, we have learned that staying inside for too long, deprived of sunlight, will have very bad effects on some of us. On foreigners especially, and you were idle on the ship, too. I think it is finally catching up with you."

"Is that why my head hurts?" Scarlet asked ruefully.

"Probably. We will amend this today," Liall said. Appointments would have to be canceled and apologies made, but there was no other choice. Scarlet was too important to him. Liall called for Nenos.

Scarlet gaped ungraciously. "What's this then?"

The solarium was tiled in light green glass, transparent as water. Overhead, the curved ceiling rained iridescent light upon the two men in a bright wash. It was also quite empty, this one being for the queen's use alone, and Scarlet relaxed visibly.

"How's it work?" Scarlet walked to the wall and touched one of the square tiles. Beyond the first glass wall was the wall of mirrors, a second false wall that served to intensify the light from the reflector above. Scarlet peered closely at the glass, trying to see beyond it. "It's like looking into the pond back home."

"Forget the pond. Come here." Liall pushed Scarlet into a large and airy chair that sat squarely in the center of the round floor. The chair was woven from summer reeds and much too large for the small Hilurin seated in it. Scattered about the room were earthen pots containing green plants and flowering vines, and their scent perfumed the air. "You must come here a little every day at first, and sit with your eyes open. After you feel better, you can come every other day, and so on."

Scarlet looked doubtful. "I still don't see how plain light cures a headache."

Liall kissed the top of Scarlet's head and drew his hand down his lover's face tenderly, regretting that he had spared so little time for Scarlet since they arrived. They were barely lovers, and already Liall was ignoring the most basic of duties he owed Scarlet. "You have much to learn here. I will ask Jochi about your education."

That announcement did not have the desired effect. Scarlet scowled. "I ain't a fucking draft horse you can curry and primp into drawing a carriage," he said crudely. "So stop trying. I don't need Jochi to teach me anything more than how to speak your damned gibberish."

"That will take years."

"Watch and see."

All Liall had meant to do was show concern for him, but Scarlet had taken it to mean Liall wanted to change him. Liall wondered if he really did want to change Scarlet, and how much, and why.

"I apologize," Liall said, mentally shoving the tangle aside for later. "I do love you the way you are, Scarlet."

That mollified Scarlet a little. He looked up at the shining arc of the dome. "So this helps?"

"It will, if you follow my advice," Liall said, careful not to frame it like an order. "There are certain foods and herbs that will help also. I will see to it."

Scarlet sighed. "And I'll have to let you, for I don't know a thing about it."

Liall's hand sought the soft nape of Scarlet's neck as they stood together. He caressed there, easing the tight, tense muscles. "You never had a need to learn before."

Scarlet leaned back into Liall's touch, eyes closing. "But I do now." He looked up at Liall. "Right?"

Liall leaned over, bracing his arm on the back of the chair, and pressed soft, lingering kisses along the line of Scarlet's jaw and over his chin. "Remember when we first met, and you refused me a kiss?"

Scarlet huffed a sound of amusement. "Wise of me, recalling the first time we did kiss. I bit you."

"What about the second time?"

Scarlet's wicked grin made Liall shiver. "Now that was a kiss, ugly mariners watching and all."

Liall kissed the ink-black line of one eyebrow and then the other. "Now that I think on it, the kiss on the deck of the Ostre Sul was our third kiss. The second time, you were not even conscious." Liall saw Scarlet did not understand him. "When I found you with Cadan, you had ceased to breathe," Liall said softly.

Dark eyes stared back at him, and Liall marveled again how much their color could hide, how many secrets could be contained in a look, a glance.

"How did you...?"

"Like this." Liall blew a short, light breath against his lips. "A mariner's trick, for those drowned. You opened your eyes and said my name."

"Liall."

He nodded. "Your wolf of a Kasiri, as I will always be." Liall fussed the edge of Scarlet's silk collar, slightly rumpled, back into place. "It is Scarlet of Lysia I love. Scarlet the pedlar, with a patched crimson coat. Learn all you wish here, or nothing. I will love you no matter what. But can you love a fool of a prince?"

It seemed to be what Scarlet needed to hear. He gripped Liall's collar and pulled the prince down for a longer kiss, on the mouth this time. "I liked you well enough as a bastard of a bandit Kasiri," he said, his dark eyes glittering mischievously. "I guess I can love a prince."

"Rake," Liall accused, stealing another sweet taste from his mouth.

Scarlet pushed him away, laughing, and Liall followed his pointed look downwards. "I think we should stop."

"Hm. Yes. It would not do to have the queen or her attendants walk in on us, although it might be fun."

Scarlet pushed him away more firmly and tried to change the subject. "So, do I get a virca like yours for hunting?"

Liall was already beginning to regret his reckless promise. "For your own sake, you might reconsider joining the hunt. It is very dangerous, t'aishka. Will you not at least think about staying behind?"

Scarlet's answer was to grin at him. "It's not my fault if you make promises in haste and regret them later." He flopped back in the chair. "So, how long am I supposed to sit here?"

The nightmare was unformed, all shadows and blood and faces drawn in fear or pain, like the half-thoughts that devil a person just before waking. Scarlet woke, knowing only that he had dreamed of horses and snow, and of seeing Liall racing ahead on his mount while Scarlet shouted for him to stop. Scarlet's heartbeat thundered and he sat up quickly, a cry echoing in his ears.

"Liall?" he called. He pulled the bed-curtains aside, but Liall was not there.

The outer door opened immediately and Nenos stood there. Gods, did the man never sleep? Nenos approached the bed anxiously.

"Ser? *Un huna hircenge'kaya th'hus?*"

"What? No, I'm... it was a dream." Nenos shook his head, and Scarlet made a formless motion in the air. "You understand? Dream?"

He shook his head. *"Cenge'kaya?"*

Scarlet dropped his hands. "Like talking to a badger, it is." he sighed and imitated the motion he had seen Liall use, the one of dismissal. It worked like a charm, and Nenos bowed out of the room.

Rising, Scarlet found his robe and went to curl up in the chair beside the fire to wait out the rest of the night. He did not want to risk going back to sleep and dreaming again, not like that, and there was a heaviness all around his heart, as if the dream were a warning.

After an hour or so, he heard the door open again and turned to see Nenos. Nenos seemed surprised to see him still awake, and approached and bowed before speaking softly in Sinha. Scarlet understood very little more Sinha than he had before they landed, but he was getting to know Nenos's intonations. He shook his head. No, he didn't want anything.

Nenos studied his face for a moment and withdrew. He returned in a short time with a tray that held che and some cold biscuits with poppy seeds sprinkled on them. Scarlet sighed inwardly, but thanked Nenos and told him to go away again. Scarlet sat there under the window and let the che get cold, brooding and thinking.

Nenos left him alone, but came in a while later. Seeing the untouched tray, he frowned, and spoke to Scarlet softly, questioningly. Scarlet shook his head and waved him away impatiently. Nenos left again, but Scarlet could tell he was not happy about it.

Only a few minutes later, the outer door opened and he heard Nenos let someone in. The lamplight from the hall flooded the room, and Jochi, rumpled and obviously just roused from his bed, stood there bowing to Scarlet. "Can I be of service, ser?"

Scarlet sighed, exasperated and near anger.

Jochi frowned. "What's amiss, ser?" he persisted.

"Nothing. I'm fine, honestly. I don't know why they bothered you. I just had a foul dream."

Jochi smiled again and took the chair opposite Scarlet's. Nenos closed the door softly. "It is never a bother to serve a member of the royal family. Nenos knows that Prince Nazheradei cannot be disturbed at the moment, so he sent for me."

Scarlet snorted and looked at the fire. Cannot be disturbed? Why? "I'm not a member of the royal family."

"Strictly speaking, no, but in Rshan, appearances can matter almost as much as reality. You are a foreigner, yet you enjoy a protected status from Prince Nazheradei and you were accepted by our Queen."

"What does that mean, protected status?"

"Of course, a Hilurin would need to be protected in Rshan. You know we do not allow foreigners here."

"What would happen to me if I didn't have this status from the prince?"

Jochi looked vastly unhappy. "You would be killed, ser." He looked away, seeming embarrassed. "I am sorry, but that is our law. No lenilyn may set foot on Rshani soil without permission from the reigning monarch. Even then, the people do not like it."

"Why the hell not?" Scarlet was getting a little angry. "What did we ever do to you that made your people hate us so much?"

"Oh, we... they do not hate you, ser," Jochi said, excluding himself from the lot of them. "They fear you."

Scarlet blinked, trying to mask his surprise, and Jochi watched him closely.

"You did not know?"

Jochi had been sincere with him so far, so Scarlet decided to answer honestly. "No," he said. "I didn't know. I feel like I'm in a story, or a dream that I can't wake up from." He studied his hands next, tired of looking into the fire, which seemed to wink at him with mocking red eyes. "I've always had a gift with languages, but Sinha is unlike anything I've ever tried to learn before. I'm afraid it will be a long time before I can really talk to people here. And I'm used to talking to new people, being able to exchange stories and ideas with them. Now it seems all I have are you and Liall, and Liall is seldom here." Scarlet knew he sounded pouting and immature, and so he deliberately pasted a smile on his face. "It's not that I'm homesick," he said. "I'm never homesick. But at this moment, I want nothing more than to see sunsets and mountains again."

Jochi's expression was sympathetic. "Prince Nazheradei has many important matters to attend to. He had many friends and allies when he lived in Rshan. He is a trained warrior, and more than that; an adept and practiced leader, a skill that comes naturally to him. People trust his judgment."

Jochi told him nothing he did not already know from witnessing Liall with the Kasiri. "Why did he leave his home for a life in Byzantur?"

Jochi shook his head regretfully. "I cannot tell you that, ser, and I am sorry for it."

"Can you at least tell me what he's doing when he's away all the time? Is he going to be king?"

Jochi looked scandalized. "Indeed not!"

Not the answer he expected. Wasn't Liall a prince the same as Cestimir, and older? "Oh...well. Why did he come back, then?"

Jochi was silent for a long moment, and then shook his head almost angrily. "Prince Nazheradei wants you kept apart from this, but I cannot see the harm in telling you what everyone at court already knows. Keeping so much basic knowledge from you may prove disastrous at some point, as your question just proved. What if you had asked me that publicly?" He leaned forward. "See? You don't even know why that would be dangerous. I will tell you what I can, most of which is common knowledge in any home in Rshan. Prince Cestimir is the Crown Prince, next in line for the throne of Rshan. His father, Lankomir, was half-brother to Queen Nadiushka's late husband."

"Liall's father was her first husband?"

"The same."

"Did he die a long time ago?"

Jochi nodded. "Yes. A few months before Prince Nazheradei was born."

So Liall had never known his father. "How?"

"By misadventure. A snow bear hunt, so I understand. The queen married Lankomir some years ago. They had several other children together, but none who lived beyond their second year. Prince Cestimir is their only child who thrived."

Liall's father had died on a bear hunt? No wonder he seemed so unsettled by the prospect of one. *And no wonder he didn't want you to go,* Scarlet thought with a little twinge of guilt, remembering how he had accused Liall of trying to box him up. "But I thought Eleferi—"

"He is Prince Cestimir's half-brother, the son of Lankomir by his first wife, as is Eleferi's elder brother, Vladei."

Scarlet frowned again. "Liall said that name once. I got the feeling he didn't like Vladei much."

Jochi smiled a little. "No, he wouldn't. That's partly because Vladei, being a nephew to Nadiushka's first husband, the dead king, has a claim to the throne of Rshan that some might accept as more valid than Cestimir's."

Scarlet wondered if that's all there was to it. "Does he want to be king, this Vladei?"

"You may depend on it."

"Do the people like him more than they like Cestimir?"

"That's not a very relevant question when it comes to royal politics. The barons know Vladei and most dislike him, but they don't know Cestimir at all. They don't know what to expect of him, and he's still very young. Vladei is a grown man. All these currents are why Prince Nazheradei is here."

"So he can convince them to support Cestimir."

Jochi nodded approval. "Very astute. An endorsement by Prince Nazheradei, along with his promise of support and guidance as Regent, would go very far in securing Prince Cestimir's future."

"What happens if he can't convince them?"

"Then I think, ser, you will be getting your wish to see

sunsets again very quickly."

And what would that mean for Cestimir? The affairs of princes and kings were above his head, but Scarlet knew that few rulers would tolerate having another candidate for the throne alive and well. Would Cestimir have to leave? What would Liall say to that?

"But," Scarlet said, struggling to put all these kings and princes together in his head "If the queen is Liall's mother the same as Cestimir, why isn't Liall next in line? Was his father unacceptable in some way?"

"I am sorry I cannot tell you more," Jochi said softly, rising from his chair. "Is there truly nothing else I can do for you?"

Scarlet sank back into the deep cushions, looking up at Jochi coldly. "No, thank you."

Jochi bowed. "Then I will bid you a good night. Do try and rest. I am certain the prince will return soon."

Scarlet nodded. He stared into the hearth and scowled, again feeling that even the fires seemed to watch him here, like everyone else. *Glare at me all you want, eyes. You can't fright a pedlar, no matter how far he is from home.*

The night closed in on him after that, and in the wee hours of the morning the fire died down and the room grew chilly. Scarlet rose and poked at the fire, but he had neglected it too long and the coals were scarce. Piling more wood on it would just put it out, and calling for Nenos did not appeal to him. He looked around the room, making sure all the outer doors were closed, and then placed several logs from the neat stack in the iron bin on top of the guttering coals.

Scarlet closed his eyes and held his hand over the cold wood, his lips moving in a silent invocation of Deva, summoning a fire withy. The withy spell flowed from his hands like warm water, a small stream of flame that slid into the coals. The coals flared and the seasoned wood hissed as the supernatural fire kindled the hearth into a neat blaze in seconds. Satisfied, Scarlet wrapped his robe tighter around him and returned to the couch.

He did finally sleep, dozing in the chair until Liall shook him awake enough to stumble back to the bed. He was too tired to mention nightmares and vague fears to Liall, so he just curled up around the prince and closed his eyes.

Scarlet slept late that day, and when he was awake and dressed he walked into the common room and stopped in his tracks, surprised to see that Liall was still there, seated at the table with a large breakfast laid out in front of him.

"You are awake," Liall called out, smiling and motioning for Scarlet to come forward. "Join me."

Scarlet had dressed in brown breeches and a plain red hapcoat and shirt that closed in the front rather than the sides, so he needed no help with the endless laces. He suspected that Liall had provided it, knowing how he hated to ask Nenos or one of the servants to help him dress.

Liall began heaping dishes in front of Scarlet as soon as he sat down. There were pastries served with preserves, a spiced porridge, thick slabs of meat, cooked only until it was no longer bloody but still pink, smoked fish, and some kind of eggs served with a sauce.

"Try some of this," Liall said, piling more on.

"I can't eat all that," Scarlet protested, staring at it.

"You should," he said critically. "You have lost more weight, I think. It is very cold here. You must eat more than you are accustomed to."

"I haven't been doing any work, so I haven't been hungry."

Liall grinned meaningfully. "Food is fuel, and we have burned some since we arrived, I do believe." His good humor seemed to have returned and he grinned at Scarlet boyishly. "Try some of this," he said, and speared a bit of fish. He held it out to Scarlet at the end of a fork. "It is especially good for you during the winter, when the sun does not shine."

Scarlet leaned forward to take the morsel between his teeth. He chewed thoughtfully. He thought he would never touch salted fish again, but this was tender and smoky and quite good: leagues away from the leathery, cured fish they had on the ship.

They worked their way through the rest of the food in companionable silence. Scarlet did not like the eggs with the sauce on them, but the meat was good, and the porridge with thick, rich cream. The pastries were sweet, but he liked more savory foods, and the fish remained his favorite.

"Now that is a proper Rshani meal," Liall finally pronounced as he sipped at a steaming cup of che.

Scarlet was so full he was afraid he would roll if he got up. He told Liall as much, and the prince laughed and made a joke in Sinha that Scarlet understood a little of, save that it was crude. He kicked Liall a little under the table. Nenos came in as Liall was feigning hurt and the old man chuckled and shook his head. Nenos gestured to the servants to clear and left them alone again.

Scarlet sipped his che. "I will be useless as a pedlar if I get used to luxury."

"Scant luxury in the Byzan hills," Liall agreed, but not unhappily.

Scarlet glanced at the thick, silken-soft wool of the draperies and the warm furs piled on the couch. "If only your people were not so determined to stay isolated. I've never seen such fine things, not even in Morturii. If only they would trade with us."

"We do some trading with the Minh, mostly through

the Morturii in the port of Sondek, and on the other side of the channel with the Volken and the Arbyssians."

"Why not with Byzantur? I find it odd that so many of the royal court speaks Bizye, but there are no Byzans here and you do no trade with us."

"It is a long story. Ask me some other time," Liall evaded, draining the last of the che from his cup. "Perhaps in the future, Rshan and Byzantur will be reconciled. For now, I must go."

"And secure Cestimir's future?"

Liall froze, and then turned to Scarlet with a hard line etched between his white eyebrows. "Someone has been talking," he said.

"It's no more than every housewife in Rshan knows, according to Jochi."

"I will have a talk with Jochi," Liall said ominously.

"You're being a want-wit," Scarlet said, putting his cup down and rising. "I can see keeping some things from me, secrets and the like, but you're taking it too far. What are you afraid I'll find out?"

Liall looked like he had been struck. "I am not... afraid. I am merely protecting you."

"For Deva's sake, from what?" Liall's reaction puzzled him. "Liall," he began, but Liall abruptly turned away and went into the large cupola adjacent to the bedroom, a dressing room he called it, and set about garbing in his court plumage: a long, sky-blue silk virca that hung in folds around his knees, a gold ring in his ear and more on his hands, and a necklace dripping with crystals that Scarlet swore belonged on a woman. Liall had to tuck his homely necklace of a leather thong strung with two cheap Byzan copper coins inside his virca to wear the crystal necklace, and the very sight of those coins made Scarlet wistful. Scarlet had given them to Liall to pay for his toll through a bandit road. He longed to see Liall again as the

man had been on the Nerit: a bandit atya with a tribe of
Kasiri at his back. That Liall had been rough and arrogant
and ill-mannered, but Scarlet was beginning to believe he
preferred a bandit to this cold prince.

"Now that you know why I am here," Liall said
distantly, smoothing his silken clothes. "You will forgive
me for leaving so quickly. The future of a kingdom is
important."

Liall strode past him to the door. Scarlet had half a
mind to go after him, but wisdom prevailed. If Scarlet
had not known better, he would have said that Liall really
was afraid.

With Liall gone, Nenos tried to deck Scarlet out in
much the same way as Liall had dressed. Scarlet objected
to the long, green velvet virca shot with red beads that
Nenos tried to stuff him in. Nenos kept insisting, an
opinion seconded by Jochi when he arrived.

"Many of the barons are at court now," Jochi said
gravely, "And Prince Nazheradei would have his affection
and respect for you be noticed. One way, ser Scarlet, is in
your style of dress."

"And just when would they see me?"

"Today, when I give you a tour of the Nauhinir."

"Oh." A tour! Even through his excitement at the
prospect of getting to see the palace at last, Scarlet felt
misgiving. "Why can't I just wear a hapcoat over a shirt
and breeches?" The long coats were much less fancy and,
he thought, looked more suited to a man.

"Hapcoats are less formal, ser. Vircas are more
appropriate for audiences."

"My sister has a dress like this, did I tell you that? For
that's what it is, you know, a dress! I feel like a mummer
in this get-up. Or worse."

Jochi's eyebrows went up, as if to ask what could be
worse than a mummer.

Scarlet jerked the hem of the green virca on the bed. "I'd look like I was selling in this!"

"Selling what, ser?"

Scarlet began to think Jochi might be making fun of him. Jochi grinned and bowed from the waist, his right arm folded over his midsection in the Rshani gesture of politeness Scarlet was beginning to recognize.

"Forgive me," he said. "I was only teasing you. You have a very open smile, did you know?"

Scarlet wouldn't answer him, feeling very misused by his mocking, and Jochi tried to paste on a sympathetic expression.

"There's no hope for it, ser. This is what stands for formal male garb in Rshan. Shall we begin?"

Scarlet cursed in gutter Falx, which he knew Jochi would not understand: "I'll look like a poxed bhoros whore, but I'll wear it!"

So he submitted to the ridiculous green virca, red beads and all. Later on, in the corridors, Scarlet found he was glad of all the layers. Gilded cage or not, they were only a few feet away from their apartments before he realized how much warmer Liall kept his quarters than other Rshani. Scarlet suspected it was on his account. The air in the corridors was cool enough to turn the tip of his nose pink, and before long he was glad he had eaten a large breakfast, for Jochi kept him moving for hours, taking him into room after room full of the tall, pale-haired, glittering folk who nodded and bowed and called him *Keriss* in their soft voices.

The Nauhinir would be difficult for even a poet to describe. There were walls and floors and ceilings, like any dwellings, but of such strange design and such unusual materials and colors that they scarcely appeared to be real. A wall was not a wall here, not simply a brace to hold the roof up, but a chance to illustrate and dazzle, to make one stare in dumbstruck awe.

Of all the things Scarlet saw that day, one stood out sharply in his mind: the midnight-blue floor of the entrance to the Inner Court, which was made entirely of small, painted tiles, each tile different and distinct, and together they made a vast mural of the floor. It was a rendering of the night sky of Rshan, with each star a painted bit of gold or silver, and through it all threaded a web of cloudy blue and pink and luminescent green strands. He asked Jochi what they were.

"That is the ostre sul, the light in the darkness."

"We traveled here on a ship by that same name."

Jochi nodded. "Many ships bear a variant of that title. It's considered lucky. As for what it is, it is a celestial phenomenon that occurs often, though it is only visible when the sky is clear."

It had been overcast and snowing almost constantly since they made landfall. Scarlet peered at the floor, stepping back and forth across the blue tiles to see it from different angles. "How can there be threads of light spread out across the sky? Who hangs them there, and how?"

"It is a long account," Jochi said patiently. "Later, if you are still interested, I will try to explain."

Which meant that Jochi wanted to keep moving. Scarlet followed Jochi through massive arches of gilded columns weaving together at the crown like the limbs of trees, past screens of fine iron scrollwork, so thin they were like spider-strands, and into a round, domed chamber that reminded him slightly of a castle room he had seen once in Morturii, although it was nothing as fine as this. The walls were hung with wool tapestries dyed in many colors and there were dozens of the blue crystal lamps he had seen so many of, hung from the ceiling and perched on tall pedestals built just for them. A fire blazed in the most

massive fireplace he had ever seen. There were many court
folk in the palace, all dressed in the elaborate Rshani style
that Scarlet was beginning to gain some knowledge of.

They entered the Inner Court and the drone of chatter
came to a standstill. Jochi murmured to Scarlet, reminding
him that he must bow to them only slightly.

"You must not bow lower than that," he had told
Scarlet previously, in the corridor, after yet another
blunder. "For you are the prince's t'aishka, his twice-
chosen, and as such, you hold rank higher than theirs."

Scarlet was dismayed and almost told Jochi that he
was only a pedlar who had lived in a four-room cottage
all his life, but something wiser warned him to keep his
mouth closed.

Facing down a new pack of unknowns, Scarlet bowed
slightly and waited for Jochi to introduce him around.
Meaningless names were put to him, Rshani sounds
without the depth of familiarity that a Byzan name would
have yielded. He nodded and tried to keep them straight,
but it was impossible. He also repeated his stock phrase –
edsite' hnn? – so many times that he was sure that *I don't
understand* would be the only words he would ever be
using correctly in Sinha.

"Tesk," said one tall courtier –they were all tall!– in
a silken virca that seemed to be made entirely of intricate
embroidery. He stuck out his big hand for Scarlet to shake
and spoke without preamble. "I am an artist. You must
allow me to paint your portrait."

Scarlet was so taken aback at hearing Bizye and being
given a name that was not nine syllables long that he
shook Tesk's hand before Jochi could stop him. "Scarlet,"
he answered, remembering that at least.

"Oh, you need no introduction, ser Keriss. We all
know who *you* are." Tesk glanced at Scarlet's hand, which
was engulfed by his, and turned it this way and that. "So

small. Such color. Are all Anlyribeth like you?"

"Your pardon?"

Tesk said something in Sinha and Scarlet could only look at him blankly, a little intimidated by the line of people waiting behind Tesk, and wondering if there were going to be more misunderstandings with language. Scarlet tried to gloss it over. "Well, anyroad, nice to meet you."

Tesk smiled and Scarlet saw that he was handsome and resembled Liall a little.

"Just Tesk?" Scarlet asked, retrieving his hand.

"First meetings are so fragile. Why burden them with impossible names?" Tesk shrugged and the green peacocks embroidered on his collar moved up and down.

He was the first Rshani who admitted his language was unpronounceable to Byzans. Scarlet smiled back at him. "I'll never remember them all."

"No one expects you to." Tesk glanced over his shoulder, seeing the mass of people still waiting to greet Scarlet or stare at him. "Oh dear, I'm holding up the line," Tesk sighed. He gave a deep bow that Scarlet returned. "And please, dear boy, cease repeating the names spoken to you," Tesk murmured, when their heads were close. "You called the man in front of me a wet, hairy chair."

Scarlet laughed and Tesk winked at him before moving off. In the corner of Scarlet's eye, Jochi hovered close, seeming not pleased at all. Scarlet suspected Jochi would have words for him later.

They wended their way throughout the morning like that, and then, just as Scarlet was almost wishing to be put back in the damned cage again, they reached another door.

Jochi drew himself up and looked at Scarlet seriously. "This is your most important audience," he said. "But do not try to speak Sinha at all. I will translate for you."

Scarlet felt a sliver of apprehension. "Audience?" he asked, but Jochi opened the door on a room full of women who turned as one and looked at them with their alluring, blue-painted eyes. One of these was Lady Shikhoza, who smiled thinly at Jochi but ignored Scarlet. All bowed, nearly as deeply as they had to Liall, and Scarlet strove to execute the short, perfect bow that Jochi had lessoned him at.

He must have succeeded, for Jochi smiled at him sidelong and guided him to an inner door painted with red lacquer. "This is the second tier," Jochi said almost in a whisper.

Scarlet could feel the Lady's eyes on him, sharp with malice, and shivered as he went through the door. The room within was astonishing, scarlet and gold everywhere, and he blinked in the lamplight. A woman's voice spoke and Jochi bowed very, very low. Scarlet turned in that direction and his heart nearly stopped. It was the queen.

He began to bow as low as Jochi, but Jochi flicked a hand out to stop him. "Remember," he murmured.

But she was the queen! Still, Jochi had not misled him yet, and so he followed the advice and bowed shortly. She motioned them forward, speaking to Jochi again.

Jochi smiled faintly. "Queen Nadiushka welcomes Keriss kir Nazheradei to Rshan na Ostre."

Scarlet gave Jochi a puzzled look, clearly out to sea about the whole thing. What *was* that damned thing they kept calling him? Keriss? What did it mean?

"That is your court name, ser Scarlet. Keriss. The queen has decided this, and it is what I must call you from this moment on. Please do not take offense at this. It is meant to be an honor."

"Tell her, um, thank you very kindly." Scarlet felt like a fool and slightly annoyed. Change my name and not ask me? Not so much as a by-your-leave? What's wrong with my own name?

Nadiushka was a beautiful woman, albeit frail in appearance, but there was nothing frail about her power of will. It burned in her like a flame, so bright that Scarlet almost felt he could warm himself by it. Liall had her eyes, which were a bright but pale azure, like the descriptions of the Southern Sea.

Scarlet remembered his manners and bowed again. "Your Majesty," he said, a little uncertain. They called the Flower Prince so, as well as Divinity, but he was not sure how to address a monarch here.

Jochi looked both amused and impressed and translated. Her laugh was musical but not unkind. She gestured to a nearby chair.

"The queen says you are very gallant and desires that you be seated," Jochi said quietly. "And be comfortable."

Scarlet sat in the large chair that dwarfed his smaller frame. It was deeply padded and felt wonderful to sink into, and he had to remind himself not to slouch. The queen gestured to Jochi, and Jochi bowed and moved across the room to a door, where he spoke softly for a moment to someone unseen.

Jochi returned. "We will have refreshment momentarily," he told Scarlet.

Scarlet hoped it was not the eggs and sauce dish again. The queen spoke and Jochi listened, then turned to Scarlet. "The queen wishes to know if Lady Shikhoza has been less than courteous."

Scarlet's tongue clove itself to the roof of his mouth. He stared at Jochi mutely.

"You must tell her the truth," Jochi said. "You see the ring on her hand? We call it the Stone of Truth, and legend says that whosoever wears it shall have the gift of discernment."

Scarlet felt another sliver of superstitious apprehension run up his spine. The Shining Ones, Liall had said. Perhaps she had the ring from them. "She seemed to be courteous," he said cautiously. Jochi translated.

The queen studied him, stretching her hands over the arms of her chair. Her eyes grew less kind, though one corner of her mouth curved slightly. She spoke to Jochi in a different tone, almost like a command.

"Queen Nadiushka says you are to be commended for your tactfulness, but she would have all the truth, not merely part of it."

Hells. Scarlet began to sweat. "Majesty, I can't be sure, I don't speak your tongue and I may have misunderstood her."

Jochi translated and arched an eyebrow at Scarlet. "Please, continue."

Scarlet swallowed hard. "Or I may not. She gave me a phrase to answer the Baron who sat across from me, and he wasn't very happy with what I said."

Her eyes did not release Scarlet. Jochi spoke, and then she to him, turn and turn again, ignoring Scarlet for the moment.

The door opened and a woman came in bearing a tray. To Scarlet's relief, the queen and Jochi continued conferring as the woman served him. Not the eggs, but the little dumplings he had liked. He did not eat, however, and the queen broke off from her discussion and gestured at Scarlet.

"Please, ser, you must enjoy," Jochi said. "The queen made special inquiries of Nenos."

"But," Scarlet began, and Jochi shook his head very fractionally.

Stifling a sigh, he took a bite of the dumplings –they were even better than the ones he had before– and Jochi and Nadiushka continued their conversation. Jochi's tone was calm, comfortable, as if he conferred with queens every day. What did he know of this palace or these people? Scarlet wanted to learn about them but they were the oddest folk. He could get more warmth from a stone at the bottom of a cold river.

"The queen wishes you to know something about the Lady Shikhoza," Jochi finally said, turning to Scarlet with a warning look in his eye. "She was, many years ago, betrothed to Prince Nazheradei, but the engagement was broken."

Scarlet blinked. "Oh."

Nadiushka's eyebrows went up.

"Oh?" Jochi was interested now.

"I was just thinking, perhaps it explains her deception, if it was deception. Did she love the prince very much?"

Jochi was definitely amused. He bit his lip and spoke to Nadiushka again, and she answered him in clipped tones. "The queen says that Lady Shikhoza loved the prince's rank more than she loved him, and now her pride is stung. You must not take account of it or waste sympathy upon her."

Well, that was plain speaking. Scarlet relaxed. Nadiushka gestured again.

"She asks also if it is merely rumor that you did not know Nazheradei's true name and rank before you came to these lands." Jochi's expression was bland.

Scarlet stared at the man, desperate for a hint. It was Jochi himself who had warned him to avoid giving out too much information about Liall. But this is his mother, Scarlet thought. Will she be angry at Liall if I tell her the truth? Will Liall be angry at me if I give something away? How can I know?

"The truth," Jochi murmured.

"I didn't know," he said, hoping he was doing the right thing. "I knew him as Liall, only."

The queen looked at Scarlet silently for a long moment, and then asked a question.

"She wishes to know if you were angry when you discovered the truth," Jochi asked.

"No... or not all that much. I was shocked and puzzled, and we do quarrel sometimes," he blurted, Jochi translating everything smoothly and instantly. "Liall says it's because we are both proud and have sharp tempers."

Nadiushka leaned forward. She touched Scarlet's hand delicately and spoke several very somber sentences.

Jochi translated: "The queen offers her sympathy. She says her son is willful, proud, arrogant, and indeed has a sharp temper. She asks if it makes you angry when he grows too overbearing, and how you prevent him from repeating the behavior."

"I... uh," he stammered. *How in the hells do I answer that?* "Well, I'm working on it."

Nadiushka turned and reached for something atop a table draped in silver silk. The lamplight gleamed on it, scattering blue light, and Scarlet realized it was a necklace like a spider's web of silver hung with precious blue stones. Sapphires, he believed, like the one Liall wore in his ear. She spread it with her hands so Scarlet might see it, and then beckoned him forward.

"You may go to one knee," Jochi whispered, and Scarlet did, though he resented it. All these rules about bowing and scraping. No wonder Liall tired of it.

She held the necklace up in front of him and spoke to Jochi at length. Scarlet blinked as she lowered it over his head to arrange it over his shoulders and neck.

"What's this?" he muttered aside to Jochi. "What am I supposed to do?"

"It is an heirloom of the queen's family. It was to be given to the Lady Shikhoza on the occasion of her wedding, but that day never came."

Scarlet almost jerked away. "Why in hells is she giving it to me?" he hissed.

"One does not question a Queen's motives."

"One does not but I by-the-gods may! I've seen enough of Shikhoza to know I don't want her as an enemy."

Jochi's face was immobile. "You have no choice in whom Shikhoza decides to dislike, and you cannot refuse a gift from the queen."

Scarlet sighed and bowed his head, cursing inwardly. If he could only speak to her!

Nadiushka's expression softened and she gestured for Scarlet to rise. Jochi spoke to her for a moment.

"I have told her that you feel some anxiety over the gift, ser Keriss."

He bowed. "Not anxious exactly, your Majesty. I'm a common man and I'm unused to being given without earning. I also don't know why I should have so great a gift, but... but I thank you for the honor," he finished awkwardly. The cool weight of the necklace felt strange on his neck.

Nadiushka spoke a last time to Jochi and leaned back wearily.

"The queen wishes you to wear her gift tonight in the great hall," Jochi said.

Scarlet felt a prickle of misgiving and resentment as he bowed again. The whole audience had been strange and fraught with foreign nuances he did not yet understand, and he knew the necklace was either intended to test him or buy him, for what ultimate purpose he could not guess. Her mention of Shikhoza threw him, as did the fact that the Lady had once almost been Liall's wife.

This old queen is too wily for me, he thought.

With a faint smile, she raised her hand in dismissal. Jochi bowed, Scarlet bowed yet again, and Jochi guided him back out.

On the way, they passed the group of chattering ladies again, and Shikhoza's eyes went immediately to the glittering necklace. Nor was she the only one to notice. She turned aside to one of her companions and whispered something that made the woman cover her mouth in shock, her eyes wide. Shikhoza glanced back to Scarlet, her painted mouth curving, and he was suddenly glad he didn't know what was said.

Scarlet fingered the necklace doubtfully during the long walk back to their apartments. The nagging feeling remained that he was a staked goat in this palace, with everyone waiting to see which way he turned towards danger. It made him resentful and angry, and he grew more so with every step back to the apartment. Liall was there when they arrived, standing in front of the fire and holding his hands out to the warmth.

Scarlet took off the necklace and dropped it into Liall's hands. "Your mother gave me this. I'm not sure why."

Liall shot Jochi an unreadable look. Jochi bowed low and immediately withdrew, closing the door behind him.

"What is this about?" Liall asked calmly, sliding the jewels across his palm.

"Why didn't you tell me who Shikhoza was?"

Liall went very still. "I didn't think you would need to know so soon," he said at last. His voice had gone coldly blank in that way he had, the way that told Scarlet that he was not open to questions. "It was a very long time ago. Let us be calm while you tell me what happened."

It was far from apology, but Scarlet had a feeling he would not offer that anyway. Liall listened as he described his audience with the queen.

"And she didn't speak Bizye, Liall," Scarlet fumed. "I couldn't think how to explain that I didn't want her necklace, not without knowing why she gave it." He looked askance at Liall. "She asked me things about you, and again I didn't know what to say."

Liall frowned. "My mother speaks perfect Bizye."

Scarlet froze, casting his mind backward. Had he said anything offensive? He couldn't remember. "Oh, Deva," he moaned, sinking into a chair.

Liall was thoughtfully running his fingers over the smooth stones, the silver webbing as flexible as silk in his hands. "This belonged to my grandfather, King Lukaska. My mother adored him," he said quietly. "Perhaps she just means to show her favor to you."

"She means to put a broadside into Shikhoza, you mean. And at my expense. Just don't seat me next to any more fat barons."

Liall sat beside him. "Little fear of that. If I know my mother, she will want you to sit at the high table tonight, right where your pretty necklace can sparkle the lamplight into Shikhoza's eyes."

Scarlet made a strangled sound. "Gods, does she hate me?"

"No. But she does not know you. Strange as it seems, this is her way of finding out who you are." Liall smiled a little. "I do not endorse her methods, but I am proud of the way you acquitted yourself today. She would not have given you this if she did not approve of you."

"I'll let you know my opinion of her."

His eyebrows went up a little. "When might I expect this report?"

Scarlet elbowed him, not gently. He *oofed* and chuckled. They sat in silence for a while until Nenos entered the room and bowed.

"Time to dress," Liall said to Scarlet's questioning look.

"What, again? Hells!"

Nenos had more velvet and satin for him, which was beginning to feel less stifling. Liall, already dressed and glittering in a pitch black virca with silver trim, watched silently as Scarlet was laced and chivvied into another black virca that felt like it weighed a ton. Scarlet's clothing was smaller and there were differences in the swirling silver embroidery on the front pleats, but they were near enough to matching that Scarlet did a double take when he saw Liall and himself side by side in the mirror.

Liall turned to admire Scarlet with his own eyes. Liall ran his hands over the soft fabric covering Scarlet's chest, and his arms slid around Scarlet's neck. Only then did Scarlet realize that Liall was fastening the necklace around his throat.

"Keriss kir Nazheradei," Liall said softly, as if trying it out. "I like your true name better, and I like your red pedlar's coat, but we must wear different skins while we are here."

Scarlet sighed, giving a little against his will. Liall had that effect on him. "This is very strange to me. Not at all what I expected to find."

"What did you expect?"

He shrugged. "What I've always known, I think. A good, hard road during the day, and at the end of it a simple meal and a bed if I'm lucky. New faces, new lands, new things to see."

"Well, you have the latter at least. And much more than a simple meal and a plain bed. Does that truly displease you?"

Scarlet hesitated. "I don't know," he confessed. "It's very... interesting here, but I'm not sure I could get used to it. And you're not exactly yourself, either."

"Explain."

"You're colder."

Liall paled a little. "I do not mean to be, I am just... I am afraid, Scarlet."

That nearly made Scarlet laugh. What could fright

Liall? "You? Of what, for Deva's sake?"

Liall bit his lip, looking down at Scarlet, his hands on Scarlet's shoulders. "I value your opinion of me very much."

Hells, what was this? "It's still in one piece."

"What if people were to say things about me? That I was not a good man, or that I had killed someone?"

Cadan had called Liall a brigand and accused him of murder, too, and Scarlet saw what a snake Cadan was, and how wrong. He shrugged. "I'm no stranger to insults. Did you believe everything the crew of the Ostre Sul said about me? Then stop fretting. Besides," he added "even if you have killed someone, I'm sure they deserved it."

Liall did not answer, but his face turned sad as he arranged the heavy, glittering blue stones with his fingers. "Shall we go?"

They arrived some minutes before the queen and were seated –as Liall had warned– at the high table. Scarlet saw incredulous looks from all across the hall, but he let them slide off him without harm. That is, until he saw Shikhoza's eyes, poisonous with malice, fixed on him intently. Even Oleksei's hate had not been so pointed, so personal.

Liall did not look at the Lady, but he closed his hand over Scarlet's. All rose when Nadiushka arrived, but she smiled soberly and kissed her son on both cheeks. She held out a hand to Scarlet, and he bowed, this time remembering Jochi's admonitions.

"You are very brave," she told him in that musical voice, in perfectly fluent Bizye. "And very honorable. I see now what captured my son."

"Thank you, your Majesty," Scarlet said, but it was halting and resented. He did not enjoy being her barb to prick Shikhoza with, and whatever Liall said, he knew that was a big part of her extravagant gift to him.

Scarlet sensed the queen reading him as easily as a hunter tracking a desert deer. "You are welcome here, as I have said, Keriss," she said pointedly, and took her seat beside the striking young man that Scarlet knew must be Cestimir, the Crown Prince. Cestimir lifted his glass to Scarlet and smiled cordially, but they could not talk with the queen and Liall seated between them. That would have been rude.

Cestimir was younger than Scarlet, and Scarlet had supposed this prince would be like any other Rshani he had met, either subtle and quick or hostile and curt. He had sharp eyes for a lad, though. Piercing, Scarlet decided, but there was no subtlety or art in his gaze. Cestimir's pale eyes thrust his glance like a weapon. Not the finesse of the slender Morturii long-knives either. Perhaps an axe.

Cestimir's clothes also caught his attention, for among all these glittering folk, the heir-apparent was dressed as plain a servant in a dun-gray wool virca with a piping of blue silk. The very absence of finery, in his position, made him stand out. *Here is a serious boy,* Scarlet thought. He wondered if Cestimir ever laughed.

Scarlet ate, watching the hall with interest. There were many courses of food and altogether too many pieces of silverware. Some of them completely baffled him, including one fork that was no bigger than his finger. He stared at it, wondering what it was for. Liall slid a glance to him and carefully speared a very tiny salted fish with it. Scarlet copied the action, and Liall smiled as if they shared a joke. Liall spoke sometimes in Bizye and sometimes in Sinha to his mother, but all the while Scarlet was aware that they were being watched carefully.

After a time, Scarlet managed to pretend that the hundreds of eyes on him did not exist. He narrowed his world down to the people at the table with him. By the time the meal was over and they could withdraw, he was growing sleepy. Scarlet had walked so far and stretched his mind so much to remember everything said to him that he felt as if he had done an honest day's work for the first time in months. The feeling was welcome. If they stayed here very long, he would have to get Liall to set him to some task or other, just so he would not feel useless and idle.

4.

A Bit of Music

It was customary in Rshan to stay until the host of the table, in this case the queen, retired. She remained longer than usual that night and when she rose, Liall did the same and put his arm out for Scarlet to take. As they filed out of the bright hall among the sound of clinking glasses and the mingled smells of food and incense, Scarlet flashed Liall a tired smile.

"I hope we don't have to repeat this any time soon," he said lowly.

"You did perfectly."

"I half expected someone would ask me how we met again."

Liall covered Scarlet's hand on his arm with his fingers. "Not that I give a damn what they think, but you could always put forth something else, Scarlet."

"Lie?"

"Maybe only a little," Liall soothed, knowing the Hilurin dislike for falsehood.

"Well, I could, and I did broaden the truth a little to Prince Eleferi when he prodded me for tales, but the queen was at the table."

"And?" They passed a large knot of courtiers and ladies at the far end of the hall who were chatting and drinking wine from long-stemmed glasses. They bowed to Liall and Scarlet.

"And she has that ring," Scarlet said.

Liall frowned, his pace slowing.

Scarlet looked up at him innocently. "What's wrong?"

"What ring?"

"The ring your mother wears."

"My mother wears many rings."

"No," Scarlet said impatiently, in sincere earnest. "The stone of truth."

Liall did a double-take, tried to hide what he felt, and failed.

"Oh, I see." Scarlet might be naïve, but he was never slow. "It's not a magic ring. Is it?"

Liall was chuckling openly now. "Do you believe in fairy spells and light o'the wisps, too?"

"Liall." A warning.

"Honestly, love, *magic?*" They passed another group of diners nearer to the great arched doorway, all glimmering with crystal and brightly shining silk. They stared at the prince's grinning face, openly interested.

"Stop it," Scarlet said from the corner of his mouth, his ink-dark eyes glittering, but Liall had the matter in his teeth and would not let go.

"What about toadstool imps and nightflyers and goblins and— *oof!*"

There was an audible and collective gasp from the watching courtiers, and ahead of them the queen turned to see what it was and found Liall nearly doubled up with laughter, holding his ribs where Scarlet had jammed his elbow quite hard, and the courtiers staring in absolute shock. *No one* struck a prince of Rshan, not even in jest.

"Witches?" Liall inquired, still laughing a little. "Sprites? Dragons?"

Scarlet thumped him on the shoulder, which drew more gasps as well as disapproving glares. Liall saw his mother on Cestimir's arm, and the highly diverted look she had on her face. It was worth having Scarlet's ire washing over him just to see how much she enjoyed the scene. Jochi was clearing his throat, attempting not to laugh, and the scandalized look of delight on Cestimir's young face was priceless. Before Scarlet could discipline him again, Liall threw himself at Scarlet and wound his arms around the Scarlet's slighter frame, immobilizing him before lifting him off his feet. Scarlet struggled, his expression outraged.

"Rutting lunatic, put me down!"

"No, you will chastise me again."

"Damn right I will if you don't put me *down!*"

"Mercy!" Liall begged.

Someone tittered laughter. Scarlet was as red as a flame-flower but no longer struggling.

"Nazheradei," the queen called, her tone light, "if you are quite through pawing my dinner guests?"

Liall set Scarlet on his feet. Scarlet jerked his clothing straight, not looking at Liall.

"For now," Liall said meaningfully, and there was more humor.

Liall again offered Scarlet his arm. Scarlet took it, though it plainly galled him to do so. As they resumed their progress, Scarlet dug his fingers deep into Liall's bicep, hoping it would give him a cramp.

"You are in so much trouble," he vowed under his breath.

"I certainly hope so," Liall murmured in return.

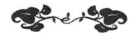

Three days later, during a lull in the Baronial negotiations due to a Feast day, Liall returned to the apartment when twilit afternoon was wearing into twilit evening. Finding the common room and bedroom empty, he peered around the corner of the dining nook and into the kitchen. "T'aishka?" he called.

Nenos appeared immediately, his bright blue tunic smudged with flour and his white hair pulled back from his face. "Jochi has escorted him to the library," he informed Liall as he dried his hands on a towel.

Liall's heart sank. "The library. Why?"

Nenos looked apologetic. "My Bizye has always been very terrible, but I believe your t'aishka made Jochi believe that if he did not take him out of the apartments today, he would leave on his own."

Liall sighed and thanked him and paced off through the long hallways and corridors of the palace. The library. Nadei and he had played there endlessly as boys. He remembered they used to hide behind an enormous bookcase incised with the heads of wolves, snickering behind their hands as servants poked in the corners, looking for them. It was not a place he wanted to see again.

Liall paused at the entryway of the library, hearing many voices issuing from the large, vaulted room.

A royal library is not a small, cozy affair, but an imposing and opulent theater where the plays being acted out by the occupants are ones of intellectual snobbery and hubris. Liall could not imagine why Scarlet had wanted to visit it, and he quailed at entering and stirring up all those old memories. Shikhoza's voice, issuing in a silky stream from the room, made him go still as a hare. Liall listened, half hidden by a solid wall of heavy, brocaded black tapestry placed near the entrance.

"I am no judge of Byzan literature, to know what might appeal, but you might enjoy this." Shikhoza held out a little gilt-edged piece of parchment to Scarlet.

Liall saw that Nenos had dressed Scarlet in muted tones today, gray boots, dark blue breeches, and a simple knee-length virca that had touches of both, with only a plain necklace of milky blue topaz for adornment. He looked small and interesting among all those pale giants, a little dark bird from the south.

"It's an old Rshani poem, from a very large and popular volume. It's in Bizye, ser Keriss. I had it translated for you."

Scarlet accepted the poem from Shikhoza, though all could see it nettled him. Then he looked at her and –Liall supposed– saw the avid way she scrutinized his response, like a cat about to pounce on the interloping bird. Her satisfaction was evident even from Liall's hidden vantage point. She was confident Scarlet would fail, would be humiliated and shown up for the peasant upstart he was. Liall's hand gripped the tapestry tighter and he began to move forward, wanting to spare Scarlet.

Then, Scarlet smiled. It was a careless, easy grin that lit up his features. He shrugged and offered the poem back to her. "It might as well be in turtle or snow bear, for I can't read it."

Scarlet, you are too honest.

Shikhoza's face went deliberately bland, pretending she had made an unforgivable blunder.

"Oh. I *see*. My deepest apologies." She turned, holding the parchment out to Jochi. "Jochi, please recite this poem to ser Keriss. Apparently, he cannot *read* it."

Jochi came forward, tense and discomfited. "Lady Shikhoza, please."

Scarlet saved him. "Please do, Jochi. I'd like to hear it."

The look Jochi gave Scarlet warmed Liall's heart: sad and admiring at the same time, and plain anger at Shikhoza's perfidy. Jochi recited the thing, a convoluted poem, elegant and complex with plays upon words that only a master would be able to decipher fully. Comparing it to Byzan poetry would be like comparing a paper boat to a galleon. Perhaps insulting Byzan arts was also part of her plan, but Scarlet made no comment other than to thank Jochi politely.

"My apologies, ser Keriss," Jochi said.

Scarlet laughed, perhaps a little too brightly, but Liall could not tell. "Whatever for? It's not your fault I can't read. Nor mine."

Jochi bowed rather lower than he needed to, and moved away from the knot of courtiers who had begun to close in on Scarlet.

A dandy courtier in a virca of yellow silk –was it Tesk the painter?– cleared his throat and leaned close. "Your parents... did not insist?"

Scarlet turned to look up at him and smiled again, rather too charmingly, and Liall felt a little twinge of jealousy when he saw the way it affected Tesk, how the man straightened his clothing and tried to appear taller than he was.

Ah, careful, Scarlet, Liall thought. Too many desire you already and Tesk is on the list of spies that I need to cultivate. Having him fall in love with my t'aishka will not do.

Scarlet gave a short, honest laugh. "What, that I learn to read? Who was I going to read to, a horse? Any lass who had a lick of sense would have thought me daft for spending my time with a book when there was work to be done, and she would have been right. You can't eat a book, after all. It doesn't help you survive or keep you warm or get crops in on time. I'm afraid none of my people read, or very few. My mother could, but she believed it brought her bad luck and she would not teach it to us."

Scarlet looked down as if embarrassed at so many words coming out of him at once, lowering his eyes. "Still," he said hesitantly, his voice very wistful, and (little minx!) looking up at Tesk through his dark lashes. "Still... it seems to me a wondrous thing, to have all those words just waiting for you, all that beauty, and you can reach for it anytime you want. It's like magic, isn't it?" Then he looked embarrassed again and waved his hand as if chasing away the words. "Don't mind me, I'm being a fool."

Tesk was highly affected. "No," he said after a moment. "That you are not."

Now their curiosity was engaged and they were on the scent. Another hesitant courtier, one whose name Liall did not know, sketched a little bow to get Scarlet's attention.

"Ser Keriss, it is said... it is said you were a traveling pedlar, before you left Byzantur."

"I'm still a redbird – that is what we call a pedlar back home – for I'm going back to Byzantur." There was some stir at that. "One day," he amended. "It's for Prince Nazheradei to say."

Liall nearly snorted out loud. *Dub me the master to my back and fight me tooth and nail on everything else to my face? Oh, little one, you are learning far too fast.*

"But how can you find your way on the road if you cannot read?"

Scarlet dug in his pocket and produced the little glass and metal compass. "In need, I use this, but I don't need it often. The routes were well known by the pedlar before me, and he taught me them."

"Routes?"

"The roads between Omara and Ankar."

Tesk could not hide his astonishment. "What, all of them? But how, since you do not read?"

"He spoke them to me, and I memorized them."

"Impossible," Shikhoza said. Her voice was too tense, for several heads turned to her, and one lady tittered behind her jeweled hand. There would be fresh gossip tonight, of poems and pedlars, and bitter court ladies with spoiled plans.

Scarlet called her on it. "Excuse me, lady?" Scarlet asked, meeting her gaze. "I'm 'fraid I didn't hear you."

"I said impossible. There must be hundreds of roads in the region you speak of. No one could memorize them all."

"You could if you had to," Scarlet said. "That's the thing, isn't it? What a body has to do instead of just wanting?"

Did he intend it the way she took it? It did not matter, for the court gossips would take it and run with it and by tomorrow the story would be that Shikhoza had cursed and spat and Scarlet danced a jig naked on the table. Shikhoza's lips thinned unpleasantly and the look she gave Scarlet chilled Liall's heart. But she did not get the chance to cut Scarlet to ribbons, for Tesk was motioning to Scarlet from the tall bookcase by the window, the one with the carved wolves that had so fascinated Liall as a boy.

Scarlet bowed slightly to Shikhoza and joined Tesk. A servant brought down a large, rolled map, the leather kind taken on campaigns, and unrolled it across the wide table with a flourish.

"Show me," Tesk said.

Scarlet looked at it, but frowned. "Do you have one without writing on it? One with just the land?"

Tesk snapped his fingers and another map was produced. "We call this a topographic map, ser Keriss," he informed gently.

Scarlet grinned. "We just call it a common map."

Tesk shrugged, smiling. "Your way is less of a

mouthful."

Someone quite near Liall's place of concealment whispered – ... *wager he'd like to make a mouthful of him* – and Liall gritted his teeth.

Scarlet placed his finger on the map directly where Khurelen would have been written in. "This is Khurelen." His index finger sketched lines east and west. "From here there are nine routes to the sea, fourteen to Omara, six back to Lysia and beyond, and four across the mountains to Morturii and Minh, but of those four only two are open in the winter months. This road here," he pointed above Khurelen "is one I travel often. It's called the Snakepath, or the North Road, from Khurelen to Lysia. There are eight small settlements on the road. Just steadings really, groups of families living off one farm. They often need small things like needles and cloth and soap and such, and can't spare the time to get to Khurelen to fetch it on their own. That's where I come in."

"Needles?" a pretty girl laughed, her Bizye heavily accented.

Scarlet laughed with her. "You'd be surprised what you can charge for a needle to a farm wife who hasn't got one."

There was a round of good-natured laughter.

"How long is the road?" asked Tesk, clearly interested.

"The north road, from here to here, is eighteen leagues. Four days on foot. (*On foot!* some whispered) From here, fifteen leagues to the junction of the east fork and the south road to the sea, but I wouldn't take the Sea Road in spring. Mosquitoes the size of rabbits!"

More amusement. Oh, they were entertained, they were. And not in the mean, spiteful way that Shikhoza had intended. Liall stepped from behind the concealing tapestry and entered the library casually. There were turns and bows and the inevitable greetings, but Liall's eyes were all for Scarlet.

"Keriss," he called softly, the court name they knew him by.

Scarlet saw him and grinned, almost forgetting to bow, not that Liall cared. Liall strolled over to Scarlet and deliberately took his hand.

"Are you enjoying yourself?"

"Very much. Your people are wonderful."

"We think the same of you, ser Keriss," Tesk said. Liall briefly courted the mental image of flattening Tesk's nose, and then decided that would be impolite.

"Well, I think you are wonderful, too," Liall said, pitching his voice low. "And I am lonely, so come have dinner with me."

There were several murmurs of protest around us. "But, we were just..."

"No, no," Liall said, looking around him. "You have had him long enough. It is my turn. There are sacrifices I will gladly make for Rshan, but not tonight!"

Clean laughter washed over them, and over it Liall met Shikhoza's livid eyes. Liall put his arm around Scarlet. "Say goodnight, ser."

Scarlet bade them good evening with perfect manners, and they left the library that held so many bad memories for Liall.

The corridor leading to Liall's apartments was nearly empty. They took their time getting back, strolling arm in arm and gazing at the paintings that lined the walls. Liall answered Scarlet's many inquiries as best he could, amused at how interested Scarlet was in everything. The paintings, ancestors all, had been there before Liall was born, and it had been part of his schooling to remember dates and facts about all of them. He related these facts to Scarlet and recited from rote, not really listening to himself or to Scarlet's responses.

"Hello?" Scarlet reached up and waved his hand in front of Liall's face. "You in there?"

Liall smiled wanly. "I was thinking of your performance."

Scarlet's smile fell. "I was only–"

"You were only defending yourself. I saw."

Scarlet shrugged. "Doesn't matter much. It was just bile and spite from a woman who used to love you. Old Hipola the midwife was full of such, back home."

Liall could smell the scent of Scarlet's hair. Nenos had combed it with some spice or cologne. It took Liall a moment to recognize the scent of the flame-flower that grew by the sea. Keriss: Scarlet's court name. It made him sad for some nameless reason.

"Do not confuse Shikhoza with a meddling midwife," Liall warned as gently as he could. "She is capable of things you could not imagine. I should know."

The last must have sounded too bitter, even for Liall. Scarlet turned to him. "Is something wrong?"

"Nenos said you were bored," Liall answered said, looking away.

"I'm usually bored," he sighed. "It's not only this place, Liall, I was bored a lot at home, too. That's why I became a pedlar, so that I would always have something to do."

"I am beginning to realize," Liall said softly, his fingers curling around Scarlet's arm. "Just how difficult our relationship will be, for neither of us will ever be content anywhere." No, content nowhere. He remembered too much of exile and Scarlet remembered too much of home. Always, they would be at opposites: in temperament, in nature, even in appearance. Scarlet was honesty and innocence and the vital energy of youth. In contrast, Liall felt brittle and overused, cynical and hateful. And yet, he could not help seeking Scarlet out time and time again, could not help running his fingers through that glossy black hair, touching that flawless ivory skin, devouring that red mouth.

Scarlet gave Liall a quick, odd look for his soft words, and for a moment there was fear on his face.

"No," Liall hastened to say, before doubt could elbow its way in. "I only meant that we must work harder to be pleased in where we find ourselves in life."

"Either that, or we need to stop paying so much attention to where we are, and more mind to who we're with."

The simplicity of the statement was so characteristic of Scarlet that Liall stopped and gave him a quick, impulsive hug, and suddenly the uncertainty of the future –both theirs and Rshan's– weighed heavily on him.

"You are wiser than your years. If only we had met in peaceful times, when I could be a plainer man. One who could make you happy enough to forget your wanderlust."

Scarlet pulled away, his dark brows drawing together. "There *is* something wrong. Tell me."

"It is nothing. I am merely jealous that Tesk has asked the queen for permission to paint your portrait, and she has allowed it."

Scarlet looked so worried that Liall had to kiss that lovely mouth again, seeking to wipe that anxiety away.

Scarlet returned the kiss enthusiastically, slipping his tongue between Liall's lips and tickling the roof of Liall's mouth and the back of his teeth, exploring. Scarlet gave a humming little moan that sent sudden heat through Liall's groin. Liall cradled Scarlet's face in his hands and kissed the delicate chin, the soft cheeks and closed eyelids, and suddenly the journey back to the apartments seemed far too long.

"I've got a wicked idea," Liall murmured into Scarlet's ear, licking the spot just under the silken lobe, warm and slightly-furred with tiny, delicate, translucent hairs.

Scarlet hissed in pleasure when Liall sucked on that spot, and pulled him closer. "Idea?" he asked, sounding breathless.

"Here," Liall said, backing up to one of the many doors that lined the hall. He pushed the heavy wooden door open.

Scarlet peered inside the small, dim chamber. "What's this?"

Liall tugged him into the room: a velvet-lined affair with a small che table in the center and several sturdy, cushioned chairs, their wood carved to be deceptively delicate-looking. At the stone casement, a round window overlooked a snow-bound garden that was perched on the roof of the apartment below.

"Nothing," Liall said, closing the door. "Another salon. The palace is full of them."

That puzzled Scarlet, and Liall guessed that Scarlet must never have seen a room that served only an occasional purpose. Liall remembered Scarlet's cottage in Lysia, the compact neatness of it and how every little space had seemed to be used to maximum efficiency and multiple purpose. Well, they were not in Lysia anymore.

Liall kissed Scarlet until he was breathless again, and only when Liall's hand dropped to unlace the front of Scarlet's breeches did the man pull away. "Liall...not here."

"Yes, here." Liall drew Scarlet into another tight

embrace and jerked at the front of Scarlet's breeches impatiently. Scarlet seemed a little unsettled, but did not try to prevent Liall from attaining his goal, and gave a shaking sigh when Liall's hand curled around him intimately.

"My t'aishka," Liall breathed, "I love to touch you. I love to see how you desire me." Liall gripped a little harder, making Scarlet gasp in delight.

Scarlet dug his fingers into Liall's virca and kissed him, sliding his hand around Liall's neck to pull the prince in for a deeper kiss, and thrust his tongue between Liall's lips.

Liall moaned in delight. So bold! Before Liall knew it, he heard Scarlet's boot-heel bump the leg of the small table, and he realized he had been backing Scarlet up all this time. So much the better.

"Hey!" Scarlet exclaimed when Liall cupped his hands around Scarlet's bottom and lifted him, depositing his rump on the polished surface of the table.

Liall pushed Scarlet's legs apart and dropped to his knees.

"Liall," Scarlet moaned. "What—"

"I could eat you up," Liall growled, and proved it by leaning forward and licking Scarlet's cock from base to head. Scarlet shivered and Liall's gaze turned predatory. "In fact, that is what I will do." Liall pulled at Scarlet's breeches, tugging them down his hips. Mine, he thought almost savagely. This is mine, this beauty, this sweet, halting reluctance, these layers of innocence that I have only begun to explore and peel away, one by one, never in haste, never carelessly. He would take Scarlet in many ways, but never carelessly, never without realizing what a treasure he held in his arms, and how rare it was, how precious, how he must protect it always.

Scarlet squirmed. "Liall, what if someone comes in?"

106

"Then they will go back out very quickly," Liall answered, pulling Scarlet's breeches down to his knees. Scarlet was not being very helpful. Liall wrapped an arm around Scarlet's waist to hold him still, leaned forward, and took him in with a deep groan that seemed to reverberate through Liall's toes.

Scarlet's backbone went rigid and he made a startled little grunt, and then his hands were in Liall's white hair, fingers gripping tight. "Gods," Scarlet breathed in a high, harsh whisper.

There, Liall thought, feeling the quick response of his own body. Merely the sound of Scarlet's voice, lifted in passion, had the power to stir his lust. Now he had what he sought clasped firmly in his mouth, warm and hard and slightly musky, heady to his senses. Liall swallowed Scarlet down until his nose was pressed against dark, silky hairs, then sucked softly as he pulled back, until he had the head between his lips. He twirled his tongue on it and sucked it like it was the sweetest strawberry. Beautiful, he thought fiercely, feeling as though he had drunk strong wine. Scarlet could have that effect on him, able to overload his senses until he was nearly intoxicated with awareness.

Scarlet shuddered and threw his head back, his eyes squeezed shut and his lips clamped together.

Trying so very hard to keep silent, Liall thought, watching Scarlet intently through his lashes, how his chest heaved and he struggled not to cry out as Liall sucked him hard. Liall's other hand moved to circle and stroke in time with tongue and lips. Then Liall stopped stroking and slid his fingers into his mouth, getting them very wet. Liall slipped his hand beneath Scarlet's scrotum, nudging and curling to find the closed entrance of flesh there, and slid one wetted finger inside him.

Scarlet's hands tightened in Liall's hair and he uttered

a strangled shout, his thighs tensing as he arched up from the table. His hips bucked wildly and Liall felt the wet, silken flesh nudging the back of his throat just before Scarlet's semen bathed his tongue. Some of it spilled out over Liall's lower lip and dripped onto the fine silk of his shirt as Scarlet shuddered hard.

Scarlet's fingers were still tightly wound in Liall's hair, and Scarlet made a noise of contrition and smoothed his hands over Liall's scalp and around his neck.

"Sorry," Scarlet whispered, sounding like he had just run a very long way.

Liall looked at Scarlet, observing how he was flushed and sweaty, his dark eyes wide with the experience. Scarlet looked down and brushed his fingers over Liall's mouth, tracing through the glistening moisture. Liall smiled up at him. Gods, so beautiful. No wonder they coveted him. Who among the men and women in the library tonight would not?

Liall knew that answer, and he thrust the thought away before it could sour his mood. "Good?" he asked, forcing his voice to be light. He rose and gathered Scarlet in his arms.

"*Good?* Deva save us." Scarlet rested his cheek on Liall's shoulder to recover. "There shouldn't be words for how that feels," he said into Liall's collar. His lips touched Liall's neck and kissed his way to Liall's mouth. "I can't even describe it."

Liall shared the taste of Scarlet's seed with him slowly, then more insistent as he trapped Scarlet's leg and rubbed it between his thighs. Already Liall could feel an uncomfortable dampness in his breeches, and he longed to just open them here and bend Scarlet over the table, to feel that slender form writhing under him, to bury himself in that young body and feel the responding heat and passion coursing through his blood. He felt that if Scarlet were a drink he would have drowned himself in it willingly. Alas, that would spoil his plans for later. Regretfully, Liall broke the kiss and began to put Scarlet's clothing to rights.

"What about you?" Scarlet protested.

"It can wait. I have a surprise for you," Liall said, and was amazed at his own flush of gratification when Scarlet grinned hugely.

"Oh, another one? Tell me!"

Musicians who can play Byzan music were rare in Rshan, but being a prince carried its advantages. Scarlet listened to the familiar melodies a pretty Rshani girl played on the tal vielle and laughed when Liall proved he knew a Byzan song or two himself. They were together in the formal room. The tables and chairs had been removed and replaced with a long, low padded chaise and trencher, so the pair could take their ease half-reclining on pillows and eating while the bright, lively music was played on box harp and dittern and pulled from the taut strings of a tal vielle with a curved bow. Liall was determined to forget everything outside his apartments tonight. There would be no barons, no court intrigue, no ghosts nipping at his heels.

Liall also ordered the dinner himself. Scarlet seemed to like fish and seafood greatly, and there was no dearth of that in Rshan, so he ordered lavishly with an eye to salted and piquant dishes, and be damned if it was too much. Dvi, the cook, could set a feast for his fellow servants later.

Wine had been a problem. Scarlet did not like it much,

preferring plain bitterbeer and honest Byzan ales, neither
of which were available. Liall recalled a vintage that used
to be popular ages ago, brewed from tart berries rather
than grapes, and sweeter than men are wont to like. He
instructed Dvi, the cook, to find a few bottles of it and
ignored the glance the cook gave him.

Scarlet liked the wine. He liked the food too, and since
it was salty, the wine went faster than Liall thought it
would.

Liall poured the dregs of the second bottle into
Scarlet's glass and laughed at his flushed face and the
way he sang off-key to the mournful Byzan love-song the
girl was crooning. Scarlet normally had a very fine voice
but the wine had taken its toll. Scarlet leaned closer to
whisper something into Liall's ear and tumbled against
him, clumsy with drink. Liall's back hit the pillows and
a moment later Scarlet's hand was on his thigh, fingers
kneading gently as the Scarlet breathed hotly into his
ear.

Not wanting to break the spell, Liall raised his hand
in a subtle signal and the music stopped. Nenos bowed
as the musicians immediately rose and filed out, silent
as ghosts, and the servant closed the doors after them.
Scarlet and Liall were alone with the blue lamplight and
the smoky incense curling to the ceiling.

Their mouths met with a clash of teeth and tongue, and
then Scarlet's hands clasped Liall's arms and the prince
was shoving him off the low couch onto the thick carpet.
Scarlet tried to take the aggressive role, but Liall deftly
pushed him off and pinned his wrists over his head.

There did not seem to be enough oxygen in the air.
Scarlet struggled under him and Liall released his hands.
Immediately, Scarlet began to tug and pull at both of their
clothes, stripping layers of fabric away to get to bare
skin.

"Scarlet," Liall laughed breathlessly. "If I had known a little wine would have this effect, I would have gotten you drunk much sooner. What has gotten into you?"

Scarlet grinned, jerking at Liall's belt and trying to shove his breeches down his legs, hindered as he was with Liall on top of him. "You. Several times. And I want you again." He nipped Liall's chin with his teeth. "Now."

Liall rolled his eyes to the ceiling as if seeking divine guidance. "I am a dead man."

"Too old for me?"

Liall could never resist a dare, and Scarlet was hot and willing under him, and more than a little wild. "I'll show you *old!*" he growled. Scarlet laughed and they rolled on the carpet, struggling and nipping like wolf cubs, knocking the wine bottle off the table and spilling dregs into the fine weave, and neither of them gave a damn if the world ended outside, just as long as they had this.

"Scarlet," Liall moaned into Scarlet's mouth, when he could speak at all, as if the simple name tied him to earth and he must not let go of it. They had lost so much of themselves here. The bandit and the pedlar were fading, and what came next Liall did not know, and feared.

Liall's touch had turned gentle, but Scarlet gripped the prince's hands and pressed them hard against his skin. *"More..."* he pleaded.

Liall was always so careful with him, mindful that there were vast physical differences between them. "No, I will hurt you," he murmured, almost in pleading. "I must be careful. You are too precious to me."

"I won't shatter, damn you, I'm not made of glass." Scarlet bit Liall's lower lip sharply.

Liall felt his resistance crumbling. "You must not tempt me in this way. Please." He rolled over again, taking Scarlet with him, feeling Scarlet's warm body draping him like a blanket. He pressed his nose into soft, straight hair, fragrant still with that touching scent, and sighed deeply. "You have no idea how much I love you, how it frightens me to think of anything happening to you. I must be watchful always."

Scarlet's echoing sigh and the slight sagging in his muscles let Liall know that Scarlet had relented. He would not demand that Liall give in to his more brutal nature. Scarlet would allow himself to be loved, he would surrender to it, and in doing so, conquer Liall more thoroughly than he ever dreamed.

I am lost, Liall thought almost in gloom. Lost, and I do not care at all. Not a bit.

The fire had burned down to red embers when at last Liall shuddered and moaned as Scarlet moved on top of him and straddled his hips. Liall watched Scarlet closely, his eyes narrowed to pale slits and a look of intense concentration on his face as he gripped Scarlet's waist and helped him move.

Scarlet's head was thrown back and the pale column of his throat ran with sweat. The firelight cast flickering shadows over Scarlet's bare skin, flame colors over white, as he murmured Liall's name over and over again, soft and with hope, as if it were a magic chant against harm.

"Glorious," Liall grated out in a raw voice, before his eyes closed and his own orgasm took him. "Glorious..."

5.

An Audience

Scarlet felt terrible when he woke. His mouth tasted like what he imagined a sewer must contain, and his head throbbed in time to his heartbeat. A groan escaped him before he could stop it.

"Are you awake?" Liall asked, rather more loudly than necessary.

Scarlet put his hands over his ears. "Oh, Deva, what did I do last night?" Perhaps, in seeking to set aside Liall's obvious worry and fear, he had gone along with the diversion a bit too much!

"Aside from singing very badly and very loudly and fondling me in front of the musicians?"

It's really not necessary to talk so loudly, Scarlet thought, and then realized what Liall had just said. He flung himself upright and top of his head threatened to come off. "Ai!" he moaned and held his forehead. "Tell me I didn't, please."

"But you did. Several times."

Great. Not only suffering, but mortified. "What did I drink last night? Wine?"

"Quite a bit of it." Liall's tone was amused. "I ordered it especially for you, and you seemed to like it very much."

"Demon's brew!" Scarlet moaned. Something crashed to the floor and he rolled up into a ball of misery. "Aaaargh."

"Oh, dear," Liall said apologetically. "Sorry about that." Another loud bump and then he called –loudly– for Nenos.

"Heartless bastard," Scarlet moaned into the blanket.

Liall snickered. "It is reassuring to know that I am not the only one who gets randy when he drinks."

Scarlet was never going to recover from the embarrassment. On the other hand, he did have some very nice memories of the night before, or they'd be nice when he was feeling well enough to enjoy them. Nenos entered holding a pottery cup, and Scarlet heard the old man say something to Liall in a reproving tone. Liall patted Scarlet's back.

"Nenos has fixed something to remedy your wine-sotted head. You must drink it very quickly."

Scarlet unwrapped some of the blankets and sat up.

"Hold your breath," Liall warned as Scarlet took the small cup and drained it.

Scarlet tasted something slippery and something tart and then his throat and tongue were on fire, and the fire was spreading from the inside to the outside. He spluttered. It tasted like bird dung! On fire!

Laughing, Liall gave him another cup filled with water. Scarlet drained it, then fell backward, gasping. The fire on his tongue was dying, but he had begun to sweat.

"What was that?" Scarlet panted.

Liall was still chuckling. "You really do not want to know. The raw eggs were the least of it."

Scarlet made a gagging sound and pulled the blankets over his head. Liall only laughed louder, and Scarlet heard Nenos saying something sternly to the prince.

"Maggoty, sheep-raping bastard," Scarlet croaked in Falx, which only made Liall laugh again. Nenos shooed Liall off and they allowed Scarlet to go back to sleep for a while. The next time he woke, he felt much better. He got up and peered through the door to see Liall reading in the common room. Taking a soft robe from the beside, Scarlet went to sit next to him to apologize for calling names earlier, but Liall waved it off.

"You are a very ardent and sweet drunk. No apology is necessary. You have seen me ill-tempered from drink at least twice before."

Scarlet thought back. "Oh, that's right. I'd forgotten the morning at the Pass."

"And on the ship, and you were vile to me!"

"You deserved it!"

Liall pushed Scarlet's shoulder, and the pedlar suddenly felt that his Wolf was not all lost beneath the prince. It comforted him.

Liall instructed Jochi to keep Scarlet busy for the next few days. The third day, Jochi informed Scarlet that he was to be lessoned in Rshani history, but as they left for the library, Scarlet saw that a tiny red box secured with a gold ribbon had been left on the little table next to the outer door.

"What's this?" Scarlet asked Jochi.

"It looks suspiciously like a present," Jochi said. When Scarlet put it down, Jochi picked it and up and dropped it into his hand. "I'm sure it's meant for you, ser. These are your apartments."

Scarlet's look was doubtful, but he untied the tiny gold ribbon and put it away in his pocket, an action which made Jochi smile.

"Waste not," Scarlet said sensibly, then removed the lid. "Well. No guessing where this came from."

Land of Night

Jochi peered over his shoulder, and Scarlet took the little thing –a silver pin in the shape of a running wolf– and held it up to show his teacher. The silver was not even pure, but yellowed a little from dross, and Scarlet smiled. It was not a princely gift: no jewels or gold, but for the lover of a hill-dwelling bandit king? It was perfect.

"From the prince?" Jochi guessed.

"Of course, since it's a wolf." Scarlet saw that Jochi did not understand. "The Kasiri word for wolf is his common name in Byzantur: Liall."

"Ah," Jochi said. Scarlet let him hold the pin and he admired it a bit before giving it back.

"Very nice," Jochi commented, his amusement plain. "I never pictured Prince Nazheradei as a sentimentalist."

Scarlet was a little embarrassed. "It's just a pin," he said, fastening it to his collar, where Liall would be sure to see it at dinner.

"No, this is a personal gift, ser," Jochi argued. "Wolves are not highly regarded in Rshan, especially not for jewelry, so he must have had this made especially for you."

Scarlet smoothed the material around the pin and said nothing, but inside he felt a rush of warmth for Liall. "Are you ready?"

They found a quiet section in the huge library where the two of them could sit and talk without being observed. And talk Jochi did. Scarlet was itching to learn more of the language, but Jochi nattered on forever in Bizye, rattling off dates and the names of kings, queens, battles, trade skirmishes, and border disputes. Scarlet listened politely for an hour, then began to slump in his chair and examine the fold of the draperies until Jochi sharply asked for his attention again.

"Sorry." Scarlet listened as Jochi resumed a long, rambling speech on feuds between baronial houses and the Tribeland Campaigns and uttered a long list of unpronounceable Rshani names and gods his head was going to split!

"What do you do people *do* here all day?" Scarlet finally interrupted, desperate for diversion. "Or night, or daynight, whatever you want to call it. When you're not telling fables about magic rings of truth, that is." He was still stinging over that deception, but Jochi only gave Scarlet a mild look. "Surely you don't just sit around all the time and *talk* about things?"

Jochi closed the book he had been quoting from and signaled for a servant to bring che. "That is precisely what we do, ser. The talking, not the fables, I mean," he said with some salt, and Scarlet saw that Jochi was not sorry at all that he had tricked Scarlet about the queen's ring. "You must understand, ser, that it is winter now, and this is a royal court. We cannot travel in winter, or not very far, and there is no manual labor to be done that is not already being taken care of by someone else. The queen employs a huge household."

"So you just... do nothing?"

"No, we spend our time learning," Jochi explained patiently. "Trust me, once the roads thaw and the ice melts from the fields there will be activity beyond belief. Our growing season is very short, and it takes all of us to work very hard to grow enough grain and vegetables to feed ourselves and our animals all winter long. Even the Prince Cestimir will be expected to thresh the grain and carry hay."

Scarlet found that amusing. "Did Liall work in the fields?"

"Naturally, he did."

"And the queen?"

"Even the queen, in her day."

"Huh." Finally, something Jochi said had thrown him.

He tried and found out he could not picture Liall doing farm work. "So all winter long, you bury yourselves in books?"

"There is little else to do, if you are not a craftsman. You may have noticed, ser, that the Prince Nazheradei and yourself have more servants than you strictly need. There is not very much for them to do either, but they stay on here during the winter because we need them in the growing season so badly. The Nauhinir Palace is more than a fortress, it's a community."

Scarlet thought he was beginning to understand. "What kind of things do you learn?"

"Languages, for one. The long season of indolence is the reason why so many of us speak Bizye and Falx and such, though not the only reason. Bizye, well, you may say that only the old aristocrats think it a strictly necessary part of a noble's upbringing to learn Bizye."

That puzzled Scarlet, and Jochi saw and chuckled as the silent servant –a very young man in the same blue livery that Scarlet had seen many of the palace servants wear– served the che very quietly and bowed as he backed away to his post by the door.

"Do not look so surprised. You know that Hilurin once lived among us."

"I thought it was just a tale..."

"So it is, but most legends have some truth in them."

"But when—"

"Ask me another time," Jochi said kindly. "For now, I have been ordered to see to your instruction in Rshani history."

"By who?" Scarlet grumbled, reaching for a cup of steaming che. Maybe he shouldn't have called Liall a bastard, after all.

"The queen."

Scarlet nearly spilled the che. "What in Deva's shrieking

hell for?"

Jochi opened the book again, ignoring his lapse. "I think she believes it improper for the prince to have a consort who knows nothing of our culture. Besides, it is only fair, is it not? The prince knows a great deal about your culture and country."

"But I'm a commoner," Scarlet groused unhappily. "You'd think that would leave me out."

Jochi did not like that reasoning. "You are Keriss kir Nazheradei," he said primly.

Scarlet made a rude sound.

"At the very least, this is true while you are in Rshan," Jochi amended. "As for my own feelings, completely aside from what it would take to win Nazheradei –and I have known him since I was a boy– I believe you are worthy of inclusion into the Camira-Druz household."

Scarlet resisted the urge to roll his eyes. From what he had seen of Liall's family, he was not particularly honored by that. "But guarding me is a dull job, isn't it?"

"It is not so simple as that, ser, I am not just a bodyguard. I am a guide, and, as you see today, a teacher."

"Still sounds dull."

"Far less so than you would imagine. Besides, I am trained to this, nearly bred to it." He smiled genuinely. "I am one of the Setna, the Brotherhood."

Scarlet must have looked strange, for Jochi frowned. "Have I said something wrong?"

"No. Just... setna. That's another word for snake, isn't it?"

He was not offended. "Serpents are wise, are they not? Knowing when the weather is right to come outside, having enough of their own defenses to be feared, being able to detect their enemies just from vibrations on the ground? In Rshan, being called a snake is not necessarily an insult, unless you are called an *essima*, an assassin."

Jochi closed his book (hopefully for the last time) and sat with it on his knee. "We are sworn to the royal family from ages past. We serve them, in part, as bodyguards and teachers and guides, at least when they are young."

Scarlet was caught by what he had said earlier. "You said... bred to it? You mean you have no choice? Like slaves?"

"No, no, I said that poorly. There are no slaves at all in Rshan, ser. It is just that the Brotherhood was founded long, long ago, and their descendants have continually served the crown since then. I chose to enter the Brotherhood, as did one of my own brothers, but my eldest brother did not, and has a fine family of his own."

"You can't marry?" Scarlet was too startled to realize what an impertinent question it was, then bit his lip when he did. They have no slaves, he thought. Why is that, when every other country in the world has them? "I'm sorry, that really was rude."

"No, merely curious. We can marry, if we choose, but our duties to our charges come first. When they no longer require us, we may also choose to take a wife. When Prince Nazheradei's father was killed, my own father withdrew from court and married and then sired three sons and four daughters." He grinned. "It is not a punishment, ser, I promise you. All who enter the Brotherhood do so willingly. And since there are far fewer members of the royal family than there are members of the Brotherhood, those are not our sole duties. We enforce the law in the more distant parts of our land, and we preserve knowledge where it would be lost." He made a gesture that may have been one of dismissal, as if talking about his life was unimportant. "It is complicated."

"Sounds like it," Scarlet said, and went back to his original point of curiosity. "But you served the queen before she asked you to look after me?"

"We all serve the queen, but no, not personally. I was at court, and the queen made a request of me. I confess, I am one of those odd Rshani who is fascinated with foreigners and foreign lands, and frankly, you seemed rather lost here. I was glad to accept." Jochi shrugged. "And I find you far more deserving of my time and attention than, say, Lady Shikhoza might be."

Scarlet laughed a little, seeing that Shikhoza was not well-liked. "Well...thanks for that."

That was all the discussion Scarlet had that day that did not involve history. Liall was nowhere to be seen when Scarlet returned to the apartments, but Nenos had supper ready and was waiting by the table with a smile, so he indulged the old man and ate, though he had no appetite.

By the time Dvi came to lower the lamps in the bedroom, signaling that the Rshani night had arrived, Liall still had not returned. Scarlet went early to bed without him. Sometime in the night, Liall finally crawled in beside him and woke him a little. Scarlet moved into his warmth, and Liall sighed and pulled his fingers through Scarlet's hair until Scarlet became drowsy and slept again. By morning Liall was gone, swift as a redbird, before Scarlet had even had time to greet him, and smiling Jochi was there again, eager to bore him to death.

Scarlet still managed to find something to distract him. "You said your people had legends like mine. Will you tell me?"

Jochi narrowed his golden eyes. They had found another section of the library outfitted with its own fire grate and hung with draperies the color of the Nemerl sun, brassy and yellow and cheerful.

"Am I to suppose that you have little interest in politics?" Jochi said, as if everyone in the world would naturally be interested in such, and Scarlet was an oddity because he was not.

Scarlet looked at his boots as the fire popped, not wanting to make Jochi –one of his only friends here– annoyed with him, but Jochi only nodded.

"Very well." Jochi closed the book with a snap and put it away. "We do have a legend very like yours," he said briskly "except that ours tells of the elder ages, when the Shining Ones ruled over all of Rshan. There were pale nomads living on the ice in those ages, and the Shining Ones took some of them as wives. Legend says that we are the result. They also say that this land was the first home to your people, the little dark ones, only the Shining Ones were cruel to your folk, enslaving them and using them badly. The Anlyribeth –what you called yourselves back then– rebelled and fled, taking powerful talismans of magic with them, and when they reached what is now Byzantur, the iron in the mountains protected them from the Shining One's pursuit."

Jochi got up from the library table and went to fetch a cunningly carved and inlaid globe that whirled around a spindle, no bigger than an apple.

"Here and here are the ancient boundaries," Jochi said, sketching an outline on the globe with his little finger. "Legend says there was a great catastrophe after the talismans were taken. A flood shrank our land as the waters rose, a punishment from the gods for the cruelty and ruthlessness that brought down the last of the High Kings." He pulled the map they had earlier used back to compare with the globe. "You see how much larger Rshan was in elder times? This valley, now far under the sea, was the seat of the kingdom."

"Did everyone in the city drown?" Scarlet traced the larger land mass on the globe with a fingertip.

"No one knows for certain. Some stories say all perished, some stories insist that a few escaped by ship and made their way to other parts of the world, where they lived on the sufferance of people they would once have enslaved. Myself, I doubt that last. If they had survived, there would be another kingdom. While there were certainly good rulers in the lineage of the ancient High Kings, there were equal numbers of cruel and exigent ones. The Brotherhood was formed to prevent our kings and queens from ever taking that path again."

Scarlet's eyes widened. "What would you do if they did?"

Jochi arched an eyebrow. "Not by open rebellion or regicide, but by teaching and guidance and example."

Jochi was right, it was complicated. And Jochi was tricky. "You're turning us back to politics."

"And I thought I was being subtle."

Scarlet liked Jochi, he liked him a great deal. Jochi was one of the few people who accepted him for his own self, not for who he was to Liall or what hold they thought they could get over the prince by pandering to his lover. The next few days, however, Scarlet liked being with Jochi much less, for Jochi had him moving into the smaller rooms that he called *salons*, rather than the larger gathering chambers.

Scarlet could have sworn that they walked a length equal to the distance between Lysia and Patra winding in and out of the interconnecting rooms that honeycombed the palace. It was a lot less interesting than journeying to Patra, too. Not that he did not enjoy the luxurious surroundings, but with no sun and only torches and lamplight, even the most lovely surroundings can become melancholy. Now add bored and malicious court-folk –although not all were, he admitted– and he finally rebelled a few hours after the midday meal as Jochi led him to yet another one of the glittering cells.

"I don't want to go in there."

Jochi stood poised in the doorway. "No?"

"No." Scarlet frowned at the sound of laughter. "I'm tired of meeting people I can't talk to, or who pretend not to understand me, only to move on to the next batch and then the next and the next. I'm not a gods-rotted sideshow. No more today. I want to go outside."

"Ser Keriss, it is very—"

"Cold. I know. I can see that through the windows. Why can't we take one of those things, what are they called... sleighs? Out for a ride."

"That would be very unwise, ser."

"Why?"

Scarlet could see Jochi struggling silently with an excuse to convince him, but a page suddenly scurried out of the blue shadows further down the corridor and approached Jochi with a folded piece of parchment. Jochi took it, frowning a little, and read. The page, a boy of perhaps twelve or so, stared at Scarlet, which was a pleasant change from sidelong glances and whispers. Scarlet stuck his tongue out at the boy when Jochi was not looking, and enjoyed the pop-eyed response.

"I must attend the queen," Jochi said and folded the parchment again. "Come, I will escort you back to your apartments."

"I can find my way back," Scarlet said, and he was sure that he could by now, after days of wandering all over it.

"No, that will not do. I am your escort."

"I'm not a baby," he insisted, "And you're wanted somewhere else."

"As it was she who assigned me to escort you. The queen will understand," Jochi said patiently.

"It's quite all right, Jochi, he can stay here with Alexyin and me until you return."

The youthful voice came from behind the wall and

they both turned in surprise. The page hurried off.

A panel of the wall slid away, revealing a small, dim chamber like the salons, lit only by a few blue lamps turned down low. Seated on a low chair faced away from them was the striking young man with the plain clothes who sat at the queen's right at dinner, the Prince Cestimir. Beside him was a very large, older man with a square face and a hooked nose who wore his long silver hair in a simple braid that hung to the middle of his back. He was clad in a heavy wool virca that was plain by Rshani standards, and carried a single long-knife on his hip. Scarlet assumed the man was a bodyguard, by the size of his frame and the way he sized Scarlet up. There was a book opened on his knee.

Jochi murmured something under his breath that sounded suspiciously like a curse, at least in tone. He bowed and Scarlet followed suit uncertainly.

"Prince Cestimir," Jochi murmured, then, "Ap kyning, may I present to you—"

The boy beckoned without looking around. "Yes, yes. I know. Who does not? Keriss kir Nazheradei. Come in."

Jochi looked at Scarlet, then shrugged. "I see no harm in it," he said. "And if you will wait here until I return, ser, I am content."

Well, he had survived the queen, and while Cestimir might be Crown Prince, he was still only a boy and Liall's younger brother. Given his mistakes the first time he had appeared in the great hall, Scarlet could understand Jochi's concern. He nodded and ducked into the room. The panel closed and Scarlet stood with his back to it as Jochi's footsteps grew more distant.

"Your Majesty," Scarlet said. He was not nervous of this boy as he had been of the queen. Cestimir was facing away from him, kneeling backward on a chair with both elbows perched on the headrest, peering intently through some kind of transparent disc set into the wall.

"Shhhh," Cestimir whispered, and looked sidelong at Scarlet. "Come sit with me." He patted the chair next to him. "Did I hear you say you liked sleighs? I must take you out on mine soon."

The older man seated in the corner closed his book. His thick white eyebrows drew together as he frowned at the prince.

"Ap kyning, I feel certain this is not what your mother would consider decorous behavior."

Cestimir flapped a hand at him. "Perhaps not, but it is instructive. Come, Keriss, sit with me."

Scarlet gnawed on his lower lip and dragged a chair close to the prince, but not facing the wall.

"No, no, you must see," Cestimir insisted, motioning.

Scarlet turned in the chair and peered through the disc, which seemed to be made of gray glass, murky but transparent enough so that he could perceive that it looked out into another room. Not a salon, but the large domed chamber with the iron screens that he had met Tesk in. The chamber was brightly lit, and the hidden alcove was dim, so Scarlet had no need to use his Hilurin sight to peer into the room. He could see very well. Lady Shikhoza sat in one corner under a flickering lamp, stitching on a piece of cloth while several men attended her. She seemed to be ignoring them.

"Now watch," Cestimir murmured. "You see the girl in the silver brocade tarica?"

He pointed and Scarlet looked before nodding. She was very beautiful, perhaps his age or younger, and was presently on the arm of a bearded man who had hair the same ruddy-gold shade as hers.

"Lady Ressilka. She's new to court, but very well-trained by her father, the Baron Ressanda. That's him holding her arm, by the way. She just became one of my mother's attendants. Now... watch Lady Shikhoza as Lady Ressilka draws near."

Interested, Scarlet rested his chin on the back of the chair. As Lady Ressilka was escorted by her father to a chair, the center of the room seemed to shift and even Lady Shikhoza's admirers turned toward the newcomer like flowers toward the sun. Scarlet could see even from this distance that Shikhoza's mouth grew pinched and tight.

"She's a bitter woman," Cestimir said, "And yet, I could feel pity for her if she were not such a poisonous bitch." His mouth curved in amusement. "Call a worm a worm and don't insult the snake, as Alexyin always says. What do you think, Keriss?"

Cestimir looked much younger when he smiled, which Scarlet sensed was not often. Scarlet hesitated, not knowing if he should say anything at all.

"I am sure," Alexyin broke in quietly, "that I never intended that reference to recommend vulgarity."

"My apologies," Cestimir said, but he didn't look sorry. A voice came from very near and Cestimir frowned, listening. After a moment, his mouth thinned out and he shook his head. "Gossips," he muttered.

"Can they hear us?"

"No." Cestimir shifted sideways in the chair to look at Scarlet. "It's the way the ceilings were built; the sound travels into this alcove, but not out, at least not if we're speaking normally, like this."

"You looked bothered," Scarlet said bluntly.

Cestimir lifted his shoulders in an elegant shrug. "The main topic of conversation for days and days has been my elder brother. I've heard many things and my nerves are a bit sensitive."

He could imagine. "Do they... do they speak ill of him?" If so, Scarlet was grateful not to speak Sinha.

"Some do. It frustrates me because I know so little of him. I cannot even argue with them about it, because I don't know if they're telling the truth or not."

"He has been long away?"

"He left Rshan before I was born. My mother has told me of him, of course."

"But you know him now."

"No," Cestimir said wryly. "He has been too occupied on my behalf to meet with me just yet."

"He *has* been busy," Scarlet said helpfully.

Cestimir looked amused again. "And you hate it and wish you had him all to yourself."

This charming guess was not entirely true, but it made Scarlet uncomfortable, telling as it did that Cestimir was interested in his relationship with Liall. Scarlet looked back into the dome chamber to see that Shikhoza's courtiers had begun to move toward the younger woman and gestured instead of answering him.

Cestimir looked once, but only quickly before turning his attention back to Scarlet. "Is it very different here from your home?"

Scarlet heard only curiosity in Cestimir's voice, and no mockery. "Very," he said. "It's very cold here and there is no sun."

Cestimir leaned his cheek on his palm and his eyes –pale blue and sparkling with intelligence– narrowed. "And did you have many lovers there?"

Scarlet was taken by surprise. Not so much by the question, but the questioner. "You're a little young for that kind of talk, aren't you?"

"Oh, we are an ancient society," Cestimir waved it away with a motion like airing a tendril of smoke from his face. "And such decadent cultures are both worshipers and despoilers of youth. I have seen much that I am too young to see, and done much that I am too young to do."

He should have guessed that a boy so burdened with duty and the hopes of others would long for a childhood he never had. Scarlet felt a pang of sympathy for him. "I'm sorry," he said without thinking.

"Do not be. But we were speaking of you. Have you slept with many men? What did you do before you found... occupation... in my brother's bed?"

"Cestimir," Alexyin called out in a tone like a whip, then spoke several low words in Sinha. Cestimir bowed his head to Scarlet, looking not the least bit chastened.

"Alexyin reminds me that you are my brother's t'aishka and it is unforgivable to offer you insult. This conversation is improper."

"No harm done," Scarlet said, though he was stung by Cestimir's words. "I'm not going to roll up and die from it." After the crew of the Ostre Sul, even insults felt like polite conversation.

"You are kind."

"No, I mean it." Scarlet met the young prince's gaze straightly. "You don't know me. I haven't done anything yet to earn your respect, so you give me none."

Cestimir stared at him for a long moment, then dropped his gaze and bowed his head in real apology. "But manners should prevail even if respect is absent," he said. "Your pardon, ser."

Scarlet shrugged. Strangers can assume much from looks alone. Liall had taught him that lesson in depth. "No harm done," he repeated.

Cestimir hesitated, and then scrutinized Scarlet closely, as if he was rearranging Scarlet's shape in his head. "They told me you would not be what I expected."

"They?"

Cestimir smiled a little, the cold smile of youth forced too quickly to wisdom. "The ones who watch and plot. Yes, they." He jerked his chin in the direction of the concealing tapestry. "My beloved people."

Scarlet grinned. "Funny. You don't sound in love."

"We know each other too well for romance, though there is enough at stake for elaborate copulation. And you; are all Hilurin so forthright?"

"Only when we're sober, which is often."

"Then I will assume you have no need of drink to goad your partners to the sheets. Congratulations."

That made Scarlet laugh, and Cestimir joined him, like two veteran soldiers on a battlefield, counting their cuts. Alexyin went back to his book and the two young men resumed spying on Cestimir's subjects.

"Ressanda," Cestimir said, again pointing out the large man with the reddish beard. "Who may one day be my father-in-law. He is very wise and brave, and so he has many enemies. There is to be a bear hunt soon, and Ressanda will be in the lead team. Perhaps the bear will do him a favor and rid him of a few of them," he added mischievously, and then his face clouded. "I should not say such things. It's very unlucky."

"The bear hunt," Scarlet said with foreboding, remembering what Jochi had told him about Liall's father. Men were often killed on these hunts.

"Oh, were you told? It's a grand affair, horses and hounds and banners and many sharp spears, and we must all wear silver in our hair: another old tradition from the Shining Ones. Oh, look, there's Tesk, who asked to paint a picture of you. He's such a gallant."

They watched a while longer, and after a bit, Scarlet remarked to Cestimir again about the lack of sun.

"We are only sunless in the winter," Cestimir assured. "Does it get very hot in Byzantur in the summer?"

"Not where I live. Lysia is in the mountains. It gets warm, yes, but not like it does in Morturii, and not as cold in the winter."

His eyes widened. "You've been to Morturii?"

"Many times. The first time when I was fourteen, with a merchant caravan."

"That is my age! You must tell me," Cestimir demanded, his face lighting up. "I envy you and my brother, to have seen such lands."

"I thought your folk didn't like foreigners?"

"Oh, we do not." Cestimir frowned, and a little of the boy in him showed through. "It's tradition for us to stay here walled in ice and never let anyone in, ever. I hate that. It was not always this way, you know. We used to travel everywhere and foreigners were allowed to walk freely in Rshan. Small wonder our court is a hotbed of plots and whispers, since we must cannibalize ourselves for fresh entertainment. Now... tell me of Morturii," he commanded in a regal tone.

"I was just a boy," Scarlet said, smiling a little. "A caravan came through from Omara bound for Morturii. They needed a wainwright when they arrived, and my father worked that trade, so I got to know Rannon, the karwaneer, and he asked me if I'd like to see Morturii and off I went," he finished, like it was as easy as that. He did not mention how hard it had been to convince Scaja and Linhona to let him go. "My people said I had the Wilding, so they never tried to keep me penned in. We usually stay close to home, otherwise."

"Wainwright?" It was evident that Cestimir's education had not included that term.

"One who builds or repairs wagons," Alexyin said without looking up from his book.

Cestimir gave him an apologetic look. "My Bizye isn't as fluent as my brother's, I'm certain, but at any rate there are few wagons in use in the winter here. Sleighs are the more logical choice of travel, for both goods and people."

"Your brother has had longer to practice Bizye." Scarlet said, hoping Cestimir wouldn't ask him much about Liall's travels in the Southern Continent, for he knew little of them. He was coming to realize that there was a great deal about Liall he did not know.

"That is very kind."

"Just truthful, though I honestly don't know how much longer." I don't even know how old Liall is, Scarlet realized, and was a little annoyed. I should know the age of my lover, at least.

"We are all close-mouthed, we Rshan," Cestimir said with great seriousness. "Now, I've interrupted your tale. Please continue."

Scarlet talked until his throat was dry. Cestimir interrupted only to ask questions or details, and Alexyin was silent but attentive, absorbing every word.

"You must tell my lady mother some of this," Cestimir said when Scarlet was talked out. "We need more contact with other lands, I truly believe this. And trade. We do not do poorly the way things are, but there is no growth, no change, I think Rshan will grow more and more stagnant without that infusion."

These were matters of state, matters for kings, not for pedlars, but it seemed good sense and Scarlet said so very cautiously. He was also curious. "Li... Nazheradei says that you do no trade with Byzantur."

"This is true."

"Why?"

Cestimir frowned. "I'm not sure, exactly. It's an old prohibition from the elder times. We once traded with many nations, and foreigners were allowed to walk freely among us. There's a legend that the Hilurin used to live in Rshan na Ostre during the time of the Shining Ones. They were slaves."

It matched what Jochi had said. Now it was Scarlet's turn to frown. He did not like the idea of Hilurin being slaves to anyone. Cestimir touched his arm.

"It's just a tale, Keriss. Anyway, the story goes that the Nauhin, the Shining Ones, held dominion for a very long time, and were known throughout Nemerl, until they made the mistake of letting the Anlyribeth –that's what the little people were called– use their magic. The Anlyribeth stole the magic of the Nauhin to break free of them and fled beyond the ice, but the departure of the Anlyribeth sundered the kingdom of Rshan and brought catastrophe. It split the land in half between the Kalas Nauhin, the southerners, and the Fanorl Nauhin, the northern kingdom. It was a very dark time and little is known of it. Since then, Rshan has had nothing to do with Byzantur, because that is where the Anlyribeth were said to have settled."

"But... Byzantur is thousands of years old. Do the Rshani hold grudges so long?"

"Not that I'm aware of, although you could not prove it by this royal court. But no, it is more of a superstition now than a punishment or fear of any real threat."

The tale amused and irked Scarlet. "Surely there's no harm in a great and powerful kingdom like Rshan trading simple goods with peasants and villagers."

Cestimir grinned. "I agree. Yet if one should suggest in front of the Barons that we open up trade with Byzantur, you would believe it was a plan to turn the world upside down and shake all the people off."

"You have to make the idea taste sweeter to them," Scarlet suggested. "Show them they'd profit from it." He pretended to weigh an invisible coin pouch. "From the stories I've heard back home, even our Flower Prince has to do that before he can get his nobles in the right mind."

Cestimir's expression turned polite. He was indulging him in listening, Scarlet saw, but he was also interested. "How?"

"Well... I know enough of business to know you buy low and sell high, otherwise I'd never make a copper. If you have trade with the Morturii and the Minh, how do you know all the goods actually come from there?"

Cestimir's brow arched. "They don't?"

Scarlet saw the ornamented long-knife on his belt. "That's Morturii scrollwork on your blade, but where do you think they came by the iron to make it?"

His mouth quirked. "Byzantur?"

"Just so. And I'm sure there are other examples. You've probably been trading with us second and third-hand for generations and just didn't know it. Probably been paying twice what you should, too, because to get Byzan materials you've had to use a middleman instead of going straight to the source. Even stinking middleman merchants have to eat."

"That's very astute, Keriss," Alexyin had closed his book and was watching them with interest from the shadowed corner. He looked very imposing in his plain wool, a stark change from the usual silks and velvets, and with that stern brow like a shelf over his eyes.

"Shining Ones save us," Cestimir said, looking from him to Scarlet. "We live in a vacuum. I have no more brain than a woodlouse or I would have realized that already. It makes perfect sense."

Alexyin's stern manner softened. "Don't swear, Cestimir. I happen to think you have a very good mind, and so does your lady mother."

Cestimir pinned the older man with a look. "And my elder brother, what does he think of my mind?"

Alexyin simply folded his hands, and Cestimir turned the same look on Scarlet. "Well?"

Scarlet cleared his throat. "I... I really don't know. He doesn't discuss his business with me."

"And that bothers you?"

"Yes, but not in the way you might think." Scarlet traced the scrolling design of the chair back with a fingertip. "It's not that I care so much about what goes on in the palace or with his family. I only want him to trust me enough to confide in me."

"You really didn't know he was a prince, did you?" Cestimir asked. "I think that's marvelous. It reminds me of some of the old romances, a disgraced prince meets his true love in a far land where no one knows who he is."

Scarlet looked at Cestimir blankly. "But he's not a disgraced prince. Is he?" he asked in confusion.

Cestimir blinked and paused. "Oh, no, those are the old romances."

"Oh." Scarlet was at a loss, at that moment very certain that Cestimir was hiding something from him. "Well, I don't know if it's like a romance or not, but I do love him," he said defiantly, as if Cestimir would mock him for the admission.

Cestimir grinned. "Good. You are worthy of a prince's love."

The panel squeaked a bit as it rolled away from the wall, and Jochi was there. "Ser Keriss," he said, his tone relieved. "Forgive my long absence, but Prince Nazheradei awaits you."

Since he had not been able to see Liall in days, Scarlet rose hastily and bowed. "It's been an honor to meet your Majesty. Truly it has."

Cestimir inclined his head. "Promise you will come and talk with me again. I want to hear more about Byzantur."

"I will."

Jochi gave the closed panel a backward look as they left the alcove, then he studied Scarlet. "I believe you have won another friend."

"I like him. He seems very straightforward. For a Rshani."

"I believe that he is," Jochi agreed. "And much underestimated."

Scarlet's mind was on the awkward pause between he and Cestimir, and he intuitively sensed that it had something to do with the question Jochi would not answer before. "In Byzantur, the firstborn inherits the throne," he said innocently. "Is it different here?"

Jochi's expression went bland and he gave Scarlet a droll look that told Scarlet that his teacher was not deceived. "You have a quick mind, ser."

Close-mouthed Rshani's indeed. "I crave your pardon," Scarlet said wearily. "I meant no offense."

"Hm, no. You just meant to catch me in an unguarded moment in the hope I would reveal something I have pointedly been told not to tell you."

"Told by Liall?"

Jochi sighed again. Jochi's manner may have been mild, but he was no fool. He put his hand on Scarlet's shoulder. "Perhaps the prince will choose to explain this matter to you," he said, his tone suddenly sympathetic.

"Can I ask you one thing, at least?"

"I will endeavor to answer," Jochi said carefully.

"Keriss kir Nazheradei . What does the kir part mean?"

Jochi's face went neutral again.

"Ah," Scarlet said, sounding very much like Liall. He had trespassed again. "I see."

"Here we are," Jochi said brightly and with relief, and opened the door to the antechamber. He escorted Scarlet through, as if an assassin might be lurking there.

Inside, Liall was reading a book on the lounge with a silver cup on the table next to him. He looked up at their entrance and asked Jochi a question in Sinha. Jochi shot a look to Scarlet and bowed and answered Liall shortly before withdrawing.

Liall sat up and studied his lover. "What have you been up to all day?" he asked casually, as if they had just parted company a few hours before, and as if there had not been words between them. "Jochi did not go into detail about his plans."

Stinging at his cold greeting, Scarlet wished he had some way to nettle Liall back. He'd also spoken Sinha to Jochi with him in the room, excluding him from the conversation, which was rude. "I met your brother."

Liall went stiff. "Vladei?" he growled.

Scarlet took a seat beside him. "I don't know any Vladei. I've never met him. I'm talking about your brother, Prince Cestimir."

"Cestimir?"

"Cestimir. He's not near as stuck on himself as most of the nobles are. I liked him."

"You like almost anyone who isn't unkind to you," Liall groused, shoving his book further aside.

"Well now, that makes me sound simple."

Liall's expression did not lighten, and Scarlet could see that he was irritated and out of sorts.

"Well, you are simple, and I mean that in the best possible way. You have a kind and clear heart and you tend to think the best of folk until they prove otherwise."

"I'm a good enough judge of character to know when I'm in danger from thieves and murderers," Scarlet retorted, stung by Liall's words.

"Which reminds me; you never did explain what murderous thieves you encountered on your way to

Volkovoi."

"Oh, the crew of the cargo ship that carried me across the channel," Scarlet said, dismissing that. "It was months ago. Anyway, I like Cestimir. He seems very direct. And he's got a wicked sense of humor."

"Does he? That's good to know."

Then, because Scarlet's pride had been dented often since his arrival, he added; "And Alexyin said I was astute."

Liall was startled. "Alexyin?"

"Yes, and stop repeating every name I give you. Why do you sound so surprised? Is it really that amazing that one of your folk would think I have a quick mind? Without you there to make them say it, that is."

Liall withdrew and looked ashamed, his attitude losing the edge of anger that had been skirting his mood all day. "I may be overprotective of your safety here, but I never said you were stupid."

"Do you know Alexyin?" Scarlet asked, deftly changing the subject.

Liall paused for a moment before answering. "I do, and from Alexyin, what he said to you was a great compliment. He used to rap my knuckles when I made mistakes at sums."

Scarlet tried to imagine anyone rapping Liall's knuckles. "Oh. A very brave man, then."

Liall narrowed his eyes. "I believe someone has regained his capacity for impudence."

"I'm never impudent," Scarlet said, and elbowed him.

"Stop that, you little thug," Liall said, laughing as he took hold of Scarlet's wrists. His grip was firm, but his eyes were gentle at last. This was the man Scarlet knew. "So, you liked Cestimir," Liall said. "And he was well behaved?"

"He called one of the ladies a poisonous bitch."

"Dare I hope it was Shikhoza?"

"It was." Scarlet leaned against Liall's chest and stretched his legs out. "My feet hurt and I'm beginning to recognize the corridors by the tapestries. I've spoken to more people who don't understand Bizye than I can count. Or who pretend they don't," he added, remembering the queen's deception.

"If they are pretending, it is their loss." Liall shifted so that they were stretched out together. "The less I must share you, the better." Liall caught Scarlet's elbow this time before it hit the target and poked him several times in the ribs.

Scarlet yelped. "No more, I surrender."

"Very wise. Now tell me of this conversation with Cestimir."

"He wants to see Morturii," Scarlet said and settled in to tell him all of it.

Scarlet was not sure what Liall thought of Cestimir when he had finished, but overall Liall seemed pleased. "I have been avoiding Cestimir," he admitted. "I should speak with him this evening."

"Must we eat in that great, drafty hall tonight?" Scarlet asked, yawning. "I don't feel like figuring out all that silverware again."

"You will not dine in the hall tonight and, thankfully, neither will I. I have a private meeting with several barons and I want no crowds to influence them." His fingers slid through Scarlet's hair. "And no beautiful Hilurin to distract them."

Scarlet's eyelids were getting heavy with the warmth of the room and the comfort of Liall's arms. "Uh huh."

"I shall wake you when I return?" Liall ventured.

"And I'll hit you with a pillow if you do. My feet feel like I've just walked to Rusa in slippers. I didn't do enough walking on the ship. My soles have grown soft."

"Do not wait up, then. I will dine with the barons and attempt to re-forge some of those old ties. You would be surprised at what deals can be made over a good plate of stew."

"No I wouldn't." Scarlet yawned again. "I've made a few of those m'self."

6.

The Hunt

Gentlemen," Liall called loudly. "Please, we must have order."

The ceiling of the great hall was vaulted like a dome, painted blue with many patterns of stars etched in silver and gold. Liall stood on a high dais before a great stone casement that overlooked the lands below, the draperies thrown back to reveal the blue twilight of the Rshani day. Before and below him was a sea of brightly-garbed nobles and barons and courtiers, all talking at once, all angry or demanding or frightened of what the future would bring.

And they have only me to comfort them, Liall thought drolly. Well, he had disappointed them before. *"Order!"* Liall thundered from his high place.

The quibbling of the Barons died down and all eyes turned to Liall. Disgraced or no, he was still the Blood Prince. Talk had gone from to trade tariffs under the old king and whether they would remain the same, to disputed borders between Maekva and the Lower Kingdom, and even to irrelevant remarks about Cestimir's youth and style of dress. Truly, they would argue over anything. Liall was weary of it, and yet he knew the Barons said these many lesser things because they were unwilling to say the greater thing: that they did not trust Liall to hold the reins for Cestimir and then hand them meekly over when his time was done.

Liall could not blame them. After all, he would have been king in Cestimir's place if fate had been kinder. Or crueler, depending on how one saw the matter.

The Baron of Tebet –Ressanda by name, a bearded, heavy-set man with a blunt manner– sat with his pretty daughter Ressilka at his side, as unlike her as moon to sun. The presence of such a young woman in a Baron's council was unusual, but Liall understood Ressanda meant for her to inherit his title, so none objected. In Rshan, one did not necessarily inherit by gender. The young girl was lovely, tall and slender, with golden hair that held just a hint of strawberry. She was also obviously intelligent, watching every inhabitant of the great hall with solemn, discerning eyes, and Liall foresaw a great stir at court with her at its center.

She saw the prince looking at her. Instead of lowering her blue-painted eyes, she blinked slowly and held Liall's gaze, seeming in no particular hurry to look away. Liall was distracted when Cestimir, seated at his right hand, slid him a scrap of paper. He broke eye-contact with the fetching young woman to look at it.

Pretty?

Cestimir was looking at his brother unsmilingly, and Liall sensed a ripple of displeasure coming from the boy. He crumpled the paper in his fingers and reached for a pen, dipping it in the pot of ink to scrawl his own message back.

Cestimir looked down at the little flame-flower Liall had drawn and hid a smile as he deftly crumpled the paper in his fingers.

Baron Ressanda stood heavily –he was a great, barrel-chested man with a shock of pale and unruly, red-gold hair– and bowed his head to Liall. "Prince Nazheradei," he began "I know tempers are short and we all grow weary of this long debate, but I must ask: provided the barons rule to support Cestimir's claim, when would he be ready to ascend the throne?"

Liall glanced to Cestimir. As his advocate, he was positioned in the center of the long, raised table that overlooked the hall. Cestimir's young face was tranquil, a small-half smile arranged on his features and one still hand poised on the table: perfect, princely composure, and it had not wavered for over two hours.

"In truth," Liall said, looking at Cestimir, "he is almost ready now."

Cestimir's eyes flickered with mild surprise, and Liall wondered if any had given him cause to doubt his brother's confidence. "I cannot predict the future," he went on, "but I see no reason why he could not inherit before his twentieth year."

A murmur of satisfaction moved through the barons, and many nodded as if they had settled something in their minds. They needed a timetable to decide which way to follow the wind. There had never been a great deal of support for Vladei, and none loved him. Yet, change and uncertainty foments unrest and Vladei could still play that to his advantage, if he dared.

Many barons were stirring and there was a sense of finality in the way some gathered up their papers and shifted their hapcoats. Liall took the chance to end it on a good note.

"We will adjourn for the evening," he announced, and gave the hall a pleasant smile. "Prince Cestimir extends his gratitude for your attendance." He bowed to the hall and was relieved that Cestimir stood and bowed with him. Nadiushka had trained the boy well.

"Stay but a moment, Nazheradei!"

The voice that rang out was calm, controlled, and haughty. It was the voice of a prince. Vladei rose from his seat, resplendent in gold and red, his House colors.

We look so much alike, he and I, Liall thought. Almost, I can look at him and see Nadei.

Almost, until Vladei opened his mouth and any pity Liall might have had for him vanished.

"Princes of Druz," he said, addressing both Liall and Cestimir at once. He made a show of a bow, a little thing so deftly tossed that none could mistake it for obeisance. "If we are to be ruled by an untried boy, a youth who has not once spoken at the Council of Barons or made his voice heard at any meeting of the Moot Lords, might we at least know his mind in *some* matters?"

Liall wondered what Vladei was getting at, and held up his hand when Cestimir would have answered the older prince. "Be plain, Vladei. What is it you want to know?"

"Only that which is most important to Rshan; whether or not we are safe in this *boy's* hands." Vladei drew himself up to his full height and pitched his voice to its full power, full of subtlety and nuance, silken in its persuasion. "The Barony of Uzna Minor houses one of our most sacred shrines to our ancestors. In grandeur, it is surpassed only by Nauhin. In the hearts of our people, only Fanorl –the oldest of our dwelling-places, the very birthplace of the Shining Ones– stands higher in esteem. Uzna Minor is my charge. What she stands for is mine to protect, and only death can relieve me of that duty. What I would hear from this prince is this; will he honor what our ancestors intended for their sons and daughters? Will our lands remain sacred and apart, or are we –like every other land of Nemerl– to be infiltrated by foreign influence until the very memory of our culture is destroyed?"

"Yes," called out a man in red. He had a voice like a horn and Liall recalled that he was some captain of Vladei's. "This we must know. Will our most sacred laws be safe? Let the silent prince tell us!"

Cestimir flinched and Liall made his expression amused.

"These laws you speak of have not been questioned by any ruler since Ramung's time. And, I remind you, Vladei, that Ramung the Usurper was your ancestor, not Cestimir's. Why do you believe that my brother would threaten our legacy?"

"You give me reason," Vladei said meaningfully, pointing at Liall. "Is it not our law that no lenilyn may set foot on the mainland? Even those Arbyssian captains who we trade most closely with have never been allowed closer than the island of Sul-na. Yet, you, Nazheradei, have brought a Hilurin to our very court." Vladei turned to address the barons, walking up and down in front of the tables. "And I hear our Crown Prince is quite taken with this outlander. Who knows what lenilyn filth that creature has polluted the boy with?" He stopped in front of Baron Ressanda and looked down, clasping his hands behind his back. "Who knows why the lenilyn was sent here, or to what purpose?"

"He was not sent here," Liall grated out, controlling his temper. "I brought him with me, and even that was not intentional. He was to be put ashore in Morturii, but he fell ill and could not be left alone. By the time he had recovered, it was too late to turn back."

"He appeared to fall ill," Vladei countered, as quick of tongue as ever. "How do you know his illness was not feigned, so that you would have to bring him here where he could get close to the throne? For what purpose? To bring it down! How do we know he is not an assassin?"

Liall hid a laugh behind a cough. "Pardon me, Vladei, perhaps you have not met ser Keriss." He placed his hand below his shoulder to approximate Scarlet's height. "He can be fearsome when roused, but as long as you keep a civil tongue in your head and your hands to yourself, you will be safe enough in his presence."

A titter of laughter chased around the room. From the corner of his eye, Liall saw Lady Ressilka smiling and whispering something aside to her father. Apparently, she had as little love for Vladei as for Shikhoza.

Vladei gritted his teeth, and Liall wondered at the man's anger. It took Liall a moment to comprehend that Vladei actually believed what he was saying, and he was shocked. He wondered how a man as educated as Vladei could see menace in someone like Scarlet, simply because of the color of his skin.

"This bigotry does not become you, Vladei," Liall said. "Keriss has a gentle spirit. He would never harm anyone, save to preserve his own life."

"Gentle spirit." Vladei smiled thinly through his anger. "So gentle that one mariner aboard the Ostre Sul is disfigured for life, and three others suffered harm at his hands."

"Only after he nearly suffered rape at theirs," Liall shot back, but he was worried that Vladei apparently knew so much about the events that occurred during the voyage from Volkovoi. That alone told Liall whose hand had been behind the bravos at the port and the pirate attack at sea. "And it was Oleksei who scarred ser Keriss's face as well. For that alone I should have killed him."

"And how do we know even that is true?" Vladei said. "The mariners denied it."

"I saw them at it with my own eyes. Now, Vladei, call *me* a liar."

Vladei bowed only enough to deflect the challenge, again giving the Druz princes that trifling gesture that said anything but politeness. "I would not insult you so."

"But you will insult my t'aishka quickly enough."

Again, the red-garbed man with the loud voice stepped forward. "He's only saying what everyone is thinking."

Liall decided he had had enough of him. "Everyone, or merely the mercenaries in his pay?"

The red man subsided and cast his eyes to the floor. Vladei could look for no further help from there. It alarmed Liall to see a powerful man like Vladei so hostile to Scarlet. Vladei was a determined man with great intelligence, which meant he would make a formidable enemy.

We were close once, Liall thought. There must be some way I can reach him.

"Vladei," Liall began, stretching out his hand in a gesture of friendship.

Vladei turned on his heel and pushed past the barons in the hall, leaving a stir of whispers behind him.

Liall sighed and Cestimir shot him an apologetic look. As the barons and their attendants filed out, Cestimir helped Liall to gather the papers he had scattered about the table.

"I have never been a neat scribe," Liall said.

"They like you," Cestimir mused, nodding towards the retreating barons. "And at least one of them likes looking at you," he added, flashing a smile.

He is an astute one, this unknown brother of mine, Liall thought.

Cestimir was young, but not frivolous, and with that aura of seriousness and devotion to duty that reminded Liall of Nadiushka. Yet, as Liall saw from the flash of his teeth and the wicked gleam in his eyes when he smiled, there was still a streak of mischievous youth in Cestimir.

"As a novelty, perhaps. Like an heirloom that everyone talks about," Liall said, hoping to deflect any ideas Cestimir might be harboring that Liall found Ressilka desirable, or vice versa. "But you are their heir. They have high hopes for you."

"But they respect you, which is a rare thing. You seem

to have won them over, which brings me to a point I did not raise earlier: You are the Blood Prince of Rshan, the only one alive with a right to the throne that none could doubt. Why do you not simply claim it and end this uncertainty?"

Liall froze. "Never. I will never claim the throne of Rshan."

Cestimir gave a sigh and looked suddenly depressed. "And why would you? Why would anyone? Even now, as we speak, Khatai Jarek has taken a battlefield to the north. She carries my name on her banner. To many of my people, that name will mean death. That is not what I would have chosen, but it is what I must do if I am to keep what my ancestors have passed down to me in trust." He held his hand out to the last members of the hall as if offering them a plate. "They would all want to be king. Do you know what it means to be king, my brother?"

Liall did, but he kept silent. He had also not known about Jarek winning the field in Magur, but she was Cestimir's general, not his. It made him worry: the more defeats Vladei received, the more desperate he would become.

"It means being born with the power to do whatever you want, but none of the freedom. I will never see the kingdom of Minh or the high mountains of Morturii. I can't even go on a sleigh ride when I feel like it. I am hemmed in here, and I will be a prisoner of my crown until I grow old and die or someone kills me." Cestimir shrugged. "So I take small pleasures when I can: my books, racing my horses, eavesdropping on the court, which is sometimes better than watching a horse race. You are the same. I've seen you with your t'aishka. I've heard of the small things you seek out for him, the Byzan music for example."

"Cestimir…"

"No," he said, shaking his head. "Don't feel sorry for me. Tell me about the music."

"It was more difficult than I thought," Liall said, honoring his wish. "There are no Hilurin musicians here. In Byzantur, Hilurin families are what we would call virtuous: very proper and chaste. The only Byzan music I could find was erotic love songs and street ditties that would not be sung in public."

Cestimir was silent for a moment. "Ser Keriss is this way? Virtuous and proper?"

"Yes. I had a devil of a time even getting a kiss for months," Liall grinned, saving that story for another time.

"Oh," was all Cestimir said.

Now Liall was curious. "What?"

Cestimir looked embarrassed. "It just makes my first words to him all that more insulting," he said apologetically. "When Keriss and I first spoke, I insinuated that he was a paid lover."

"Then it is a wonder you do not have two black eyes." Liall was amused that Cestimir used the more polite term rather than whore. "Why did you say that?"

"I don't know. Perhaps because I was angry at you. You've been away all my life, but ever since I could remember, I've heard stories about you and I've wanted to meet you. Finally you came, but you had no time for me."

"Oh, Cestimir," Liall said, greatly ashamed. "I never meant—"

"The little pleasures," Cestimir interrupted, as if Liall had not spoken.

Cestimir was turning the subject, but it took Liall a moment to realize he meant the music, or perhaps more than that. He could not tell. Cestimir was at turns subtle and direct, and Liall mused that his brother would be a ruler that many trusted, but few understood.

"They are all that a king can really expect in life," Cestimir continued. "Keriss wants to go on a sleigh ride, did you know? I've promised him an excursion in my new one."

"When it can be arranged," Liall said, not wanting to forbid it, but the thought of Scarlet and Cestimir alone, outside the palace, made his heart beat faster. Assassins live in hope of just such an opportunity.

Cestimir sighed, knowing the adventure had been put off. "If you ever leave Rshan, I will long to go with you."

There was little he could say to that, yet Liall was glad for his brother. Cestimir would have no period of short-lived bliss after he ascended the throne. No aborted happiness destroyed in bits and pieces by the slow, dawning knowledge of what it truly meant to rule. He was going into kingship with his eyes open. "I am sorry."

Cestimir waved that away. "Not every eye will shed tears for me. Poor lad, he must stop his whining and become a king." Cestimir laughed and touched Liall's arm. "I will be fine, Nazheradei."

"I think you will be," Liall said honestly.

"I will. But be assured, Nazheradei... if I do ascend the throne, I will not be the ruler that my mother is. She wanted progress and change in her rule. I want only what was once ours. In this, Vladei and I are very much alike. We differ only in the times we wish our people to return to. Vladei longs for the days when we fired on foreign ships that were sighted closer than Sul-na. I don't want that. I want a return to the age when we feared no one and nothing, least of all the color of a man's skin."

Liall stared at Cestimir for a long moment. "Spoken like a king," he murmured.

"Or perhaps a fool," Cestimir said, grinning suddenly. "I would not be the first king who was more charmed by an idyllic past I had never lived than by a present I found myself trapped in. You must lesson me against false nostalgia."

Liall linked his arm with Cestimir's, liking the boy greatly. "Come. It grows late and there is an interminably boring day ahead of us tomorrow. I will see you to your room."

As it turned out, Liall was not able to seek his bed just yet. Baron Ressanda was waiting for him in an alcove not far from Liall's apartments. The Baron was alone, his daughter presumably retired, and he had come without guards, a matter which did not escape Liall's notice.

"Ser," Liall greeted casually.

Ressanda bowed deeply. "Blood Prince," he said, his voice weighted heavy with foreboding. "I come on a grave matter."

"Oh?" Liall looked up and down the hall meaningfully. They were empty, and Ressanda and he were alone.

Ressanda touched his ear with a fingertip. "Even stone walls can hear," he quoted. Liall took his meaning and turned on his heel. Ressanda followed. There was a room not twenty paces from the apartments, a small salon that Liall had searched thoroughly the night before. It was safe as any room could be in a palace.

Ressanda stood watch by the door as Liall found a lamp and struck a spark for its wick. Blue light flickered around the room as he settled the glass over the flame, then motioned for Ressanda to come forward. Liall found

a chair and pulled it up to the small table. This was a bare
room with only a little furniture and no ornament, no
tapestries or paintings, nothing to hide behind. With a
final, suspicious look at the room's contents, Ressanda
sighed and heaved his bulk into the single remaining chair.
It creaked under his weight and the wooden legs popped
and groaned before submitting to support him. Ressanda
put his elbows on the table and folded his arms.

"There is a matter," Ressanda said. "I would have
brought it to you before, but I was not sure of you yet."

"And now you are?"

The Baron held up a hand. "Not so quickly, my prince.
I may be reassured, but I am not totally reconciled with
your return. I knew Nadei from the time he was a boy."

Liall felt his teeth wanting to clench. "Then you knew
how he naive was, how delicate his pride and how easily
he could be lead, or insulted."

Ressanda nodded, his ruddy hair tumbling across
his forehead. "I did, but he was still my prince. That he
would have made a poor king does not excuse you."

Liall bowed his head. "No. It does not."

He was surprised to feel Ressanda's hand on his arm.
"But there is nothing you can do to recall that. What's
done is done, and we are here and Nadei is burned to
ashes, and whatever future he would have taken us to is
dust. Now we must look to you to carve a new future."

"Not to me," Liall argued. "Cestimir—"

"Is a boy, still," he finished. "I, for one, believe you
when you say you will turn the throne over to him in
swift manner, but many do not. Not truly. Yet... they are
content to have their prince back, disgraced or otherwise.
It is enough, after so many years of uncertainty, to have
a strong man of the pure blood to look to. Vladei!"
Ressanda said the name with loathing. "There is not one
man of honor in all of Rshan who would back him, but

we both know that honorable men have never been in the majority."

"So he has followers," Liall said slowly. "More than I have been led to believe."

Ressanda nodded. "Much more, though they are gathered to the north. We all saw Khatai Jarek and her army leave the Nauhinir, but we were told she was headed south. Now my spies tell me different." He leaned a little forward. "Is this true? Has she gone north to clean out the rat's nest?"

Liall knew how much was riding on his reply, and what a mistake it would be if he misread Ressanda.

True, he thought. The army belongs solely to the queen and she may aim it where she will, but if word gets loose that fighting has broken out and none of the nobles are notified, there will be a bloodbath within the court. "You ask a lot of me when you ask for my trust."

"Then take this as proof of my trust," Ressanda said at once. They understood one another. "I am not of the pure blood. That is easy to see, with my red hair and my uncouth body. I am not a pale-haired and elegant Druz prince, but I did manage to marry a woman who is: Winotheri."

The name was known to Liall. "My cousin," he said in surprise. Many things had changed in his absence. He had not even known they were kinsmen. "I did not know."

Ressanda patted Liall's arm brusquely before withdrawing. "And as Winotheri is an only child, my daughter, Ressilka, inherits her titles, which includes the name of Druz. She, like you and Cestimir, is a vanishing breed. How many Druz are left now? Seven? Eight if you count that rag-tag second cousin of yours who went seafaring. And Ressilka's youth and unmarried status –not to mention her wealth– make her a very valuable commodity."

This was too rough-spoken, even for a man like Ressanda. "You daughter is not a cow at market, ser."

"That is exactly what she is!" Ressanda snapped. He took a deep breath. Snow hissed against the window in the silence. "And she knows it," he added, much calmer. "She is a prince in her own right, a great woman already. I would not see her given to a dog of a man who snarls for scraps at a royal table he has not earned a place at by deed or character."

Vladei. "Ah. And has such a dog been sniffing around your daughter?"

"He has," Ressanda growled. "But he shall not have her. I am saving her for another."

"Cestimir."

"No other is worthy of her," he said grudgingly, as if he privately thought that not even Cestimir would do. "When you returned, I had hoped, just for a moment..."

Liall sat back. "My heart is elsewhere," he said. "And even were it not, I would saddle no child of mine with a crown. But I am flattered," he added. He meant it as a courtesy only, but when Liall said it, he found it to be true. The girl was obviously Ressanda's jewel and he had meant, however fleetingly, for Liall to have her.

The Baron nodded, unsurprised. "Well, I heard as much. But a man always hopes, yes? Anyway, I wanted you to know my will; that if Vladei sues for leave of any queen or regent or prince the right to wed my daughter, and wins it, I will take it as a mortal offense."

So that was it. By ancestral right, a Druz married only at the pleasure of the queen, whomever she chose, whenever she chose. However possessive his words may have sounded, Ressanda had no legal choice in whom Ressilka married, though he could always rebel and face the consequences.

"Royal blood and royal name are too precious to bestow lightly," Liall said carefully, wanting time to think.

"My daughter is too precious to bestow lightly," Ressanda said meaningfully. "Not even as the scrap that will keep the wolf from seeking blood."

Liall was silent for several moments, pondering. Not for a moment did he believe that Ressanda meant him when he said wolf. It was true that Ressilka would be a powerful foil to calm Vladei should he lose his bid for the crown, which he would if Liall had his will. A Druz prince as his wife would insure that Vladei's future generations, at some point through marriage, would sit on the throne of Rshan. If Vladei himself could not be king, at least his granddaughter might rule at the side of one of Cestimir's heirs. Ressanda had good reason to fear.

But those assumptions were made upon a guess that Vladei would be content with his heirs inheriting power and nothing for himself. It was logic, made upon the premise that Vladei was a logical man. Liall knew that Vladei was not.

Liall pushed back the chair and rose. Startled, Ressanda, got to his feet as well.

"Fear not," Liall said before the man could speak. "Vladei will not have your daughter."

"How—"

"Ask me nothing," Liall said curtly, and the Baron closed his mouth. Liall put his hand on Ressanda's shoulder and pressed it, hoping Ressanda could find the strength to trust him. "I can only give you my promise; Ressilka shall belong to Cestimir, or she shall belong to no man."

Liall saw that Ressanda did not know how to interpret that. Outwardly, the Baron was not a subtle man and perhaps he thought Liall was being cryptic, yet the promise must be enough for him. Ressanda's eyes grew stony and Liall saw that he realized which way the prince's thoughts must run.

"So even she would not be enough for Vladei," Ressanda said slowly. "Very well, my prince. My lot is now cast with yours, and if you should fail, we must fall as well."

"There is a way out of it for you," Liall said gently, for he did not wish Ressanda to lose hope.

The baron shook his head. "We cannot all be as brave as you, to accept exile in unknown lands, for that is how far we would have to go to escape him. No, I'm afraid that death would be a much more welcoming embrace."

Ressanda left without another word or glance at Liall, which somehow was worse. Though it had been there from the moment they landed on Rshan, Liall felt keenly the heaviness Ressanda had placed on him. If Cestimir failed to win the throne, Vladei would still seek to have the boy murdered. Once in power, Vladei would never tolerate such a threat to exist. Cestimir would be forced to flee or fight, and he would never run. Conversely, if Vladei failed, he would not rest until power was his. Civil war was looming on the horizon.

His shoulders slumped under the new burden, Liall put out the lamp and went to seek his bed. Scarlet was already asleep, his eyes closed so peacefully that Liall could not bear to wake him. Through the window, the blue morning twilight looked the same as evening twilight and every other hour of the day.

It is beautiful here, Liall thought suddenly, wondering when he had forgotten that. He had forgotten what it was to wake and part the gauzy bed-curtains and see snowflakes cascading past a gilded window in the half-light of the Rshan winter, with the bright stars wheeling in a sky the color of faded indigo.

It is wondrous pleasant to sleep with the smell of incense and flowers in your nose, he thought, to feel silk against your skin and open your eyes to blue lamps cut from a crystal that only grows in your homeland.

Scarlet slept deeply, one hand curled under his cheek and his dark eyelashes like frayed silk on his cheeks. Liall looked at him for a long time, standing by the bed, marveling at how a chance meeting on a mountain road could have brought them together here, and terribly alarmed at how strongly he felt the sudden urge to send Scarlet away.

Yes, there was beauty here, but every instinct Liall had was telling him that what he found the most beautiful was in serious peril. His heart said that he should send Scarlet packing before Fate grew tired of Liall's flirtation with disaster or his enemies grew luckier. The pirate attack had been a warning. It had shown him that Scarlet could innocently be caught in the crossfire of kings and be killed for it. One misstep: that is all it would take. A poisoned cup, a dagger in the night, a broken neck on icy steps, and Scarlet would be gone. Liall's hard heart, so long unmoved by anything but regret and guilt, would again turn to stone.

The scene played itself in his mind; Scarlet on the blood-soaked deck of the Ostre Sul, ducking under the Minh's sword, only this time he moved too slowly and the blade caught him under the chin and that beautiful face vanished in a spray of red. Scarlet's black eyes would be open when Liall found him, still caught in an expression of endless surprise and accusation at how Liall had failed him.

Send him away, the wise part of him whispered.

Liall undressed and crawled silently into bed, not wanting to wake Scarlet. When I wake in the morning, Liall told himself stoutly, I will feel better and be more optimistic. There is no need to send him away.

He would realize later that it was, as in Volkovoi, pure selfishness that made him forget any thought of sending Scarlet away from the Nauhinir. With Scarlet, his blood had come to life again. His heart was not a lump of cold seeping into his veins.

I want him with me.

It was decision he would have cause to regret within a day.

"Kaya hast kyen min fer s'ctath!" Liall swore, his voice rising.

"Same to you," Scarlet quipped, not at all impressed with Liall's anger. He sat up in the bed and moved a little away from the prince. "And I'm still going. You said I could."

"Scarlet, a bear hunt is not like fishing for trout. Bears bite back!"

"I'm going. Try and stop me and you'll regret it."

It was two days since they had quarreled. The morning of the bear hunt had come and Liall still had not been able to convince Scarlet to stay behind. Liall had mentioned it gently when they awoke, cajoling Scarlet with caresses and soft words to do as he asked. When that had not worked, the words had become more forceful and Liall had grown exasperated.

Liall opened the bed-curtains and swung his legs over the side of the bed before stomping naked into the privy. The servants turned and bowed politely as he passed, and he heard Scarlet utter a Bizye curse and throw the covers aside. Typical of Hilurin, it annoyed Scarlet when others saw Liall's body.

When Liall returned, Dvi had brought a tray to the side of the bed and Scarlet sipped hot che with a thick robe belted around him. Scarlet gave Liall a sour look and eyed the robe that Nenos held out for the prince. Liall stepped into the robe and avoided Scarlet's glance as he took a cup.

Liall sipped it. "Stop being such a prude," he said lowly. The che was dark and doubly strong, which was welcome.

Scarlet muttered and rose to go to the table. Liall followed, but not before Nenos had pulled him aside and questioned him about the wisdom of taking Scarlet on the hunt.

"He has had no real exercise in months, since before you set out at sea," Nenos said, his jaw set mutinously and his bright blue eyes sparkling with anger. "If he were my charge alone I would forbid him to go in such a condition. He grows weak and listless in these rooms, and boredom preys on his mind. He has nightmares. Did he tell you that?"

Liall shook his head, shocked. "He has said nothing about nightmares."

"He is in no shape for a bear hunt." Nenos's tone was truculent and almost rude. "You must forbid this."

If only he knew. "I have tried!"

Nenos glanced at Scarlet worriedly and insisted on getting Liall's promise that Scarlet would be kept in the rear guard of the hunt, and not allowed near the spears.

"He is safe with me," Liall said, stiff with insult. Nenos turned and spoke in a scolding tone to Scarlet, who did not catch a word of it.

"What did he say?" Scarlet asked, resigned.

"Aside from telling me that Hilurin are reckless, stubborn fools, he says you should listen to me and keep your stubborn arse in this room before you get yourself killed chasing bears."

"He never," Scarlet scoffed, disbelieving. "He's too polite."

Then Scarlet did an odd thing. When Nenos put the che pot on the table and before he could leave, Scarlet took Nenos's gnarled hand in both of his and pressed it to the side of his face in a very old gesture of gratitude. Only another Hilurin would have understood the gesture fully, but Nenos interpreted it well enough.

Nenos stared at Scarlet, startled, then summoned a smile and patted Scarlet's cheek with his free hand. Liall watched Scarlet thoughtfully as Nenos left.

"Why did you do that?" Liall asked. He had only seen Scarlet do such a thing once before, and the gesture had been offered to Liall himself on the mountain road near Lysia, in gratitude for saving Scarlet's sister from death.

He shrugged. "You probably don't realize it, but that old man could have made my life a misery here. Any good servant knows how to make a guest feel unwelcome. Instead, he went the other road and made me feel like this was my home."

"I thought redbirds had no home."

Scarlet only smiled a little, not answering, and after a long moment Liall leaned over and shoved a plate in front of him.

"Eat," he commanded. Scarlet dug in, seeming content for once to comply without argument. "How do you know so much about servants? You were a pedlar."

"I had a friend, Kozi, who was a servant in a Morturii house before becoming a pedlar."

"The boy who disappeared one year? Were you close?"

Scarlet speared a piece of the salt fish. "If it's so risky, why is Cestimir going?"

A nobleman knows when a subject has been turned. "Hunts are always perilous, especially with rivals like Vladei and Eleferi skulking about, but if Cestimir is to be king, he cannot sit in his chambers and hide while the world spins around him."

"Is this another thing that only another Rshani would understand?"

"Possibly," Liall said, nettled at the jibe. "Let me just say the Hunt is a matter of honor, and as matters stand now, well... Cestimir cannot refuse to go, and neither can I. You could," he added hopefully.

Scarlet ignored the hint. "Has Cestimir hunted snow bears before?"

"That shocks you?"

"From the way you described the beast, yes. Hard to believe that a fourteen year old, no matter how tall, would be allowed to track and kill it."

Liall nodded. "My mother says that Cestimir has been on many hunts, but not on the spear team."

Scarlet gave him a blank look.

"He rides in the rear of the hunting party and observes, but does not participate," Liall explained. "Which is where you will be, if you are truly resolved to do this. Jochi will be at your side, and you must stay there."

Scarlet opened his mouth to say something and Liall gave him a black glare that made him shut it quickly. "On this point, I will not yield," Liall said sternly. "I regret that I have been overprotective and you feel coddled, but I really will have you locked in this room if you do not promise to stay behind the spear line."

Scarlet laughed a little. "You could try, but I promise. I'd rather be beside you, though."

"Too dangerous."

Scarlet nodded. "And the queen?"

"She is not well enough to join us." Liall looked away

for a moment. "But I remember a day when she trailed the hunt as fiercely as any warrior. It is difficult to see her so frail." Then he saw that Scarlet's dark eyes were suddenly misty and sorrowing. "What is it?"

"I was thinking of my mother, Linhona."

Liall took his hand and held it. Linhona and Scarlet's father, Scaja, had both died in the Aralyrin raid on Lysia. He wondered if Scarlet would ever be able to talk about it. Scarlet had not mentioned them more than a handful of times since their murders.

They finished breakfast in silence and washed up before Nenos dismissed everyone and brought the hunting clothes. The servant gave Scarlet a handful of silver ribbons while giving Liall a baleful eye. Liall saw that Scarlet had no idea what to do with the ribbons, so he plucked them from Scarlet's hand.

"Here, turn around," Liall said brusquely. He was still angry at Scarlet for insisting on going, and resentful at being cast as the villain in the whole affair. "They are meant for your hair," he said, quickly weaving a ribbon into Scarlet's black locks. Liall caught Scarlet's horrified expression in the mirror and could not repress a sudden smile. "Is this another thing that only women do in Nemerl?"

"You should know," Scarlet complained. "You were there for, what, how many years? Did you ever see a man in a dress with ribbons in his hair?"

"Never on the street anyway," Liall chuckled, avoiding the slanted question about his age. "There was a bhoros boy in Rusa, though..."

"I don't want to hear it."

Liall weaved three or four more into his hair. "It suits you." But when he took Scarlet's shoulders and turned him into the mirror, a chill raced down Liall's back and his smile faded.

"Liall?"

Liall shook his head, trying to clear the vision. "Nothing. A will o'the wisp, nothing more. I fancied for a moment that I had seen you with silver in your hair before."

"Only snow," Scarlet said, looking at him with puzzlement.

They finished dressing, and Scarlet marveled at the skill of Rshani weavers as he drew on layer upon layer of the thin woolen hunting gear. Over all this went the glittering court vircas of blue and silver and black. Soon, they left the apartments and went down to a lower hall and thence to the courtyard, where Jochi awaited. Scarlet was given a white fur coat to match Liall's and it fit him snug and warm, as well as fur-lined gloves and a conical fur hat that was the standard Rshani outdoor dress. Scarlet examined the hat and saw that it had been thoughtfully embroidered with a little crimson flower with saw-toothed green leaves. Liall wondered who had ordered that, but forgot it when Jochi brought the silks.

"Pull this up to your nose while riding," Jochi told Scarlet, showing him how to wrap the long length of tightly-woven silk around his neck and the lower part of his face. "It will protect your face from the wind." The silk was woven of blue and silver –the queen's colors– and also served to denote which team they rode for in the hunt.

"Hunting silks," Jochi answered Scarlet when he asked. There were others in the hunt wearing similar scarves, but only a handful in these colors. Others were in red and gold or green and silver, which Jochi explained to Scarlet were colors of other noble Rshan houses. Liall was silent while this education progressed, still shadowed by the vision of Scarlet with silver in his hair.

The courtyard was a hubbub of noise as hounds and

grooms darted between the horses. A few of the nobles were already mounted. Eleferi and his brother Vladei were in red and gold hunting colors near the head of the line, as were Alexyin and Tesk and also two of the courtiers that Scarlet had spoken to in the library. There were some forty or more horses saddled and ready, splendidly groomed and decked, and twice that many spectators and court ladies and little lads running underfoot everywhere and laughing. The horses were well-trained and did not shy even when one of the children ducked under a horse's belly and shrieked laughter, playing a game of tag with his friend.

A groom marched up to Liall carrying a white-painted wooden pole that was twice his height. One end was blunt and had a wide grip and guard fashioned for the hand, and the other end was sharpened into a point and covered with a thin, beaten layer of silver hardened with nickel and lead. At least twenty other riders were holding similar implements, and Liall accepted his and settled it easily into a grooved slip fashioned into the leather of his saddle.

"What is that?" Scarlet asked in awe, still unmounted. "That's never a spear."

"It is. The rider must hold it during the chase, like so." Liall showed him, one hand on the reins and the other steadying the stake.

"You've got some cheek, calling that a spear," Scarlet said. "It's a sail mast, at least."

Scarlet did not have to ask what the spears were for, for several of the tips were still stained with old blood the color of rust. This was how the bear would be hunted: ran down with dogs and horses, corralled into some narrow ravine or the base of some hill, and then impaled by many of those great stakes.

"Doesn't seem like much sport to me," Scarlet

commented.

"Then you can rutting well stay behind!" Liall growled in gutter Falx, which bought him a laugh from Scarlet. Not exactly Liall's intended reaction. A groom led another saddled horse up to Scarlet. Liall spoke to the groom in Sinha, wanting the man to double-check the saddle, but Scarlet stepped up and checked it and the bit as well, and then put his foot in the stirrup. He swung up, no easy task for a small rider drowning in fur, and settled himself easily in the saddle. He caught Liall gaping at him.

"What?" Scarlet laughed. "Close your mouth lest something fly in, want-wit."

"I did not know you rode."

"Of course I ride. Well... at least enough to stay in a saddle. My dad fixed wagons for a living. What do you think pulled them, mice?"

Liall scowled, still wishing there was some way he could forbid Scarlet to go, but it was too late. "You and Jochi will stay in the rear of the hunt, with the watch-riders and youths," Liall said, bringing his mount alongside Scarlet's and reaching down to check the stirrups of Scarlet's horse one last time. "Neither of you will be hunting today."

"We will still be able to see any excitement," Jochi reassured Scarlet, and Liall turned to see Jochi mounted on a fine dappled horse.

Liall sighed and glanced at Scarlet a last time. "You look splendid," he said, suddenly regretful that he had been in such a foul mood. He was also nearly ill with anxiety. All that morning, he had had a sick feeling in the pit of his stomach, a hole that was slowly being filled with a nameless dread. He felt the shamed urge to pray to gods he didn't believe in, just on the thin chance that it might do some good. Liall mentioned none of this to Scarlet.

"I must join the others," Liall said unsmilingly. "Jochi, I leave him in your hands."

Jochi inclined his head. "Depend upon me, my prince."

Scarlet gave Jochi a saucy wink. Liall guided his horse through the melee to the edge of the courtyard. He turned and Cestimir was beside him, mounted on a gray horse similar to his own.

"Well, brother," Cestimir smiled "Are you ready to hunt?"

Red and white, white and red.

The rules of the hunt were that the watch-riders in the rear would not come near the actual kill, but would stay far back from any slaughter or blood, yet Liall kept looking at Scarlet so anxiously that Jochi was moved to gently reassure the prince that he would watch out for the boy, and Liall's heart was eased.

And so, Liall was easy and relaxed when the worst happened, and did not see the yawning edge of death, red-fanged and razor-clawed, until it was too late.

Three bears had been spotted in the hunting preserve during the spring season, and during the night the beaters went out and drove them into the lower preserve closest to the palace, a wide, open expanse of snowy lowland field bordered by a dense forest. It was near the bear's hibernating time, and they would be fattened and irritable and in no mood to tolerate intruders. The dogs, great, thick-furred beasts with sly, slanted eyes blue as a summer sky, would run tandem with the lead horses until they reached the hunting grounds, then given their head to run on and scent out the bear.

The dogs began to bay and growl even before they

were really clear of the palace grounds. The huntsmaster sounded a note on a silver pipe and the dogs leaped forward, melting into the looming edge of the forest so fast it tricked the eye into thinking they had vanished. The riders went in after them at a fast trot, cautious and not having that heightened sense the dogs possessed, to let them know by smell how close the bear was. Forty men on horses, twenty of them with stakes, the rest either serving as flanks on the line to keep watch for the bear or bringing up the rear as youths training to the hunt or just observers.

In the twilight gloom, the horses kept pace with the dogs for several minutes, seeing their shadows up ahead, wending in and out of the trees and baying at full throat. Then the dogs surged forward and hunting party lost sight of them, pursuing the animals by sound alone. The huntsmaster blew another note on his pipe, and several of the dogs bayed loudly, signaling their location. The hunters spurred the horses and turned west back towards the open field.

The line of riders broke from the forest in a blur. Baron Ressanda was on Liall's right, a veteran of many hunts, so limber and confident in the saddle he seemed not to move at all. Vladei was behind Liall, which set his nerves to humming, for Vladei had been in the lead when they started out. Liall glanced over at Ressanda and the Baron jerked his chin over his shoulder. Ressanda was no fool. He was keeping a tight watch on Vladei himself.

Up from behind him, a rider rushed past –Tesk or Baron Tebet, Liall could not tell– and somewhere ahead the dogs began to howl and bay in a crescendo of blood lust. That was when they first heard the bear.

The snow bear is an unfriendly beast. It is a loner for much of the year, staking out and marking its hunting grounds by scent and claws. It only tolerates its own kind to mate or to fight and –for the female– to raise her young to two winters before abandoning them. It can tower four to six feet above a horse's head, and its girth measures a mature oak of thirty years or more.

The bear the dogs had pinned down near the wreck of an ancient pine was an old one, a male, his jowls and muzzle marked by long whiskers that gave him a grizzled appearance. Twenty baying, bristling dogs snarling and snapping at the bear's flanks, and the great white mound of the bear himself trapped between the bole of the dead tree and a finger of bare rock protruding from the low hill at his back. They rode up on it in two lines, one to either side of the hill, and those hunters with spears moved forward to surround the beast with a circle of sharpened death.

"Pail'aa sest Nauhin!" the huntsmaster cried over the din of dogs and bear and horses stamping in fear. It was a ritual cry –*For the Shining Ones!*– but the Shining Ones had lived long, long ago and no one remembered why the bear was always sacrificed to them.

Three spear teams, six to a team and the huntsmaster and the houndsmaster hanging back to let them work. The baiting team goes in and prods the bear to turn, and then the other teams move to turn it back with sharp prods from the spears. The maddened beast almost always charges the third time, right into the spears. Liall had seen it happen so often that it was almost rote to him. The baiting team, blue and silver for the queen, moved in, and Liall was not happy to have Vladei at his back, but it was Vladei's skin, too, if they failed, and Liall was counting on Vladei loving that too much to risk it.

As the baiting team moved forward, Vladei kneed his horse close to Liall's, his red silks fluttering. Liall slid a black glance to Vladei, one gloved hand on his reins, and then quickly spurred his horse, piercing the bear's hide enough to madden it and turn it to the other two teams. The second and third teams took their turns, shouting and stabbing the bear shallowly or deep, and the bear's pure, snowy hide blossomed with red flowers of blood.

When the bear turned again and it was up to Liall's team, the queen's colors, to take the killing shot, Vladei appeared to hang back as he must, not being on the queen's team. And then, at the last moment when Liall's stake was furthest out and his horse a full head closer to the bear than all others, Vladei spurred his well-trained mount to surge forward, getting in the way of the other horses until Liall whipped his head around –*"Vladei!"*– and saw that he was alone. The bear had his opening.

Four weak spears and one lowered one, and one horse within paw's reach. The bear roared and reared up on his hind legs, a towering wall of thick hide and teeth, and Liall's horse shied and screamed, feeling death even before Liall. One blur, an arc of sharp spikes slicing the air, and his mount's innards splattered on the snow. The gelding went down screaming and took Liall with it, rolling –thank the Shining Ones– away from the bear, but pinning his left leg under the saddle. Liall dropped the stake, his right leg already out of the stirrup and pushing, trying to shove the gelding off or himself out from under the animal's bulk, the thick stench of steaming guts and blood making him want to vomit.

Fear. He had hunted snow bear before but never this close. From the ground the bear looked even bigger, a tide of death coming toward him. Liall saw a rider on Vladei's team –Tesk it was– viciously spur his horse forward and spear the bear in the shoulder to get it to turn, but the beast had scented blood other than its own and would have it. Tesk flung his spear at the bear, shouting wildly. It might have been a toothpick, so little did the bear heed it. Liall heard the huntsmaster sound his pipe and the dogs came forward in a furious, boiling mass, finally allowed to rend and tear. They hung dripping on the bear's hide, fangs buried in his flesh, until the bear dragged two into his embrace and crushed them. Red and white, blood and snow, and the bear opened wide his mouth, which yawned open like a dinner platter ringed with small knives, and let out a roar that made Liall's eardrums ring. Someone was shouting in Bizye –or was it Sinha?– and any second now the bear would charge over the hump of the dead horse and bury those teeth into Liall, bite through his neck until the corded flesh parted and his head rolled on the ground, white and red. Liall could only stare into the bear's eyes and wait for it, his ears deadened to sound, feeling a cold sense of awe that the bear's eyes were the most beautiful shade of clear gold, like candlelight, burning up everything in his field of vision. He prepared to die, swallowed by the fire in the bear's brain, unaided and trapped under the horse.

And then, it all changed.

Scarlet, little Scarlet, whom Liall had made ride in the rear guard because he knew nothing of hunting, proved it by doing what no real hunter would ever do: he whipped his horse straight into the bear, thus cutting his mount out from under him and leaving him on equal terms with his prey. Scarlet drove his heels into the horse's flank and shouted wildly, and the mount –trained to a flawless performance– leapt forward obediently, its eyes rolling white in terror, but still charging the bear. It crashed into the mountain of white fur and teeth, bowling it over and throwing Scarlet up and over the saddle to impact with the side of the icy hill. Scarlet lay stunned for a moment as the bear turned its killing gaze from him to Scarlet's horse and ripped open its throat. The valiant horse fell dead just as Scarlet was rolling over and getting to his feet and –oh gods– he was behind the bear. The bear was between Scarlet and the hunters, and the hill was to his back. He was trapped.

Scarlet knew this, too. Liall could see it in Scarlet's eyes in the instant before the bear came between them. Red and white, Scarlet and the White Wolf, Scarlet and the snow bear, blood and snow, and the bear roared a note of pure pain and fury and charged Scarlet.

Scarlet's mouth opened and he inhaled once, eyes so black and round they looked like pits, and then he dropped to one knee. Liall thought Scarlet had fallen, and then he saw Scarlet's pale hand grope for something on the ground: Tesk's thrown spear, half-hidden in the snow. Scarlet's fingers curled around it and he brought the point up swiftly, bracing the butt against the rocky side of the hill, as the bear raced forward, blind to everything but prey, and it *struck*.

Blood splashed the snow, a great arc of it, red and steaming and smelling of iron and brass. There was constant roar in Liall's head, and whether it was him screaming at the hunters to get Scarlet out of there or him keening for his lover's death, he could not tell. Suddenly, there were men surrounding Liall, sliding friendly hands under his arms and lifting him, levering the horse away from his leg. The snow bear was conquered at last, slumped in an impossibly large heap near the foot of the hill, presumably dead.

Where was Scarlet? Liall could only believe he was under the bear, and in the same condition. Liall tried to go to Scarlet, but his leg gave out and he was on his hands and knees, buried up to the wrists in crimson slush where the hot blood had melted the ice.

Ressanda was at his side, and Jochi, trying to help him.

"My prince," Jochi babbled, his face drawn by grief into lines of ugliness. "My prince, he went... I could not stop him..." He was pale and sobbing openly.

Liall shoved them away and lurched towards the bear. *"Scarlet!"* He turned to Ressanda, who was staring at him in shock and pity. "Help me move this beast!"

It took more than Ressanda. Four men, using spears as a fulcrum, were at last able to lever the bear off the small, still body pinned between the hill and the beast. The stake had been aimed true: Scarlet had impaled the bear through the heart.

It must have been the heart, Liall thought. The bear's blood was everywhere. The beast had poured himself out on the ground. It covered Scarlet from neck to foot, drenching his furs, and his eyes were closed as though dead. Liall gave a wild and anguished cry and knelt to gather Scarlet in his arms.

Red and white. The blood-painted hill and the ivory of his skin, now stained red. One moment of distraction, long enough for Vladei to play him for a fool, and his nightmare had entered the waking world.

The dream was true, Liall thought in misery. A portent of things to come, and I knew it long before I left Volkovoi. Had I not been warned not to bring him to Rshan? I knew I risked his life, but I was selfish. I wanted him with me.

Liall lifted Scarlet and moved to clean ground, where he knelt again and brushed Scarlet's hair away from his forehead. A little blood stained Scarlet's temple, and Liall saw that a dark bruise was forming at the line of his hair.

"Your hair is always so unruly," Liall whispered in fading despair. "Scarlet...please," he moaned, wanting to deny this death, find some way to banish it, but there was none. Had the gods not warned him? "Scarlet, no."

Scarlet's cheek was still warm against Liall's hand as he cupped it and kissed Scarlet's mouth. Still warm there, too. It made Liall weep at last, something he had not done since the last time he feared Scarlet would die, and before that it was the day Nadei died.

A shower of snowflakes came on a sudden wind as Liall huddled on the ground, his arms locked around Scarlet. They rained down and settled in Scarlet's hair, turning black to frost and silver.

And then, like the magic in the stories, he opened his eyes.

"Liall?" Scarlet croaked, and then he coughed. Behind them, Jochi gave a cry of joy and began shouting orders to bring a sleigh. There were other shouts, cries of wonder and disbelief, as the hunters saw with great relief that it would not be a day to mourn after all. They had lost no hunters. The bear was dead. They were alive.

Liall held Scarlet, drenched in bear's blood as he was, and gazed in profound relief at what he had been given back.

"You... you are not," Liall stammered, more than a little afraid that this was the true dream and he would wake to find himself in the palace surrounded by sorrowful faces. "Oh, Scarlet, are you really alive?"

Scarlet reached up to touch Liall's face, and Liall realized with awe that this was the second time Scarlet had awakened from "death" to find Liall weeping over him.

"Kiss me and find out."

7.

The Gift

They rode back in a sleigh. Liall pushed Scarlet into the carriage, sticky as he was with blood. Scarlet was dazed, not only from the shock of seeing Liall trapped on the ground, but from his own recklessness in taking the damned beast on. His fur coat and his hat were mucky and growing stiff with blood, but Jochi wouldn't allow him to take anything off. Liall rode next to Scarlet, silent and pale, his hands clenched into fists, as Jochi apologized repeatedly and wept.

"Stop, Jochi," Scarlet said in a weak voice. "I'm alive."

"It is my fault," Jochi said for the tenth time. He looked to Liall. "I said you could depend on me, my prince, but he nearly died, and it was my fault."

"It was the bear's fault," Liall growled. "Cease this, I command you."

Jochi choked back a sound and nodded, wiping his face with his sleeve.

Scarlet had never seen a man so upset over a thing he couldn't prevent and had no hand in at all. The bear went after Liall, so he went after the bear. It was plain as water to him, and why Jochi could not comprehend that only Deva determined the outcome of such a thing was a puzzle he couldn't sort out. Scarlet wanted to reassure Jochi, but Liall was still staring at him. Liall's jaw was clenched so tight there was a white line under his lower lip.

"Are you all right?" Scarlet asked again. Liall unclenched his fists to touch Scarlet's face, as if he still could not believe Scarlet was alive. Scarlet was a bit surprised on that count himself. The snow bear had been the most enormous animal he had ever seen.

"Yes, t'aishka," Liall said. He moved Scarlet's outer furs aside, inspecting his lover for injury yet again. "Are you sure none of that blood is yours? How is your head?" Liall worriedly examined the lump on Scarlet's temple.

Cestimir, who had abandoned his horse to ride in the sleigh beside Liall, snorted. "How many times must you both ask the same question? No, brother, the blood is not his, and yes, ser Keriss, Nazheradei has only a bruised leg."

Liall scowled at the prince. Cestimir smiled drolly. "And I've become fond of the pair of you, so I'm glad on both accounts."

Scarlet gave Cestimir a warm look. He leaned his head on Liall's shoulder and rode the rest of the way back to the palace with his eyes closed. There was a slight pounding in his ears and the sway of the carriage seemed to make him feel queasy, almost as if they were at sea again, but he swallowed hard against the sickness and took deep breaths, terrified of shaming himself.

The courtyard was flooded with watchers. It was as if the palace had been upended and every one of its people dumped into the courtyard to witness their arrival. He was surrounded as Jochi helped him out of the sleigh, and from everywhere, from every direction, hands reached out to touch the blood on his clothes and face.

"Sange hun'esk hinir," some whispered. He asked Liall what it meant, more than a little shook by the awed looks on their proud faces, and the way they touched their bloodied fingers to their lips.

Jochi did not budge from his side, and Alexyin was beside Cestimir, with Liall limping between them. "Blooded by the bear," Liall supplied. "It is a rare thing. Usually, when a man is near enough to a snow bear to get its blood on him, he does not come back alive."

Cestimir touched his brother's arm. "Nazheradei, I think ser Keriss has broken the curse."

Liall shot Cestimir a forbidding look and led Scarlet quickly away into the great hall. When they arrived, Scarlet gladly let servants strip away the bloody furs, which were taken away reverently. Where, he did not know. He even put up with a subdued Jochi silently taking a damp cloth to his face before pronouncing Scarlet presentable enough to stand before the queen.

They took seats at the queen's table. Spiced wine was served, hot from warming and fortified with stronger liquor. Beside Liall, Alexyin and Jochi spoke quietly and urgently to the queen, and she listened, her face growing steadily colder. She raised her head to pin Scarlet with her eyes, and Scarlet was chilled by her gaze, yet he sensed her coldness was not directed at him.

The queen raised her cup and the great hall went silent. "Drink in honor of Keriss kir Nazheradei, who has not only won victory over the snow bear, but has saved my beloved eldest son."

"Again," Liall murmured, loud enough for many to hear. He raised his cup.

Further down the high table, Scarlet saw a stern man with nearly-colorless eyes rise from his seat and raise his cup with Liall, his mouth twisted in a sneer.

Liall stiffened.

"Yes," the man agreed, "Let us all drink to the royal trinket."

"Vladei," Liall growled in warning.

So, this was the brother whom Liall disliked so much.

There was little resemblance between them. *Step-brother and cousin*, Scarlet reminded himself. Still, even a stranger could see the way Liall's hackles rose when Vladei stood up, and the way Vladei regarded his kinsman with a mixture of hatred and icy contempt.

It was the first time Scarlet had ever seen this man that Liall had named several times as a danger. He could see the strong family resemblance to Liall in Vladei's hard features, but Scarlet felt an almost instinctive wariness for this cold man who bore his lover's face.

Vladei turned his attention to Scarlet and gave the young man a knowing smile. "You do know that's what you are, yes? A trinket. Perhaps that's why my brother never had you tutored to speak Sinha." He moved away from his chair and toward Scarlet. "Keriss kir Nazheradei. What do you imagine that means, I wonder?"

Scarlet felt his temper rising as Liall moved to his side, facing Vladei. Liall took Scarlet's hand and gripped it so hard that his knuckles ground together. Scarlet glanced at Liall to see his expression hewn in stone, all cold rage and danger.

"It's a court name."

Vladei chuckled. "Poor ignorant. Kir means belonging to. Or, in other uses, owned. Keriss, owned by Nazheradei. Like a jewel or a pet."

Scarlet's stomach knotted up and he looked at Liall, waiting for Liall to deny it.

Liall looked only at Vladei, and his rage was clear.

"Liall?" Scarlet nudged him with his arm. Say something, damn it, he thought. Why doesn't he say anything?

Liall finally looked down at Scarlet, and there was something in his expression that made Scarlet's heart sink.

"Scarlet, I swear to you, it is not the coarse thing he

makes it out to be. There have been many in Rshan, many honored and great people who have been known as kir."

Scarlet remembered when he had questioned Jochi about his court name and how Jochi had evaded answering him. "If it's such an honored term, why wouldn't Jochi tell me what it meant?" Scarlet looked to Vladei, forgetting for a moment that Vladei was Liall's enemy.

Vladei chuckled lowly and swirled the wine in his cup. Behind him, a woman covered her mouth with her hand, and Scarlet saw with a sick feeling that it was Shikhoza. She was laughing at him: the illiterate pedlar had finally been put in his place.

Liall put his hand on Scarlet's shoulder, turning Scarlet to look only at him. "Ignore that pig, he dirties everything he touches."

The taste of the wine was suddenly revolting to Scarlet, and he was dismayed to realize he felt the same way about Liall at the moment. He had refused to be bought when he first collided with Liall in Byzantur, and later he had not wanted the mariners to think he was a whore, yet Liall had made little of the offense when the mariner with the coin had accosted him aboard the Ostre Sul. Now an entire palace knew that was precisely what he was: a whore. Oh, prettied up in the usual fancy language, but still a whore. And Liall knew and had not told him, had not warned him! What did it mean? What was a t'aishka and what did being a Hilurin have to do with it?

"Why didn't you just tell me?" Scarlet's voice sounded thin to him, almost invisible, and that was how he felt. His chest was beginning to hurt as well as his head, now that he was feeling the bruises from the hunt. "That's twice you've lied to me."

"When did I ever lie?"

His face felt numb and stiff. "The day we met. You told me you were no prince."

Liall gaped. "I– Scarlet, surely you can't believe–"

Vladei interrupted again. Scarlet wished he could punch his smirking face right there in the great hall, no matter what they did to him later.

"Strictly speaking, he is not a prince." Vladei bowed a little toward the other occupants of the hall, all the nobles. "He's a Blood Prince, carrying the royal blood of Rshan, but he can't inherit the throne. Do you want to know why, little flower, little Keriss?"

Liall whirled on him, letting go of Scarlet. "Vladei, I swear to you..."

Vladei bared his teeth again in that unpleasant grimace that passed for a smile. "What? Will you kill me to silence me? Will it be a duel, or a knife in the back?"

"Be silent!" Liall roared and his hand dropped to the knife at his belt.

Vladei laughed again. "You have not changed, Nazheradei," he jeered, "A snow-bear, a whore, is there nothing you will not kill your kin for? I would have expected no more from the Kinslayer, the prince who murdered his own brother."

The queen rose from her chair. "It was an accident, Vladei!" she said sternly, but she was pale.

Vladei bowed to her, but there was hate and malice in his gaze. "No, my Queen, it was not, it was a duel! He killed his elder brother because he wanted to be king."

Liall went even paler. "I never wanted to be king and I never intended to kill him!"

Scarlet listened in shock. Liall had killed his own brother? That was why he could never be king. That was why Cestimir had said it was like the old romances, why Jochi told him to ask Liall about the line of inheritance. That was why Liall had been an exile from his own land.

The image of a dagger bathed in the red light of sunset

flashed before Scarlet again. He remembered how Liall had gone into a rage on Nerit Mountain, and how afraid he was that Liall might hurt him, dishonor him, kill him. He remembered that until then, Liall the bandit had kept his composure and had shown regret, and then Scarlet had called him murderer.

Liall took a step back and dropped his hand from his knife. Vladei closed his mouth and bowed to the queen, apparently done spreading poison for now.

Scarlet stared at Liall. "Why did you keep all this from me?"

Liall gestured angrily. "It was my secret to keep. You were not a part of my life then. You have no right to know every detail that occurred before we met."

Scarlet felt sick. "This isn't a detail, any more than letting the entire court call me a slave to my face when I don't know they're doing it. Gods, I've been such a fool."

Liall was cold. "There are reasons for what I do. You must trust me."

"Oh, must I?" Was that his voice, raised in anger and shouting in front of the assembled lords and ladies? Manners be damned. "Trust you? I spent four months on a rat-infested ship, sick half the time and hiding from your ill-mannered countrymen the rest. I followed your commands on the ship and I've followed them here, and at no time during all of that did I know who you really were or why you had come to Rshan. If that didn't prove that I *trusted* you, nothing will!" Scarlet was shaking so hard that his voice trembled and he bit his lip to stop the words, fearful that Liall would take it for weakness.

Liall's mouth was tight, his dark face ashen and pinched. "I did not want you to hear these things. I was only trying to protect you."

"By keeping me ignorant? I don't need protecting! I'm

not a child and I'm for rutting sure not your pet! Will you, for the gods' sake, stop treating me like a toy or an infant and start treating me like a man?"

Liall kept his silence, and Scarlet believed that he looked vaguely ashamed.

"I see," Scarlet said slowly. "You really don't think of me as a man, do you?" His voice had miraculously turned level and calm, when he felt anything but.

"That's not true, t'aishka. Will you listen to me?"

"Don't call me that. Gods know what that really means." Scarlet could feel the eyes of everyone on them, and imagined it was all malicious delight.

Liall flinched and reached out to take hold of Scarlet's shoulders again. Scarlet jerked away.

"No! Enough!" Scarlet took a deep breath and saw Jochi's horrified expression as well as the worry on the queen's face. He wanted to simply flee from the hall, but he recalled Jochi's lessons and bowed to her.

"I'm sorry for the noise," he said clearly, aware that he didn't have the tact or court manners to say what had to be said with grace. "I'd like to leave now, please."

"Keriss, I regret but I cannot permit you to withdraw." The look she gave him was not without sympathy, but it was unbending. "You will remain."

What for, so they could laugh at him again? So Vladei could mock him while Liall stood there like a lump? But the queen had spoken, and Scarlet had learned that, in Rshan, one did not defy a queen. He bowed his head and remained beside Liall, knowing it was the only place he could go at the moment, and he felt trapped and miserable. It was also suddenly very hot in the hall and he could feel that his face was flushed and sweating, and a wave of dizziness washed over him. His head ached horribly.

Please, Deva, he prayed. I can't fall down here, not in front of these fancied-up giants laughing at me. I'd rather die.

Scarlet stayed where he was after asking to leave, and Liall knew it was only because he had no other choice. The queen was not done with her game of courts and pawns, and every courtier in the hall had seen Vladei's plain and unvarnished hate on display. She was of course, hoping Vladei would hang himself further, and so Scarlet had been ordered to stay. He tried to catch Scarlet's eye and Scarlet would not even look at him.

Liall felt sick. Now that Scarlet knew about Nadei, he would want to leave, for who could love a murderer of their own kin? Not Scarlet, certainly, who put so much value on family and blood ties. He suddenly had a wild wish that he had told Scarlet about Nadei from the beginning, explained how it was, so that Scarlet would not be looking at him now like he was a stranger. A murderer. A liar.

When the crew had wanted to toss Scarlet overboard, Liall said only that it was a misunderstanding and never that he made them believe Scarlet was his property. When Scarlet asked him repeatedly why he was journeying to Rshan, Liall had refused to answer fully. He had lied to Scarlet about being a prince, and he had never spoken Nadei's name to him.

Scarlet was no fool, and Hilurin have a deep-seated respect for secrets and privacy. Scarlet had known all along that there was much Liall was keeping from him. He had, in his forthright way, simply expected Liall to be honest with him in his own time, except that time never seemed to come.

Liall tried to take his hand, but Scarlet pulled away.

"No," Scarlet said. Not snapping like before, but with

listless anger. Scarlet hid his hands in his pockets, and that tore at Liall's heart.

"Scarlet," Liall implored, trying to reach him with his voice. There were too many eyes on them, and the queen looked more distressed than ever. Liall looked after Vladei, wanting very much to follow his step-brother and pound his face into a pulp. He saw Vladei standing with Shikhoza near the queen's table, and they seemed to be arguing. Cestimir was at the queen's side, glaring at Vladei and casting worried looks in Liall's direction.

Vladei and Shikhoza's heads were bent close together in conversation, and Vladei was twisting his rings again. Shikhoza gestured angrily and said something, her red lips twisted in a sneer, and Vladei smiled unpleasantly. She shook her head and left him, and Vladei went back to staring at Scarlet in that mocking way of his.

Liall took Scarlet's arm. "Come with me." Liall pulled him when he would not come, almost dragging the Scarlet into a corner of the hall, behind a carved panel where they were less on display.

Scarlet struggled. "Let me go!"

"I will, just as soon –"

"Damn it, you're hurting me!"

Liall released him immediately. Scarlet rubbed his upper arm and stared at Liall with an angry flush of shame brightening his cheeks.

"My t'aishka," Liall soothed.

"I'm not your anything," Scarlet flung back, as if he were deliberately trying to hurt Liall.

"You do not mean that."

Scarlet wiped his forehead with the back of his hand, and Liall saw that he was sweating. "Stop telling me what I mean, what I think. Did you ever once ask me if I was *your* Scarlet? You talk about me to your servants as if I'm not in the room. You say I'm yours, that I belong to you, like something you own, your cup or your chair, but you never once asked me if I wanted to be owned. I've had enough of this."

Cold dread gripped Liall's stomach. Love is such a fragile thing. It hangs by a thread most of the time. "Of what?"

"Of lies and half-lies, of sneering Rshani nobility."

"They do not dare to—"

"I mean you, Nazheradei. I'm tired of you."

Liall was stricken, as if Scarlet had slapped him or betrayed him with another. Somewhere in his mind, he heard that thread stretched to snap. "You wish to leave me?"

"Right now I'd like nothing better. If I thought I'd get five feet out of this place without—"

"You are no slave," Liall said calmly, but his chest felt like it was cracking. "You have always been free to leave me. Tomorrow, I will arrange for you to return to Byzantur at the earliest possible time. If all you want is to be away from me, you shall have it."

"That's not—" Scarlet began, but they were interrupted by Cestimir.

"Nazheradei?" Cestimir's eyes slid from Scarlet to Liall and back again. "Can I help?"

Liall said nothing, cold and stiff as he was with hurt, so Cestimir shrugged and offered Scarlet his cup. "I thought Keriss could use a drink."

"I would not know what Scarlet needs," Liall snapped, and left them to sort it out. "I would not have the slightest idea." He did not turn back to apologize and ask forgiveness, as his heart urged him to, nor even look back to see if Scarlet was watching him.

Liall went to the queen. Bhakamir was at her side, holding a glass of clear liquid under her nose. It smelled of medicine, and she looked paler than usual, tired and thin.

"Madame?" Liall leaned over her, putting one hand on the arm of her chair as Bhakamir tended to her. "Are you well?"

"Do I look well?" she asked with some asperity, and then waved Bhakamir away. One thin hand massaged her breast in the region of her heart. "I will be fine. Worry not. See to the future king, there are vipers in the hall today."

"I know it," Liall growled. "And I will put paid to one of them soon."

Her eyes met Liall's, and he saw the finality sink into her. She did not argue, and after a moment, she nodded.

"Call him out," she uttered lowly. "What has occurred today proves Vladei's intent: he will never allow Cestimir to become king without a fight. My sons... all my sons... are brave, Nazir, but a fourteen-year-old boy crossing swords with Vladei is not a wager I would take. If it must be done, it needs be done soon. Did Vladei not betray you at the hunt? Did not every noble see what he did? Did he not insult your t'aishka, which insults your honor as well? It is sufficient cause. Call him out."

Kill him, she was saying. He stared at her, not knowing what he hoped to see, but she was implacable.

Of course, he thought. She is a queen. I know what that means, or I should know. A ruler must possess the ability to bow to necessity, no matter what the personal cost. Oh, there is a hardness in you, my mother. Did I drink that in at the breast, I wonder?

There was a core in Nadiushka that no one, perhaps not even Liall's late and unknown father, Lindolanen, ever got to touch. In that deep place she was like iron; cold and biting.

And so am I. This is why Scarlet recoils from me.

"As my queen commands," Liall murmured, apparently

submitting to her will, but she was not deceived. Liall wanted Vladei as dead as she did, and this time there would be no mistake about his intent. "I will kill him, but this is not the time."

"Nazir."

"It was you who called me back, Mother. Now you must trust me."

After a long moment, she nodded. "Very well, my son." She took a shuddering breath. "Since there is to be no blood in the hall today, other than the bear, would you tell Keriss he is given permission to withdraw?" She looked worried. "I do hope the fracture between you is not permanent."

"I do not know. He is very angry with me."

"And you are angry with him," she returned, seeing far too much. Her pale eyes glittered. "You believe he should follow all your orders unquestioningly, be ruled by you, trust you as he would a khatai."

Liall did not like the intimation that he wished to lord over Scarlet's actions like a general. "He is in danger here!" he hissed, aware that others could hear them.

"We are all in danger here. Fear is no reason to stop living."

Liall strove for words, feeling impotent and furious at the same time. "But he is so reckless, so careless of his own safety. He thinks he can do anything!"

"And you are afraid for him," she finished. "You wish to protect him."

"Yes. Naturally, I do."

She regarded him in silence for several moments. "My son... are you certain that you do not merely seek to protect yourself?"

It was not fair. First Scarlet accused him of keeping him in a box, and then his own mother questioned his motives. Liall began to withdraw in offense, but she reached for his hand and he melted.

"Nazir," she said tenderly. "You were this way with Nadei. And Nadei, if I may observe, was very much like your Keriss."

Liall closed his eyes for a moment, but she would not stop.

"You loved Nadei, but you protected him so much that he never grew strong on his own. In the end, that was his undoing." She touched his face, her iron gaze for once grown soft and tender. "You shelter those you love so much that you suffocate them with safety. It is your way of avoiding pain and the possibility of loss."

She released him and Liall blinked back tears and rose, his eyes searching the room for Scarlet. Vladei was near the doorway. He looked to be leaving.

Making good his escape after trying to kill me in the Hunt, Liall thought. Liall glanced to his mother, but there were no more words between them. He bowed and she inclined her head, giving him permission to leave. Liall left her presence to return to Scarlet, who was still tucked away in the corner with Cestimir. At that moment, he saw Vladei suddenly veer from the doorway and approach Scarlet. Every one of Liall's instincts bristled, and he hurried to intercept his step-brother.

Eleferi stepped in his way. "Nazheradei," Eleferi smiled, but there was a note of urgency in his voice. "I've been meaning to speak with you."

"Out of my way," Liall commanded, shoving Eleferi aside. Vladei had reached Scarlet. Scarlet had his back turned to Vladei, speaking with Cestimir, and the young men seemed to be arguing. Cestimir spoke sharply and held his wine cup out to Scarlet, clearly insisting he drink, and Scarlet shook his head and thrust the cup away, knocking it from Cestimir's hand. There were gasps from those who saw, and Scarlet backed away from the prince, looking distressed.

Liall saw Vladei reach for Scarlet's wrist and jerk the small pedlar around to face him.

"You dare to strike a prince of Rshan!" Vladei snapped, loud enough for the entire hall to hear.

Liall's hand was already on his knife and he was four strides away when he saw Scarlet's face change. Scarlet suddenly lost the aspect of hesitant uncertainly that had been dogging his actions whenever he had to deal with the members of the royal court, changing swiftly to plain and simple anger. His jaw tightened and his hand –caught in Vladei's grip– curled into a fist. Vladei suddenly shouted and released Scarlet, thrusting Scarlet away from him and holding his own wrist.

"Don't touch me again," Scarlet warned Vladei. "Or I'll make you regret it."

And then, to Liall's everlasting shock, a bloom of fire unfurled in Scarlet's open palm like a yellow flower opening. Fire. It was *fire*.

Liall was so stunned that his hand froze on his knife and he, like the rest of the court, stood stock-still in amazement, watching as Scarlet thrust the fire withy close to Vladei's face.

"Keep your fucking hands to yourself!" Scarlet snarled.

All around the court, mouths hung open and an enormous silence filled the room. *Magic.* Hilurin magic. The fabled and dreaded power of the ancient world come to life among them.

The silence lasted only a moment. "Magic!" Vladei shouted, his voice raw with fear. "See there! Did I not warn you all of his magic? See how he intends to murder me with it!"

Like hounds set free from a kennel, the voices of the court were unleashed all at once and they all began to speak and gesture angrily and in fear. A few courtiers surged forward, their faces flushed with alarm, intent on reaching Scarlet and Vladei.

Liall's instincts shrieked danger to him, and he shook himself from his own amazement and leapt in front of the men.

"Scarlet, for the gods' sake, put it down!" Liall shouted. He pulled his knife free from its sheath and pointed it at the courtiers. "Stay back!"

"Magic! Magic!" someone else shouted, high and excited like a yapping dog. "The Hilurin brings the magic back to Rshan! We shall be destroyed!"

"Cease this!" Liall thundered, striving to be heard above the growing hysteria. Hilurin magic. Every child's tale in Rshan was full of it, of dire warnings of it, and what would happen to the kingdom if it should ever return. Inwardly, he was struggling with his own shock and sense of betrayal. How... *how*... could Scarlet have kept this from him? How was such a thing possible? Magic? It seemed scarcely to be believed, but there was Scarlet standing alone in the center of the great hall, holding fire in his hand. A fire that did not burn him.

Liall saw Scarlet staring at him in dismay. Scarlet closed his hand, extinguishing the flame and hanging his head. Cestimir stood near Scarlet, silent and still as if frozen there.

"Scarlet," Liall breathed, approaching him on leaden legs. "Scarlet, how do you do that?"

Scarlet blushed deeply and put the offending hand behind his back. "My father taught me," he whispered. "It's my Gift from Deva. The withy magic."

"You hear!" Vladei began shouting again. "His magic! He admits he brought it here to destroy us!"

Among the many voices, Liall could hear the queen shouting for order and being royally ignored.

Scarlet raised his head at the accusation, frowning. "I don't want to destroy anyone!"

"Keep silent!" Liall hissed, and then raised his voice again and spoke in Sinha. "This is my t'aishka. He has my protection!"

"Kill it!" someone shouted.

A courtier –one of Vladei's men wearing the red badge– shoved Scarlet from behind, causing him to stumble. Cestimir came out of his stillness and caught Scarlet before he fell, turning then to shout at the offending courtier. Other voices took up the call –*kill it!*–and the fragile control of the room began to fray.

Suddenly, a storm seemed to barrel toward the center of the great hall. Melev strode in, his abnormally long legs carrying him faster than any man could walk, shunting the tall Rshani men and women aside as easily as reeds. The Ancient took up position beside Liall and dropped a plate-sized hand on Scarlet's shoulder. The voices died down and Scarlet turned and looked way, way up at the huge man towering above him.

In the new quiet, all heard the awe-filled whisper from Scarlet: *"Shining One..."*

Scarlet backed away from Melev, stumbling. An expression of intense concentration passed over Scarlet's features as he tried to keep his feet under him, then his knees simply buckled and he collapsed to the floor.

Liall cried out in dismay and fear, but Melev moved before he could, kneeling to pick up the fallen Hilurin and cradling him in his massive arms. Melev faced the watching Rshani in the great hall.

"Pail'aa sest Nauhin," Melev intoned, and his deep voice rolled over the crowd like low thunder, silencing them. *For the Shining Ones.* It was the ritual cry from the Hunt, but none knew what it signified now, or what Melev intended.

Liall reached out and touched Scarlet's face as he lay in Melev's arms, and the Ancient looked down on Liall and nodded. Liall wondered if Melev could feel the depth of his fear.

"Come," Melev said simply, and swept out of the hall, the Hilurin carried as easily in his arms as a kitten. Having no choice, Liall followed, sheathing his knife and thanking all the gods that not even Vladei would think to cross an Ancient. They were saved for now, but what of later?

Liall had to pass by Vladei, and the look his stepbrother gave him chilled his bones. My stubborn little redbird, Liall thought unhappily. Why did you keep this from me? Did you trust me so little? And how am I going to keep you safe now, when you have brought so much fear to the hearts of so many?

8.

The Temple Road

The dream told Scarlet he was drowning, warm water creeping up his neck and inching over his nose. He thought maybe it was the pond below the wash in Lysia, so he thrashed and tried to stand, knowing the water was not more than waist deep in most places, but there were hands holding him and soothing voices that whispered and hissed strange comforts. Scarlet opened his eyes and woke up in a bathtub, and everything was a blur of movement and light.

Jochi was kneeling beside him, holding onto his slippery arm as he struggled and struck out at the man, which ended in his head slipping under the water. Jochi hauled him up to a sitting position cupped his cheek as he spluttered.

"Scarlet!" Jochi shouted.

Not Keriss, and that got his attention. "Jochi?" Scarlet wiped the water from his eyes, suddenly mortified to realize he was naked and the room was full of people, Nenos and Dvi and several others in attendance. The water was warm, not hot, and no soap in it. He had been soaking for a while, for his skin was wrinkled like wizened fruit. Scarlet remembered his last sight before he fainted; a man who looked both Rshani and not, who seemed at first so still that he was like a statue carved from dark ironwood. A statue with round moonstone eyes that shone like lamps in his face. Scarlet began to tremble.

"Are you cold?" Jochi patted Scarlet's cheek, seeing he was awake and in the present, and then heaved a sigh and shook his head in reproof. "You did give us a fright, ser."

Jochi stood and gave Nenos some instructions in Sinha. Scarlet almost asked Jochi about Liall before he remembered how angry Liall had been. It made his heart ache.

Dvi began to ply Scarlet with hot che with a little sugar and some odd-tasting herbs, and then Nenos warmed the water again. Scarlet was so exhausted that he dozed, and afterward, they hauled him out of the water. Nenos bundled him into the huge bed and piled woolen blankets warmed by the fire around him.

By the time Liall appeared at the door, Scarlet had stopped shivering and the dull, hammering pain had started again inside his skull. Liall came into the bedroom silently, looking at Scarlet with a set, stony expression that made his heart sink. Liall then stepped aside and a man quite taller than any creature Scarlet had ever seen entered from the common room. It was the man from the hall, the one he had mistaken for a Shining One.

A deep silence fell over the already-quiet room, and Liall said, with great gravity; "This is Melev."

Melev was bald, which Scarlet understood was rare for a Rshani. Even their very old men were not so. This one had the same amber-colored skin as Liall, but he was two hand-spans taller and wore only a simple, rough-spun robe knotted around his whipcord-thin frame. Melev wore no furs or even shoes against the cold and no jewelry or bright ornaments, which the Rshani seemed to love adorning themselves with. He looked poor and humble, if strange. Despite that, Nenos bowed low when Melev entered, and even Liall did the same.

Melev stepped nearer to the bed Scarlet was huddled

in, and Scarlet shrank back, filled with a nameless fear.

The odd giant smiled gently and knelt by the side of the bed, bringing his eyes on a level with Scarlet's, who was perched high up on pillows and blankets. A giant, indeed. Melev had a strange face: huge, pale eyes like pearls or opals, and a large, hooked nose and square jaw. He strongly resembled the wooden carving of a Shining One that Scarlet had seen in the Fate Dealer's tent in Ankar, which made Scarlet shiver in superstitious fear. Scarlet looked to Liall for guidance, but Liall was cold and unresponsive.

Melev extended one of his monstrous hands to feel the bruise on Scarlet's forehead, and Scarlet saw that his hands were wrong, misshapen in some way. Scarlet jerked back a little before Melev could touch him, and the man smiled again. Melev's expression was most gentle, and turned his hand before Scarlet's eyes.

"It is only a little different from your hand," Melev said in a muted, soothing voice, so low that its tones almost fell under the normal sounds of the air and the palace. Deep, but comforting. Yes, he was very comforting. A sense of peace seemed to radiate from his very skin.

Scarlet relaxed a bit as Melev flexed his giant's hands. He began to notice that Melev spoke perfect Bizye, even with a touch of northern accent, like his own.

"See?" Melev said, still in that calming voice. "Four joints in each finger, rather than three, and four in the thumb." He wriggled them, his fingers twisting like snakes, impossible angles. "Physical difference," he explained softly. "Nothing to be frightened of."

"I'm not frightened," Scarlet said gamely.

"Of course not. Why would you be? Your magic is as great as mine, if not greater." Melev reached for him again. "If you will permit this...?"

Scarlet hesitated, looking to Liall, but Liall was

neutral, his expression only changing when Melev spoke of magic. So he's still mad about that, Scarlet thought. He longed to be alone with Liall, to explain how forbidden it was to reveal the Gift to an outsider, and how he had often felt guilty about keeping that secret from Liall, but there seemed little chance of being alone now.

Scarlet nodded, and Melev placed his hand –so warm!– on Scarlet's temple, right on the spot that was drilling hot needles through his brain. It hurt. For a moment, a searing pain that cut through all the other pains rocked him, and he squeezed his eyes shut and gasped. Melev quickly laid his other hand on Scarlet's shoulder, preventing him from pulling away as the healer explored the aching area of Scarlet's chest with careful, precise touches. Then Melev laid his palm flat above Scarlet's heart and went very still for a moment. Scarlet tensed, expecting more pain, but it suddenly vanished, as did all his other aches, as if taken away by the wind.

Scarlet opened his eyes to see Melev smiling at him. "What did you do?"

Melev began to examine Scarlet's hands next, pressing his fingernails to see their color. "I helped you."

"You're not a curae," Scarlet said. No curae that he had ever met could take pain away so easily.

Melev was amused. "Oh, indeed I am not."

"Are you a Shining One?"

Now that caused a stir in the room, and Melev looked at him and shook his head, showing him his enormous white teeth in a grin. *"Nauhin nen chth,"* he said, which left Scarlet no wiser, but he sensed to ask for a translation would be pushing it.

Melev placed Scarlet's hand under the blankets to keep warm and rose, turning to Liall. "The bear must have hit him harder than you realized. His skull was fractured. You were right to call for me."

Was? Could Melev have healed him so quickly? Scarlet looked at Melev with fresh awe, doubting, but he had to admit that he was feeling much better, and no longer sick. He was only vastly tired.

Liall's cold expression wavered for a moment. "And now?"

"I have repaired it. There is no bleeding on the brain, neither have his lungs taken serious damage. He is bruised and battered, but he will live."

Liall seemed to be grinding his jaw as he nodded at Melev, then he switched to Sinha and Scarlet was shut out of their conversation. Melev cast a look at Scarlet and switched back to Bizye, addressing Liall.

"Your t'aishka is strong," Melev remarked. "But you must take much better care of him. Please order him to rest."

Scarlet frowned. Most Rshani automatically assumed that Liall owned him or had some authority over him, and it bothered him no less now that it had months ago.

"He is not mine to order," Liall said slowly. "But I will ask him."

"Ah, yes." Melev nodded, as if he understood perfectly. "It is the old ways, once again."

Liall seemed distressed at that, but Scarlet was too tired to figure it out. Liall's coldness shut him out more effectively than if the prince had tossed him out of the palace and locked the gates. Be damned to him, then, Scarlet thought wearily. His eyelids drooped and he sank exhausted into sleep.

Scarlet slept most of the night and woke to find Liall gone. When he asked Nenos where the prince was, the old man only shrugged apologetically and urged Scarlet, with signs and a few words in Bizye, to get back into bed and rest. Scarlet shook his head and got up to dress, and Nenos reluctantly laid out a very nice but plain red woolen virca and black breeches and boots. Scarlet wandered into the dining room and sat along at the large table, and after a short while Nenos silently brought him che. An hour went by as Scarlet fretted, then two, and by that time Scarlet was convinced that Liall was making plans to ship him back to Byzantur, just as he had threatened to do on the sea voyage.

There was a knock at the outer door and Scarlet stood, his heart speeding up, but it was only Cestimir's page, inquiring if ser Keriss was well enough to receive visitors. Scarlet's hopes fell and he did not feel like visiting, but neither did he feel like being penned up in the apartment all day waiting for Liall to come to him, if he came at all.

"Of course I'm well enough," he told the page, who spoke very decent Bizye. "Tell him to come up."

When the boy had gone, Scarlet regretted his decision. He was going to be poor company for a prince, but anything was preferable to just sitting here brooding over Liall.

Liall had killed his own brother. How? Was it by mischance, or something darker? Scarlet wanted the truth from Liall. All of it, not just the little bits of it Liall thought he could handle. Scarlet's own father had let him keep his secrets and never pried, believing that Scarlet was mature enough to handle it on his own, and trusting that, if he could not, he would ask for help. Help, which would, naturally, never be withheld. It was the Hilurin way: blunt, proud, and loyal. Scarlet would have forgiven Liall any truth, but lies were harder to dismiss. Liall naturally saw the matter differently, being foreign-born and raised with another kind of logic: one that twisted like snakes and slid away like smoke when you tried to grasp it.

And you, he asked himself. What about you? Didn't you lie to Liall about the magic?

I did, he argued silently. But it wasn't only my lie. It's what I was raised with: never show the Gift to anyone who is not First Tribe. If they're not of the Blood, they won't understand and they'll kill you for it. Well, hadn't that wisdom been proven already? Look how courtiers behaved in the great hall.

The shouts of *kill it!* still rang in Scarlet's ears: those pretty, glittering men and women calling for his death.

Haven't we paid enough for that lie over the years in burned villages and dead kin and our bones buried in the fields?

But not Liall, that inner voice argued. Never Liall. He wouldn't have hated you.

Scarlet was beginning to despair of either of them ever realizing who the other really was, and the prospect of arguing with Liall any further depressed him beyond words. He didn't want to lose Liall, but he wanted to lose himself even less.

Alexyin escorted Cestimir, as usual, and conferred with Nenos at length before leaving the Crown Prince alone with Scarlet. Nenos stood looking at the young men for a few minutes, his hands clasped behind his back and his kind face very concerned.

"How do you feel?" Cestimir asked politely.

"Well enough," Scarlet answered, and then gave Cestimir a hard look. "Aren't you afraid like everyone else, prince?"

"Should I be? Are you going to strike me down with your little flame?"

Scarlet snorted and rolled his eyes. At least one Rshani had good sense. "You'd think that's what I threatened to do to your kingdom. Be like trying to cut down a forest with a fruit knife, that would. We don't... we *try* not to use it that way. That isn't what the Gift is for."

"What is it for?" Cestimir asked, honestly curious as he sat down across from Scarlet.

Scarlet dropped his gaze. "For living," he answered honestly. "Survival; small magics to get us by in a hard world. That's what Deva gave us." He looked down at his own four-fingered hand that so fascinated the Rshani. "Without it, we may all have been dead already, with the way the world hates us," he added almost defiantly.

"I don't hate you, ser Keriss."

Scarlet ventured a searching look at the prince. "You don't, do you?" he said after a long moment. "It makes no difference to you?"

Cestimir grinned. "None at all, except that now I have even more questions to pester you with."

Seeing that the young men were speaking easily with one another, Nenos left.

Cestimir pulled his chair closer to Scarlet's. "Did you really mean to burn Vladei?"

Scarlet thought seriously before he answered. "It was very odd," he admitted. "I'd never tried to use my Gift that way before I left home. Not as a weapon. I didn't think I could. Something has been happening to my Gift since I left Byzantur. It feels... stronger. I don't know." He sighed. "Maybe it's this place. Maybe it's being so far away from home and everything is so new and..."

"Frightening?"

"Oh, you can't fright a pedlar," Scarlet retorted primly with a little smile. "But I've felt close to it a few times. I don't like your step-brother much, if I can say so."

"You can," Cestimir grinned, folding his arms. "Others

say worse about him. He's a dangerous man."

Scarlet snorted. "Who yelps like a girl at the sight of a little withy."

"It didn't look little to me," Cestimir admitted. His eyes shone. "It looked wondrous."

Scarlet shook his head, smiling.

"You want to get out of here, don't you?"

Scarlet stared. "What do you mean? Leave Rshan?"

"No, not leave my brother, you ninny." Cestimir reached over and slapped Scarlet's arm for his foolishness. "Would I do that to Nazheradei, knowing how he loves you? No. I meant would you like go sleigh-riding with me?"

Scarlet cast a cautious look to the kitchen, where he knew Nenos was listening, but Nenos did not speak Bizye. "They won't let us."

"They won't know," Cestimir said with a rakish grin. "Or at least, they won't until it's too late, and by then we'll have had our fun and they can be as angry as they please."

In spite of his dour mood, Scarlet chuckled. "Have you always been like this, or did my coming here spark some kind of Wilding streak in you?"

"Don't worry," Cestimir laughed, rising from his chair. "They won't blame you. I've done it many times before. If anything, I will be blamed for corrupting you, poor innocent Byzan."

The prince stepped out of the dining room and into the kitchen, and Scarlet could hear him conversing with Nenos in low tones. After a few moments, Cestimir came back in and held his finger to his lips in a signal for Scarlet to be silent. The outer door opened and closed, and Cestimir grabbed his arm, hauling him up out of the chair.

"Get your coat. You'll need a hat and gloves, too.

Hurry!"

"What did you do?"

"I sent him on an errand. It won't take him that long, so we must be swift. Shoo!" He pushed Scarlet into the bedroom to dress.

Scarlet snatched up Liall's blue and silver coat and a new fur-lined hat brocaded with red flowers. The coat was far too big for him, but his own red coat had been taken after the snow bear hunt and he hadn't seen it since. He wasn't even sure they would bring it back; something about the blood of the bear being sacred.

He met Cestimir near the outer door and the prince took his hand. After opening the door and peering out, Cestimir dragged Scarlet into the wide corridor and down a flight of stone steps. The boy was so much taller than Scarlet that he pulled Scarlet easily along, which annoyed Scarlet a bit. He was getting used to all these Rshani, even one three years his junior, towering over him. He did not like it, but he was getting used to it.

They made several twists and turns throughout the palace, and Scarlet was afraid they would be stopped at any moment, but Cestimir knew his home, and they met no one in the narrow and deserted passages the Crown Prince chose for their route.

Very shortly, they were outside in the twilight cold, standing before a sleigh with their minders left behind. A fierce-looking man with a full blond beard and heavy white eyebrows stood next to the horse-drawn sleigh, holding a whip and swathed in fur up to his neck.

"Is this wise, Majesty?" Scarlet asked, suddenly positive it was not. Liall was going to be furious.

"Certainly!" Cestimir said cheerfully and climbed into the enclosed carriage of the sleigh. He held out his gloved hand to Scarlet.

Cestimir's merry grin was so infectious that Scarlet

laughed and climbed into the carriage, forgetting for the moment that Liall had warned him direly about leaving the palace. Liall fretted like an old woman. What harm could there be if he was with the prince?

This sleigh was smaller than the one that had brought Scarlet and Liall from the port, but had larger windows. "Yesuk!" Cestimir called. The prince rapped out an order in Sinha, and the driver bowed and climbed up into the seat behind the pair of horses.

"Yesuk is my driver," Cestimir explained, "and has also gotten me both into and out of a great deal of trouble. They keep trying to send him away to some other post, but I shan't let them."

Cestimir tapped on the window, and through it Scarlet could see Yesuk lift his heavy arms to snap the reins. They were off.

"Where are we going?" Scarlet asked. Yesuk clucked his tongue at the horses and the sleigh began to pick up speed. Its runners on the snow sounded like the hiss of a snake inside the carriage, and the air was very cold.

"Anywhere, so long as it's away from here for a few hours." Cestimir chuckled. "Stop fretting! Liall has gotten you as scared as he is, imagining assassins behind every door. Relax,. Yesuk will protect us, and no one else knows we have left."

Neither of the two young men saw the lone figure by the roadside that the sleigh passed swiftly. Or, if they did, they believed him to be a wind-blasted stump of a tree or a rock, so still was the Ancient and so heavy was the fall of snow piled on his shoulders and head as he stood there with his bare feet rooted in the earth, colored like the landscape, patient as the mountain.

Melev turned his head to watch as the sleigh passed, and his moonstone eyes shone with an inner light that had not been kindled in centuries.

It was a measure as to how frightened Liall was that he had sent for Melev to heal Scarlet. A Rshani healer is bred, not taught, and many considered them not quite mortal. Some, like Melev, were Ancients able to heal wounds that would otherwise be impossible for a man to recover from.

Liall sat vigil outside his apartments until Nenos assured him that Scarlet would be perfectly well by morning. He left then, wandering deep in thought through long, chilly halls and glittering atriums, finally finding his way down to the barracks, which were bleakly empty. Jarek's troops were engaged on a battlefield to the north and were not expected to return for several days. She was routing Vladei's rebel supporters, which by now was no secret. That accounted for Vladei's act of desperation on the Hunt and his attempt to publicly discredit Liall in the great hall. Time was growing short and Vladei was losing ground with the Barons. If Vladei did not strike decisively and soon, Cestimir would be king. That knowledge was bound to make Vladei desperate and Liall sleepless.

Every hour that Liall spent in the barracks was an hour that he longed to be with Scarlet, but stubborn pride held him back. Scarlet had patently dismissed Liall –a prince!– from his presence, and it galled Liall to realize that he was not quite the master here. Not that he ever really fancied he was, or that Scarlet had no influence upon him, but to have it done so publicly...

Did he mean what he said, Liall wondered. Does he wish to leave me? And –gods help me– would I allow it? What kind of man am I if I do not? Then there was the matter of his magic.

Buggering gods, Liall thought. Scarlet can do magic. He had to say it aloud several times to the empty barracks, certain that it must be some trick or sleight of hand that the wily pedlar had mastered. He even had Scarlet's clothing and packs searched and examined, but beyond a piece of black flint from the Byzan hills and a battered strip of iron, there was nothing Scarlet could have made a fire with in plain sight of three hundred people. The tales were true. Hilurin magic existed, and Scarlet had never trusted him enough to tell him of it.

Neither of us truly trusts the other, Liall realized. Not in the ways that matter, the way of mates who are destined to be together. I called him my t'aishka, and he does not even know what I mean by it, for I am too afraid to say it aloud. Twice-beloved. Twice-chosen. A lover I have known beyond life. It was his face in my dreams all those years, and yet... it was not. We have known each other before.

I must amend this, Liall thought, pacing the barracks and slapping his fist into his palm in frustration. I must convince him to stay with me, and the only way to do that is to be honest with him. Tell him everything. But how? Where are the magic words to explain the killing of my own brother? Yet I must, or we will never heal the lies between us.

Near the dawn hour, he climbed the stairs to his apartments. Nenos reported that Scarlet was well, but still asleep. The old servant's manner was so carefully blank that Liall nearly stormed in to drag Scarlet out of bed and demand that they settle things between them. Or else he would strip and join Scarlet in bed, and let their bodies speak what they could not. Sanity prevailed though, and Liall settled for growling and stamping down to the scriptorium, where he buried his head in paperwork for hours.

The first inkling Liall had that something had gone wrong was Jochi's sudden appearance. The hour was around noon or thereabouts. He still had not returned to being an accurate judge of time in the twilit Rshan winter. I have, Liall thought wryly, become a Byzan: too reliant on the sun.

Jochi appeared at the doorway to the queen's scriptorium and peered in nervously, then vanished. Several minutes later, Liall looked up from the trade treaty he was scanning and Jochi was there again, his eyes darting to the corners of the room. By that time, Liall had become suspicious and he begged leave of Glin, a nervous scribe with thin, shaking hands, and followed Jochi.

Liall found him only a few steps down the hallway.

"Ap kyning," Jochi said respectfully, but would not meet his eyes. That was unlike the teacher. Jochi fidgeted and seemed alarmed. That, in turn, alarmed Liall: to see calm, level-headed Jochi, wringing his hands like a new mother over a sick babe.

"It is ser Keriss," Jochi said at last.

Liall's heart nearly stopped. "Is he worse?" Gods, what if Melev had been wrong?

"He is not here, my prince."

Poor Jochi, set to guard a youth more willful than a king. Liall felt relieved and irritated at once. "What do you mean, not here?"

"I cannot find him."

"Have you looked everywhere?"

Jochi nodded, his features tight with shame.

Liall ran a hand over his hair, his thoughts scattering in sudden fear. It was very cold outside, and Scarlet knew nothing of the countryside. Liall was stunned that Scarlet would even consider it. The boy must have been angrier than he had realized. "He cannot have gone far, it is the middle of winter, after all. Tell Nenos to—"

"Nenos has been waiting to speak with you as well, my prince. There has been trouble."

"Trouble," Liall stated flatly, waiting for the explanation.

Jochi's face was lined and drawn, and that told Liall much. "We should go and speak to Nenos at once. *At once, ser,*" he added with a look to the walls. Such a look said: other ears could be listening.

Liall followed him without another word.

Nenos was standing at attention just inside the main door to Liall's apartments, obviously waiting for them. He held a small, red velvet box in his hands.

"What is it?" Liall said harshly, his heart thudding loudly in his ears. "What's amiss?"

Wordlessly, Nenos held the box out to Liall. The prince took it and jerked the cover off. Inside, nestled on a bed of folded red silk, was a white essima, the tiny, fanged, ruby-eyed viper of the north that ever seeks warmth, hiding under pillows and cushions and near warm chairs. So silent it was, and so swiftly did it kill, that the name for this snow-pale serpent and the name for assassin are the same in Sinha.

The essima was dead, its spine crushed into a bloody mess, red blood on its pure white scales. Liall gave Nenos a look that made the servant take a step back. "Where did this come from?"

"It was left here, my prince," Nenos turned and touched the small table by the door, the table Liall had taken to leaving small gifts for Scarlet on, such as the wolf pin. "I do not know who put it here, but certainly I have admitted no one but Jochi and, once, Prince Eleferi. Beyond that there are only the other servants, Dvi the cook, and myself."

"Who killed it?"

"I did," Nenos answered calmly. "I noticed it when I

returned from fetching herbs from the apothecary on the ground floor. Cestimir sent me on an errand, saying the queen herself had insisted on this herbal tincture being mixed for ser Keriss's health. When I came back, both Prince Cestimir and ser Keriss were gone."

Gone? One thing at a time, Liall thought, forcing himself to remain calm. "And you opened it?"

"Of course, my prince."

"For all you knew, I could have left this gift for Scarlet," Liall pressed him, merciless in his fear. "Why did you open it, servant?"

Now Nenos squared his shoulders in grave offense. "That box was not here when I left, and I am charged with all that occurs inside these apartments. I open every package, listen to every conversation, no matter how intimate. I am not charged with merely serving your che, my prince, I am your *servant*, and you asked me to guard the lad."

In the face of Nenos's righteous anger, Liall wilted. The man was right. Liall placed the lid carefully back on the box and returned it to Nenos, bowing. "I have rewarded loyalty with suspicion. Forgive me. You could have been killed yourself, opening that."

Nenos was mollified, but not much. The box was handed to Jochi, who made a sound of disgust at its contents, perhaps commenting on the situation in general.

"I was not killed," Nenos said. "But I am willing to die to protect those I serve. I would be proud to do so."

"The House of Camira-Druz values your loyalty," Liall answered formally, his heart an aching lump of fear in the cage of his chest. Someone had tried to murder Scarlet, and now he was missing, probably gone off on one of his wandering adventures, not knowing that a killer stalked him.

"This was not an attack on you, Nazheradei," Jochi said. "It is reasonable to believe that whoever left the box knew that you did not sleep here last night."

"It was not an attempt to kill me," Liall agreed grimly, "only to cripple me. We must discover who did this before they try again. And Scarlet must be found and moved into more secure lodgings at once. I will put him in with the queen and her soldiers if I have to." And sleep standing up with a sword in my hand, he vowed. They would not take Scarlet from him. "I should have done this last night, but I was angry with him and stupid. Now look what has happened."

"My prince," Jochi said reluctantly. "There is more."

Gods, what more? "Speak," he commanded.

"Prince Cestimir's new sleigh is gone, and his driver, Yesuk, cannot be found."

Now that he had an idea where the boys had gone –apparently under their own will– Liall was relieved, but somehow angrier. He poked a finger in the middle of Jochi's chest. "Come with me to the guard house. We will assemble a search party. Nenos!"

"My prince?"

"If Scarlet comes back before we do, tie him up and sit on him! Do not let him leave these apartments again."

"Yes, ser."

Liall and Jochi each took ten men and horses from the guard house and searched the sleigh paths and the farthest reaches of the grounds, both in opposite directions. Liall returned before Jochi did, having found not even a trail.

The wind is up, Liall thought. It may have eroded their path, or else they may have left through another route. There are many, many...

Two dozen or more exits surrounded the palace, each with trails leading off into the countryside and back to the port city in a spider-work of paths and roads, some well-traveled, some not. Looking for a single set of sleigh tracks among them was impossible.

Liall was realizing this and pacing the little guard room near the wide, stone steps of the palace entrance –the same ones Scarlet had found so huge and imposing when he first stepped out of that carriage– when Jochi's men rode up in a jangle of bells and harness.

When Liall saw the searcher's hangdog faces, his anger curdled up into a sinking ball of fear in his stomach.

"It is time to tell the queen," Liall said. He waved his hand at the search party. "Double their numbers and send them back out. The hour is late and the snow bears will emerge soon to search for food." As he said it, the coldness in his gut began to spread throughout his body. Something was very wrong. He felt it. Perhaps the man or woman who had aimed their venomous arrow at Scarlet had now found a perfect opportunity to remove two troublesome youths with one blow.

"Find me a good horse," he told Jochi. "I will be going again, too."

Jochi shook his head. "You cannot."

Liall rounded on him, his fists clenched. "Do not order me, Setna!"

"I am not," Jochi answered, calm and rational despite his worry. "I'm only stating a fact. After Cestimir, you are the last true prince of Druz. If Cestimir is indeed taken –and that is what you're thinking, ser– then the only hope he has is if you are alive and well in the Nauhinir, where you can strike back at Vladei."

He was right. Damn him. Oh Deva, Liall prayed soundlessly, looking out into the blue twilight and the hills of snow creeping up into the mountains, if you truly do exist, guard my Scarlet, for he believes in you and he is a good man who does not deserve to come to harm. And if you will hear prayers for the life of a Rshani prince, guard Cestimir as well.

It brought him no comfort, and he turned away heavily to speak to his mother.

9.

A Small Piece of Earth

We're going so fast, Cestimir!" The sleigh raced over the shadowy road, making Scarlet feel as if he were flying. Through the window, the white trees seemed to flash by like the wings of birds. There were hollows and glades nestled in the rolling hills above the Nauhinir, and jagged tors that looked like black spikes wreathed in snow.

"Good! After that horrible hunt and the nasty scene Vladei made afterwards, we both need fresh air and time to ourselves," Cestimir said merrily. "You're growing too pale, Scarlet. And will you please for the sake of the Shining Ones call me Cesta and not that lavish title?"

Scarlet couldn't help laughing. "You sounded just like your brother for a moment there," he said. But he did not want to talk about Liall.

Cestimir reached his long arms over Scarlet to throw a blanket over their knees, and then covered Scarlet alone with another fur.

"Just to be safe," Cestimir said. "I don't know very much about Hilurin. We Rshani tolerate cold very well, but I have difficulty judging what is too cold for you."

"Prince Nazheradei does that, too," Scarlet said. "Or too hot. He's forever stoking the fire up in our rooms, until he has me sweating and swearing at him to open a window."

Cestimir laughed. "Well, you see? He cares for you."

He pushed Scarlet's shoulder. "You have been imagining otherwise, yes? Please do not. There is one thing that everyone says about my brother: his moods do not change with the weather. He is a constant man. He loved you yesterday and he loves you today."

Scarlet looked away. "I lied to him."

"And he lied to you. You are even. Time to forget and start over. Ah, Scarlet, life is short! It is so very short, and there is so little time to do the things we yearn to do. Do not waste time on this... this useless heartache, I beg of you."

Scarlet smiled a little. "How old are you again, boy?"

"Fifty, according to Alexyin," Cestimir grinned. "And then at other times: five. Today, I believe, we are at a five."

"Where are we headed?" Scarlet asked again, peering at the front window, which was almost totally blocked by Yesuk's broad back as he snapped the reins, urging the pair of horses on.

"Just for a run," Cestimir replied, settling back. "Up near the foothills. We'll be back before my mother and Nazheradei are out of that damnable council meeting with no one the wiser. I want to show you the old temple ruins. Melev has told me so much about them that he has gotten me quite curious, and I've been thinking of going there since you told me about the statues you saw in Morturii. The legends say that the Shining Ones lived there once. We're supposedly descended from them."

Scarlet nodded. "So Lia... your brother has said."

Cestimir gave him a curious look. "What do you call him? You never say it all the way, but cut yourself off or call him Prince Nazheradei, with your tongue sounding like you've eaten briars."

"Liall," Scarlet answered, pushing back a wave of sadness. "It's his name back home."

Scarlet realized that the sleigh was moving awfully fast, even faster than the one Liall and he had ridden to the palace. He gripped the cushions with gloved hands and hoped Yesuk knew what he was doing. The sleigh began to ascend another steep hill with no sigh of slowing.

"There is nothing to worry about," Cestimir said. "Yesuk is very skilled, and he is familiar with this road."

Scarlet peered out the window. Well, he supposed there was a road somewhere beneath the snow, at least. "Does the snow ever melt up here?"

"No, not up here. In the lowlands, yes. You will hardly recognize my land then. Everywhere it is green and bright with sun." Cestimir produced a flask from his coat and opened it. "Here, have a sip, it will warm you."

Scarlet took a cautious swallow and found it was the same stuff that Liall had given him on the Ostre Sul, fiery but warming. He handed it back to Cestimir, who also took a swallow and put the flask away. "Has Liall spoken with you yet?"

"About?" Cestimir arched a too-familiar eyebrow.

That made Scarlet laugh again. "There, that's very like him. Nothing in particular. He was just going to arrange a longer meeting with you." It occurred to Scarlet belatedly that it might be unwise to make assumptions.

"Oh, that. Yes." Cestimir looked pleased, though. "He apologized for delaying in coming to visit me. I think I like this unknown brother of mine. He thanked me for being kind to you, and I felt obligated to tell him I had not." His tone was regretful. "I'm sorry for that, truly. And I'm sorry that you've been ill-treated by the court. I'd like a giant broom to sweep them all away some days."

"Some of them could take up a better job than being nasty to folk all the time," Scarlet admitted. The sleigh swayed and he clutched at the door.

Cestimir grinned and Scarlet opened his mouth to

ask the prince to tell him more about the legends of the immortal giants, and then the world turned upside down.

The sleigh swayed again wildly, swinging around almost sideways in the road. Then it jolted so hard that it rattled Scarlet's teeth. There was a terrific *crack* just before the rear end of the sleigh seemed to bottom out. Beneath his feet it sounded as if the earth was being ripped and torn apart. Scarlet could hear rocks being thrown up against the undercarriage, and then there was one more tremendous jolt and they were tumbling, end over end, streaks of starlight racing past the window.

Scarlet thumped his head on the roof and caught hold of Cestimir, purely out of terror. It saved him from being thrown through the window. Gravity vanished and he closed his eyes, dizzy and sick, just before they slammed back into the earth with a crash that was thunderous in the small confines of the sleigh carriage.

They came to rest, tipped half-way up again, neither right side up, nor upside down, but balanced precariously. Cestimir tried to sit up. The sleigh rocked and shifted.

"Don't move," Scarlet gasped, and Cestimir froze. "Wait, wait." He closed his eyes a moment and breathed through his mouth, waiting for the dizziness to lift, and then opened them again.

This is very bad, he thought as the sleigh creaked again. He heard one of the horses screaming.

"What shall we do?" Cestimir's voice was muffled by furs, but he sounded calm enough.

"Be still. Give me a moment." Scarlet moved his hand by inches and rubbed his glove over the glass to clear it. "Oh gods..." He felt sick. They were on the very edge of a cliff, the window giving him a view of black, open space below them. This was going to be difficult.

"Cesta, this is very important." Scarlet was trembling

so hard that it was difficult to speak, but then he glanced at the prince's face. Cestimir was pale and his eyes were wide like blue marbles, and Scarlet reminded himself that the boy was only fourteen. Prince or not, he would have to be the strong one here.

"We need to inch back towards the other door to shift our weight," Scarlet said, forcing his voice to be level. "We need to do it very, very slowly and carefully because we're close to the edge on my side."

"All right," Cestimir said, but did not move.

Scarlet took in a breath, willing his teeth not to chatter. "You will have to go first."

"Oh. Of course." Cestimir sounded winded, as if he had run a long ways, but Scarlet admired his calm.

Scarlet held his breath, as if that would do any good, and held very still as Cestimir shifted back, little by little. "When you get to the door, see if you can open it and slide through."

"I'm not leaving you!"

"Please don't," he returned dryly, shifting his weight over with the prince. "But one of us has to go first and you're closest. Don't argue, you want-wit, just do it."

Scarlet heard a creaking noise and the sleigh shivered unpleasantly, as if it were considering sliding off the edge anyway. The door creaked.

"Open," Cestimir said. The sleigh steadied again. "Hurry, Keriss," Cestimir said in a scared voice, sounding younger by the second.

Scarlet wasted no time and pushed himself back with more speed than sense, his legs tangled in furs that were dragged out with him. He had barely reached the open door when the sleigh began to slide toward the edge. He got one foot out and Cestimir grabbed his arm, then he dug his foot in and launched his body forward, landing face-first in the snow and splitting his lower lip on something hard hidden beneath the layer of flakes. The sleigh slid another several inches over the side before it halted there, hanging suspended over open sky.

Oh, gods, the horses—he scrambled to cut them free, but he needn't have worried. One horse had vanished, spooked into running off, he assumed at first. The other was further up the hill, clear of the wreckage. The front of the sleigh containing the driver's seat and reins had snapped clean off, and Yesuk lay very still in the snow. Cestimir was beside Scarlet as he caught the mare's bridle, and they both exchanged the same grim look, for the horse was lamed: bloodied white bone poking through her foreleg.

"Yesuk," Cestimir gasped, turning.

Scarlet handed the reins to Cestimir. Prince or no, Cestimir was still a boy. "Here, hold the mare. I'll see to him." He jogged the short distance to the curve of the hill where Yesuk lay, but it was no use. The man's neck was broken and his skull crushed against a rock jutting out of the snow, now bathed red.

"The man is dead," Scarlet called out as Cestimir watched anxiously, and the boy froze for a moment, looking blank and lost. Scarlet returned to him and put his hands on the broken reins. The horse whinnied in pain, her foreleg drawn up under her.

Scarlet couldn't help the animal, but he could put her out of her misery. "Give me your knife," he told Cestimir, spitting blood from his split mouth, but Cestimir shook his head.

"I will do it."

The prince drew his knife from his belt and did what needed to be done. Brave lad, Scarlet thought, and left Cestimir grieving over Yesuk as he collected the scattered furs from outside the carriage before joining him beside the body. Cestimir's eyes were dry as he cleaned his knife in the snow.

The wind skirled down from the hill and Scarlet shivered, realizing just how bitter it was. All was shrouded in the dim, bluish light that disrupted all normal sense of distance and depth and made objects seem closer than they were. Yet the spires of the Nauhinir Palace, wedged into the cleft of the valley below, did not look so very small. It depended on how deep the snow was. They could survive it if they made good time and stayed warm.

"I will have someone's blood for this," Cestimir said coolly. "Yesuk was my friend." He reached out to touch the fallen man's shoulder and said something in Sinha.

Scarlet marveled again at the prince's calm. "Here," he said, and wrapped one of the furs around Cestimir's head and shoulders. "Keep your face covered."

Cestimir nodded slowly and stood, hauling Scarlet up with him. "You've lost a glove," he observed.

So he had. Scarlet shook his head when Cestimir would have given him one of his. "No, it's fine. These sleeves are too long as it is. I'll just keep this hand safely inside and hold the fur closed with this one. But we need to start moving."

"Agreed." Cestimir pointed. "Your forehead is bleeding again."

"It is?" Scarlet reached up and felt the matted lump over his left eyebrow. The wound was only scraped open and hadn't bled much, but the size of the lump was still impressive. "It doesn't hurt."

"That's not always a good sign," Cestimir worried. "Come," he said, and threw the remaining fur around Scarlet's shoulders. "We must start back."

As they passed the overturned sleigh, Cestimir caught his arm. "Keriss, look." He pointed to the long, shining runners. One of them had snapped, perhaps as they rounded too fast at the curve of the hill.

"It broke," he said needlessly.

"It didn't break," Cestimir disagreed. "Too clean. It was sawn through." His expression was stony.

They stood together in silence, staring at the death that been intended for them, or perhaps just for Cestimir alone. Scarlet still doubted that anyone would go to this much trouble to harm him. He opened his mouth to tell Cestimir just that, but suddenly the sleigh groaned like a living thing and began to slide towards the edge of the cliff. Both young men backed away, and within a few seconds the underside of the sleigh rolled over very slowly, like a fish going belly up in water, and it wavered there, hung out like Linhona's washing over an open sky, before tumbling end over end to the bottom of the black gorge far, far below.

They stood for a few moments in mute shock, then turned without a word and began walking down the hill.

"Be careful where you step," Cestimir cautioned. "And let us move further away from the edge. This light can make shadows very deceiving."

Scarlet chuckled a little. "Cestimir, Hilurin can see much better than Rshani in the dark."

"They can?" The prince shook his head as they walked. "You are full of surprises, ser Keriss, but I think you have heard that before."

The first part of the trek did not go badly. The snow was only as high as Scarlet's boot tops, and they were both shaking and charged from the wreck. It was nearly an hour before the cold began to sap Scarlet's bones and his legs began to tire, but he resisted feeling it. His head throbbed and the bruise on his temple was one loud hum of agony, but that, too, he kept to himself, kept his feet moving.

Despite telling Cestimir that he would keep his gloveless hand protected in his sleeve, Scarlet had to keep using it to grasp onto rocks or the bare trunks of saplings as they navigated their way down the hill. It became numb quickly and thereafter he ceased to feel it. It was a long walk and the ghost-pale trees looming over the road from the steep embankment seemed like arms reaching over the path. White trees still seemed unnatural to him, and their presence illuminated how he felt about himself here.

It was true, what Liall said. He was the foreigner here. This landscape was alien to Scarlet, and he didn't have the slightest idea how to navigate it. He had been traveling roads in Byzantur on his own since he was seven, errands for Scaja from Lysia to Tradepoint and Skeld's ferry –and even the Sea Road to Riverpoint. Now there was a royal court to navigate, dangers he had never heard of, a people and a language and a history he did not understand. Perhaps he had been too confident since coming to Rshan, too stubborn and proud, and perhaps Liall could only see how out of his element and vulnerable he was. Despite his misgivings, there were many things Scarlet loved about Rshan: the books with pictures in them, the way that everyone lived together like bees in a hive in the Nauhinir, and how for the most part they all seemed to get along and to thrive. He liked the food and the music and the smells. He even liked the blue lamps. Scarlet realized that he was drawn to this place, without ever having seen it before. Rshan felt like a childhood home he was returning to, a place dimly remembered, but always cherished. He wondered if the land felt the same about him, and doubted it.

Then there was the tangle of Liall. Scarlet needed Liall, but not in the way Liall seemed to want him to be needed. He did not want to need anyone like that. His Hilurin pride kept reminding him that a man does for himself, and does not rely on others to make the way

easy for him. That Liall always seemed so determined to
protect him and take care of things made him feel weak
and laughable, and Liall never understood that. Liall was
always so sure he was in the right.

Look where you are now, Scarlet-lad, Scaja's voice
murmured in his ear, and he smiled. True enough. Maybe
he should have been arguing less and listening more.

They kept walking. By the end of the second hour,
the palace looked no nearer in the valley below, and the
dim light and the trees kept them from seeing anything
of the grounds surrounding the Nauhinir. Scarlet's vision
may have been keener than Cestimir's, but it, too, had its
limits.

It began to snow again, and they stopped in the lee of
the hill to rest. Cestimir pulled the flask from his coat and
insisted that Scarlet drink. Scarlet thought that Cestimir
looked much more tired than he himself felt, but some of
that may have been grief for Yesuk.

"Here," Cestimir said, holding the flask out to him.
"Drink. It's not good for your head, but neither is freezing
to death."

Scarlet nodded and reached for the flask with his
numbed hand. Cestimir hissed and took Scarlet's hand
instead. The prince flexed Scarlet's fingers and examined
the white edges of his palm.

"It's already begun," Cestimir fretted. "It's hard
to see because your skin is so pale, but you have some
frostbite." Cestimir drew his own glove off and jammed
it over Scarlet's hand despite Scarlet's objections.

"I'll live," Scarlet mumbled. His mouth felt stiff and
his head throbbed, and there was a brassy taste on his
tongue.

Cestimir gave him a long look, then uncapped the
flask and held it to Scarlet's lips. Scarlet drank and barely
tasted it, but a moment later the warmth spread in his

stomach. He sighed and nodded. "Better."

Cestimir took a drink, still watching Scarlet as the wind howled around the edges of the hill and sent small curtains of snow chasing into the darkling landscape.

Scarlet pointed to the forest and the long hill sloping below them. "We should cut across country," he said. "This road is easier going, but it's three times as long."

Cestimir glanced at the forest and then at the winding road before nodding. "I agree," he said. "But if they send a search party out for us, we will miss them."

"How long do you think it will take them to send one out?"

Cestimir glanced at the sky. "Too long. The snow is getting thicker. Scarlet.... can your magic help us here?"

Scarlet's teeth chattered a little. "I know where we are relative to the palace," he answered. "I could find our way back even if we couldn't see a thing. And I can heal a small injury if I need to, or start a fire to keep us warm or send up a smoke trail."

Cestimir shook his head negatively. "It is very hard to see smoke in this kind of sky," he pointed out. "And the smell might bring snow bears to us before a search party. They are very curious and aggressive animals, and now is their foraging time. Can you do anything against bears with your magic?"

"If I could, I'd have used it on the Hunt."

"No fire, then," Cestimir sighed. He held the flask out to Scarlet again.

Scarlet shook his head. After all, Cestimir was the younger. "You drink."

"No." Cestimir took hold of his shoulder, not too gently, either. "I am used to the weather. Don't make me pour this down your throat."

Scarlet stared him down. "Liall..." he began, intending to say something about how Liall would want Scarlet to look out for his brother.

"Will blame me for this, not you," Cestimir finished. For one so young, his tone was implacably commanding. "I am prince here. I took the sleigh out. I took you with me. If anything happens to you, Nazheradei will not forgive me."

Scarlet sighed, realizing the futility of arguing. "Fine, give me the damned stuff." There was not much left. He downed the last of it and Cestimir tucked the flask back in his coat.

"We must keep moving," Cestimir said, rising.

The liquor gave him a little more energy and they started off quickly again, this time turning east into the forest and beginning the difficult descent. The wind had picked up, and for long hours it howled and fought them. Also, the drifts were deeper in the woods, and the ground uneven beneath the snow and rocky. There were moments that Scarlet could swear he felt hands in the frigid air, pulling him back, trying to force him to lie down. He pulled the fur closer over his ears and buried his face in the ruff of his coat, and he trudged more slowly, every step seeming to require a massive effort on his part. Finally, he stumbled into a drift that swallowed him to his hips, and Cestimir was there, prodding him back to level ground and cursing.

Cestimir pulled him along, his arm linked with Scarlet's, half-dragging him. "Don't stop," he begged. "Please don't. I don't think I can carry you."

Scarlet felt like he was covered in snow, and he looked down once and saw that he very nearly was. "Just down a little further, then turn south again," he mumbled to Cestimir, giving directions through numbed lips. "We'll cross the road again there. We can rest."

They reached the road below and both boys collapsed to their knees onto the flat roadway, gasping for breath.

They knelt there for several minutes before Scarlet raised his head and stood, peering through the thick forest to the south. The Nauhinir was still a disheartening distance away.

Suddenly, through the whistling of the wind through the trees, they heard the jingle of harness.

Cestimir pulled his arm, flattening them both against the hillside. A sleigh pulled by a double team of blacks barreled up from the valley road. Painted on the carriage was a strange symbol. It was not the blue and silver starburst that adorned Cestimir's sleigh, but a blazon of crossed gold hatchets on a field of red.

Cestimir swore softly. "Vladei."

Scarlet was too glad to see the sleigh to care who rode in it. He could no longer feel his legs at all. "Are we in trouble?"

"I do not know, Keriss." Cestimir shook his head, his lips compressed and white. "Please keep silent and do not speak."

The sleigh stopped and the door opened. Vladei leapt out and stood in front of the pair of cold, frightened young men. "Cestimir!" he barked and then a spate of rapid Sinha.

"Vladei," Cestimir said in Bizye, visibly fighting to keep his voice even. "How fortunate your arrival. There was a mishap near the temple road, I'm afraid. A runner on the sleigh broke and we narrowly escaped with our lives." Cestimir turned to Scarlet, and Scarlet saw the frightened look he had hidden from Vladei.

Vladei's eyes were like two river stones, flat and lifeless, and Scarlet had the feeling that if he had been alone, his neck would have been snapped before he could count the fingers on one hand. Or perhaps, if Cestimir had been alone, the same would have been true. He wondered if someone had meant for Cestimir to be alone when the wreck occurred. Scarlet bowed as best he could, covered in furs and snow. Vladei spoke to Cestimir again in Sinha.

"Thank you, my brother. We are very grateful for the rescue." Cestimir took Scarlet's arm, his voice raw. "Come, ser Keriss, my brother has kindly offered to return us to the Nauhinir, so we may warm ourselves and find dry clothing."

As they climbed into the carriage, Scarlet was nudged and shoved and ended up between Cestimir and Vladei. At least I will be warmer, he reasoned dryly, not liking the thought of Vladei so close to him.

Cestimir looked at Scarlet's stillness and dulled eyes worriedly, and he drew his own hapcoat off to cover Scarlet. Scarlet's eyes drooped and Cestimir shook him roughly. "Sleep later!" the prince commanded. "You must stay awake until we get back to the palace."

Vladei said something more. Scarlet caught a few of the words, but they were the gutter Sinha that Liall had taught him for fun on the ship. The man looked at him so coldly that he shivered, though he was no longer truly cold or felt much of anything at all.

"Lenilyn," Vladei said, glaring holes through Scarlet. "How old are you?"

"What does it matter?" Scarlet said through chattering teeth, too tired to demand why Vladei wanted to know. "I was a man in my country years ago."

"So young," Vladei said in heavily accented Bizye, giving a look aside to Cestimir, who was calm and untouched by Vladei's dark mood. "Among us, it would be a scandal: a boy of your age with Nazheradei. But of course, you are not one of us."

"Vladei, this is my brother's t'aishka," Cestimir said pleadingly.

Scarlet wondered what difference it made, or why

Cestimir's hand sought his and tightened. "It's all right," he told Cestimir. "I don't mind his questions. I've got a few of my own." If there was trouble later, he had sooner be damned for truth as for lies, and he was tired of this man sneering at him. Vladei knew nothing about him. "How old are you? And while we're at it, how old is Prince Nazheradei?"

"Do you not know?" Vladei replied, quick as a hound scenting blood.

"Vladei," Cestimir begged, his composure cracking, and then added something in Sinha.

Vladei ignored the younger prince. "What else is unknown to you, I wonder? What secrets has he kept from you? You did not know that Nazheradei was a prince, or that Shikhoza was once promised to him, or about Nadei's murder. What else has been kept from you?"

Those cold eyes, like Liall's and unlike, made Scarlet want to bend his neck in submission and look away, let the man win, but his stubborn pride kept his chin up.

"Have you met Jarek?" Vladei smiled coldly. "The woman soldier who rode at the head of the army? She is Khatai Jarek, once Nazheradei's lover. They are very close. Very close indeed, to plot such things together. Have you heard of a place called Magur, little lenilyn?"

Scarlet's stomach plummeted, and he realized that he might never come to the end of Liall's secrets. He only stared at the mocking man in dismay, and Vladei laughed and made the gesture of dismissal one makes to servants, shutting Scarlet up for good. Vladei's show of contempt had almost prompted Scarlet to lie, to say that he knew all about this Jarek, and he was ashamed of how he had nearly betrayed his own honor just to satisfy this sneering brute. Why isn't the truth good enough? he asked himself.

Scarlet closed his eyes and pretended sleep, damning

Vladei silently to ten different hells.

Vladei began to speak lowly to Cestimir in Sinha, and suddenly the carriage turned north again, away from the palace. Despite his best efforts, exhaustion claimed Scarlet and he drifted into darkness.

By the hour that marks the beginning of the later afternoon, scouts had found the dead horses and the wreck of the carriage lying far below the mountain road. There were tracks leading off from the path into the forest, but Rshani take no chances. They wasted valuable time scaling the cliff with ropes to check the carriage, and finding no one inside nor any blood trail that would have told tales on any scavenger stealing a body, the scouts sent runners to follow the tracks. They ended in a spot near a hill where fresh sleigh tracks crossed them, and there also ended the search, for the tracks led back up into the mountain, where it was snowing heavily.

A rider in blue brought the ill news back and asked new instructions of Liall, and Liall had to physically stop himself from hitting the man.

Vladei was not inside the palace and nowhere to be found. Liall knew what had happened.

So, apparently, did his mother. As the night-hour approached, he went to give her the news and found Alexyin at the entrance to the second tier, barring the door.

"She is ill," Alexyin said, holding up his hand. "No visitors."

"I am no visitor," Liall said, deeply shocked and insulted.

Alexyin looked pained. "Forgive me, I did not mean it like that. Just... my prince, she is very old and this news has brought her low. The healers can do nothing."

Liall wondered if Alexyin were telling him what he thought he was. "She will recover," he said.

Alexyin shook his head slowly. "She will not, Nazheradei."

Liall swallowed in a throat suddenly dry. "But..."

Alexyin put his hand on Liall's shoulder, and his face was kinder than Liall could ever remember seeing. "Go back to your apartments and wait. I will come when there is need."

Liall's walk through the palace was long and lonely, and Scarlet's absence seemed like an open wound. For the first time he truly felt the cold here, and marveled that Scarlet had borne it all this time without complaint.

Scarlet. Oh, gods. Scarlet and Cestimir. Where were they? Were they dead already, or in pain, or afraid? What was happening to them? Liall had to fight the urge to go out after them on his own, armed with only a sword in his hand and a horse under him. He knew it was what Vladei wanted, and he knew it would be the death of them all if he went. The only chance he had to keep Scarlet and Cestimir alive was to stay in the Nauhinir, where he was still a threat to Vladei, and so prevent his step-brother from playing his final hand. If Vladei took Liall prisoner, Vladei would kill him as well as Cestimir and Scarlet, and then claim the throne.

Liall passed the library and found it deserted. Stepping in, he breathed in the smell of polished woods and leather bindings and paper. Scarlet had thought this place a miracle: an entire hall just for books. Scarlet had never seen a library, nor more than one or two books in his life. The jeweled globe that Scarlet had admired spun under Liall's fingers as he sat by the window, his mind mired deep in tangled thoughts.

A fragrant lamp burned in the corner, and Liall remembered how the lamps on the ship had painted blue-tinged hollows in Scarlet's cheeks and left thin streaks of indigo in his black hair. He had often looked at Scarlet as he slept, stealing minutes like coins, locking them away in his heart. Even as he swore never to let Scarlet go, he had been envisioning the day when time would part them. Hilurin lives were so brief. He was already older than Scarlet's long-dead grandfather would have been. Inevitably, Scarlet would age past Liall.

I will remain little changed while he grows older, his youth brief a mirror-flashed aimed at the sun, Liall thought. Will he love me then? Will I love him? And what is love? Is it merely bodies, a fancy for a certain face, a shape, a pair of midnight-dark eyes, And if it is more than that, if my love for Scarlet is a thing of the soul that base flesh can never change, why then does the thought of losing the sight of his beauty grieve me so? Scarlet... you should have been born one of us, but then I would not have loved you.

A storm brewed up from the northeast and hurled ice and sleet at the windows, and still the palace slept on. Liall brooded in the library until the large tallow candle burned to the marker of the second hour past midnight, and then he could delay no longer. He went back to the apartments with a heavy step, dreading what news he would find. Nenos opened the door and shook his head when Liall asked if there had been word. Liall went into the den that Scarlet had preferred over the formal common room and sat with his hands clasped on his knees, waiting.

They came for him two hours before morning. Liall had been expecting it, but his heart seized in his chest when he heard a line of footsteps approaching the door to his apartments. He heard Nenos admit them, and then they entered the common room.

Nenos bowed. Behind Alexyin was a crowd of barons and guards, Ressanda among them. Alexyin did not speak, only motioned to Liall to come out and follow. Liall rose woodenly. Two of the guards came further into the common room and took up station by the fireplace. Liall wondered at their presence.

"They will keep watch for your t'aiska," Alexyin said gently.

As Liall passed Nenos, he touched the servant's shoulder. "If any word at all comes, send to me at once."

Alexyin's face was drawn and set. He did not speak, but turned on his heel, expecting Liall to follow him. In the outer hallway, the barons fell into step behind the two men. They were some ways into the palace before Liall trusted himself to speak.

"When?"

Alexyin glanced quickly at him, and for a moment, he looked the bodyguard almost frightened. "Soon," he said, his voice rough. "Before morning, certainly. It..." he trailed off. "It is not sudden, this thing. We have seen it coming for some time."

They reached the queen's apartments, and Liall was enormously glad that Shikhoza was not among the women who huddled in a loose and distressed group of silk and velvet before the doors to the queen's third tier, her bedroom. Alexyin's face was drawn into lines of grief, and he looked much older than Liall remembered as a boy, when Alexyin was his best teacher.

"Not sudden," Liall said, pitying him. "But no easier,

I'm sure."

"No. I thought it would be. We have been friends for many years, your mother and I. We have fought for the same thing, struggled to train a king fit for Rshan, and now…" Alexyin broke off, shaking his head. His voice shook. "It cannot be. We must save him."

Liall knew he meant Cestimir, not Scarlet: Cestimir to save an empire, Scarlet to save only him. It was logical. It was what was best for Rshan. But for Liall, in that moment, all he could feel was the cold weight of his heart threatening to swallow him alive if he lost his love.

The door opened and Bhakamir bowed to let them enter. Liall began to say something to Alexyin, perhaps not to let the queen see Alexyin's suffering and guess the news they had of Cestimir, but Alexyin's face, when Liall turned back to him, was neutral and smoothed of distress. Alexyin was a Setna.

The room was dim and smelled of strong incense, and as the doors closed behind them and they approached the queen's sickbed, a curae hurried away with a basin covered by a towel.

Nadiushka was propped up on pillows, her face slack and lined, the long collar of her silver bed-gown rucked up into untidy rolls around her neck. Bhakamir came with another glass of the clear liquid and held it to her lips, then tenderly smoothed her collar, making her presentable. His eyes glimmered with tears. He had served her since Liall was a bawling child and he a gallant young man.

Nadiushka caught Bhakamir's hand and pressed a kiss to it, and the man made a small sound of protest in his throat.

"I shall not need you again, my friend," she wheezed. "Go now."

Bhakamir shook his head swiftly, but she smiled at him. "You were a handsome young courtier when you came to serve me, and I was still a beautiful queen. Spare me the knowledge of knowing you witnessed the very messy demise of an old woman. Let me die with one last vanity."

He bent his head over her hand, trembling, and she whispered some words to him too low to hear. Bhakamir sniffled and wiped his face with his hand, but the smile he gave her was brilliant.

Bhakamir left them and the doors closed. They were alone with his mother, Cestimir's surrogate father and Liall. She signaled for them to come closer.

"Sit here." She patted the bed.

Liall did, and Alexyin put his hand on Liall's shoulder as she breathed shallowly and closed her eyes for a moment, then started awake. She gazed at the two of them for a long time. He finally took her hand.

"Mother," he choked.

"Shh." Her head rolled on the pillow. "No, Nazir. It's too late for that. No tears now."

Liall nodded, his head down.

"Tell Cestimir," she said faintly. "Take care of your brother."

"I will," he said, then saw she was looking straight at Alexyin. "Tell him," she struggled to speak. "Tell Cestimir... take care of Nazir."

Liall was astonished. Him, take care of me? But Alexyin's hand tightened on Liall's shoulder and the bodyguard nodded. "I will, my lady. My queen."

She still looked at Alexyin. She seemed to have forgotten Liall was there, though he still held her hand.

"He loves him so much," she went on in that faint voice. "It is strange that the strongest of men often have this weakness, this flaw of the warrior's heart. He loves too deeply. I fear there is much sorrow ahead for Nazheradei."

Alexyin nodded. Her eyes drooped and closed, and then she opened them and saw Liall. "Nazir," she said tenderly, like a girl. "Where have you been? I missed you."

Liall swallowed. "I've been away, Mother. For a very long time."

She nodded, her brow creased as if recalling some old and half-forgotten pain, then she smiled and the years fell from her. "I have ruled a small piece of earth," she proclaimed in a bright whisper, like a secret.

Alexyin's fingers dug into Liall's shoulder. Nadiushka closed her eyes and did not open them, and some minutes later she drew her last breath. Her chest fell and did not rise again, and Alexyin, so composed before that, took a shaking breath and knelt by the side of the royal bed, hiding his face in his hands as the death bell tolled in the Shining Tower.

Liall knelt on the floor with him, and Alexyin did not chide him for weeping, for all men are little boys when their mother dies.

Blue and silver for a queen, gray and violet for the dead. There would be no elaborate robes of death for Nadiushka, as there were none for any other monarch of Rshan. In death, all were equal.

Neither would there be any peace for Liall. An hour after Nadiushka drew her last breath, as Liall sat mourning with Alexyin in the third tier where courtiers usually waited, he began to be aware of a noise in the palace that was steadily increasing. The everyday sounds of the Nauhinir rose to a new pitch and blended into a dull, diluted roar not unlike the sound of the sea, until finally Liall could not ignore it and sent a page to see what was amiss.

The page – a young boy of ten or so clad in blue and silver livery - was back very quickly, hurrying and nearly tripping over the hem of his long virca. "Khatai Jarek has returned!" he said in a voice more suited for a barn than a funeral. Alexyin hushed the boy immediately, but Liall took the boy's shoulders and drew him closer.

"Where and with whom?"

"The army, my prince," the boy said breathlessly. "She is approaching by the eastern road, and the queen's army with her."

"Queen no more, little one," Alexyin told the page. "Nadiushka is with the Shining Ones. The army is Cestimir's now."

Liall made no comment to that, though he could see that Alexyin was hoping for one. Perhaps he was hoping for Liall's confirmation of Cestimir's inheritance, but that matter was already settled in Liall's mind. Cestimir would be king.

"Go on, boy." Liall ruffled the page's hair and pushed him to the door. "Go to your mother for now." He stood up as the page scampered off, taking pains not to look at Alexyin. "After all these years, you think I would take my brother's place?"

"I said nothing, my prince."

"You said everything," Liall retorted, wounded. "Damn you. Of all the people to doubt me now, why must it be you? Can you not see that I do not wish to be king? That I never wished to be king?"

Alexyin remained silent.

"Of course," Liall said slowly. "No one could ever see that, could they? Not even my own brothers. Only my mother saw me as I am, and now she is gone." *And*

Scarlet, he thought with an ache. Scarlet sees me for who I am, but where is he? Even he had his doubts, or else we should never have quarreled and he would be here right now, safe in my arms. He did not trust me with his secrets, and for good reason.

"Let us go and greet the khatai, and hear what news of Vladei's rebels," Liall said, gathering up his cloak. His posture was stiff and offended, and Alexyin could only bow his head and follow. There were no words to be said between them. Suspicion had taken them all away.

It was not the entire queen's army that rode to the main gates of the Nauhinir as the page had thought, but only a large cohort of soldiers with Jarek at their head. On the wide stone steps that Scarlet had been so fearful to ascend, Liall received Jarek's obeisance and searched the khatai's face. Snow shimmered down in the blue twilight, deadening the sound of horse's hooves, the jangle of harness and the creak of armor.

"What news?" Liall asked.

Jarek stood there with her helmet under arm and raised her voice for all to hear. "The rebels of Magur are no more!" She stood tall and proud with her boot on the first step, three steps below Liall, and her long hair blew behind her like a white cloud.

There was a rousing cheer from the onlookers, who were few. The hour was late and many were mourning the queen or preparing for the funeral wake that was soon to come.

Jarek's face was lined with worry. "We heard the bells," she said.

Liall nodded. "And they toll, as they always have, for the passing of royal blood. It was Nadiushka, Jarek. Not Cestimir."

He had divined her fears. Jarek sagged a little in relief. "Let us go where we can speak in private," she murmured. "There is much to tell."

"This way."

Their procession through the Nauhinir was not interrupted, mainly because the presence of Jarek's young soldiers, their forbidding faces and the well-worn armor that had seen recent use in battle kept all but the most powerful of nobles away. To those Barons who would have stopped them, Liall spared only a nod and a rough "Later!" to allay their anxiety.

Liall took Jarek back to the queen's tiers. His own apartments would have been more practical, but they were further away and there were no guards to keep the curious out, no invisible veil of the taboo to stop their knocking. Even dead, Nadiushka wielded a presence in the Nauhinir.

Alexyin closed the door, and Liall poured Jarek a cup of strong wine.

"Tell me," Liall said.

Jarek stripped the chain maille glove from her hand and loosened her heavy leather hauberk. The hauberk had many little, neat, v-shaped slices in it: arrowheads turned aside by the thick metal plates inside the layers of leather.

Here is another thing Scarlet would never think to defend against, Liall thought with a pang of fear. Arrows were the weapons of cowards in the Southern Continent. He doubted that Scarlet had ever even seen a bow.

Jarek drank all of the wine in one gulp, and now Liall could see her weariness.

"Magur is no more. We have taken Vladei's ancestral

cities and his request for aid has been refused by the Barons of the east. A large band of Vladei's red guards survived and escaped. My men are chasing them down, but many eluded us." She wiped her mouth and set the cup down, nodding to Liall in thanks.

"But his men were among the rebels?" Liall asked sharply.

"Indisputably. We saw their camp and captured their flags: red for Ramung, his ancestor." Jarek's smile was wolfish. "Vladei has been caught in treason against the queen, my prince. We have him."

Alexyin slapped his hands together, his jaw set. "Then he dies," he grated out. "There can be no mercy for him."

"Indeed, no," Liall murmured, suddenly subdued. This was the execution of a royal prince they were speaking of. "Unless he outfoxes us and we die first. Then, my friends, history will name *us* the traitors. It is not so much a matter of who is right in these wars, but who wins."

"We shall not lose," Jarek stated.

"I wish I had your confidence," Liall returned, "but you do not know everything that has happened. Cestimir and Scarlet are missing. They went on a sleigh ride, it appears, but the sleigh was found smashed in a valley below the Temple Road. Their driver was found dead."

"A search—" Jarek began quickly.

"We are searching. We have been for hours. They have found nothing, no hint of where they might be."

Jarek glanced to Alexyin. "And Vladei?"

"Gone," Alexyin answered. "None knows where."

"I know where," Jarek said grimly. "We captured many of his men, as I said. A man will give up his own mother under torture." Liall winced, but Jarek went on, untouched. "They have a stronghold, it seems: the temple ruins in the mountains. They've been fortifying it for months, in case they needed a fort to retreat to. Now that they've been routed, the survivors will go there. So will Vladei, I believe. Where else does that rat have to run?"

Noise echoed in the chamber beyond, and the sound of Jarek's soldiers shouting in a rising chorus of anger.

"What in the hells," Liall growled, stalking to the doors. He flung them open to see several of the royal army holding Shikhoza and Eleferi at spear-point.

Shikhoza kicked her skirts aside fearlessly and glared at the men who couched their weapons at her. Eleferi stood beside the Lady of Jadizek, nervous and fretting, his sly face damp with sweat.

"Why do you disturb my mother's deathbed?"

"It will be all our deathbeds if you keep me away." She flicked a glance, quick as a viper, to Alexyin and Jarek. "Send them out."

"They stay," Liall said before Alexyin could object. "Speak. But I warn you, Lady, I am in no mood to tolerate your poison today."

"This is no woman's game of spite, Nazheradei." She pulled Eleferi forward. "We are here to make truce with you."

"Two vipers in one basket?" Liall smirked. "Eleferi, you have been Vladei's creature since we were boys. Do you mean to convince me you would betray him now? At what price?"

Eleferi flushed and opened his mouth to answer.

"No price. For Rshan," Shikhoza broke in. Her hand chopped the air when Liall would have spoken. "Will you *listen?* Vladei received a messenger last night, a rider from Magur."

Liall regarded her narrowly. Deceiving bitch. "And why did you not tell me this last night? Why wait?"

"It was not an easy decision, Nazir. Whatever you think of me, I do nothing lightly." Her hand dug in her skirt pocket and she handed him a piece of folded parchment. "Read it."

It was addressed to Eleferi.

Brother,
Magur is lost and we are betrayed by the West.
I make for the place we agreed upon. Tell no
one of this letter.

"But Eleferi told you," Liall said, glaring at Shikhoza. "Why?"

Her smile told him much. "For years, Vladei has sought to be my husband, but if he had not been so busy taking his brother for granted, he might have seen that Eleferi had already claimed what Vladei thought was his."

Liall sensed her words were meant more to bolster Eleferi's pride and soothe the betrayal the man was about to commit rather than any true affection on her part. "So you whore yourself with one brother while gulling the other. That is a song I have heard before from you, lady."

She did not rise to the bait. "If you want to see your t'aishka again, you will listen to me, prince. Cestimir's sleigh was found on the temple road, yes? Why there, of all places?"

"You are too late," Liall went on, ignoring her hints and giving Eleferi a hard look. He thrust the letter in his step-brother's face. "Jarek has already brought me the news that you carry in this missive. You betrayed your brother for nothing, Eleferi."

Eleferi turned pale.

"And why the ruins?" Shikhoza demanded. "Melev has been heard speaking to Cestimir of the secrets of the temple ruins lately. Many times. Think, Nazheradei. I know you like to ignore the long history of our people and pretend that our gods do not exist, but think. Why would an Ancient wish to lure a Hilurin to that place?"

Liall crumpled the letter in his hand, turning away, but froze when he saw Alexyin's face. The bodyguard was staring at Shikhoza in shock and dismay. "Surely you do not believe this nonsense?" he asked his old teacher, scoffing.

"Nazheradei... my prince, you saw what ser Keriss did in the great hall yesterday. You saw his magic." Alexyin shook his head. "You were always such a poor history student. The Shining Ones and the Anlyribeth, do you remember? One channels the power of the other. They worked together to forge the great magic that created Rshan, before the Anlyribeth fled. Think what another such union could do in a place of power."

"This is ridiculous," Liall said. "Place of power! That moldy old temple? And even if it could happen, Scarlet is not Anlyribeth and Melev is not a Shining One."

"Isn't he?" Alexyin asked. "We have never known, have we? We think Melev is descended of their first children born here, but we cannot be sure of anything when it comes to an Ancient."

"It would be a betrayal!" Liall snapped. "This is Melev! Do you realize what you accuse him of?"

"Do you realize what will happen to Cestimir if Alexyin is correct?" Shikhoza broke in.

Liall rounded on her, intending her curse her and banish her from the room, and then he realized what she meant: Vladei gone, the boys missing from the palace, the wrecked sleigh. "Cestimir," Liall repeated, stunned. "That was the price for delivering Cestimir to Vladei... a Hilurin." The only Hilurin to set foot in Rshan in two thousand years, he thought despairingly. Oh gods... Scarlet. What have I done to you?

"We need men," Alexyin said to Jarek, taking charge as Liall stood there with his eyes hollow and his expression frozen in pain.

"I don't have many," Jarek answered. "Perhaps a hundred, and what guards we have in the palace."

"Get them," Liall croaked, his throat dry as weathered bone. "Get every man and woman who can hold a weapon and get them to the gates. We ride *now.*"

10.

The Ruins

Scarlet dreamed. Liall and he were arguing again, in danger again, as usual, and Liall was trying to send him to safety. Scarlet refused to go and Liall shouted at him, but stopped when Scarlet pressed his mouth to Liall's to shut him up.

What do you do when home is a person, Liall? Don't I have the right to fight for you?

Scarlet stopped warring with it then, and admitted how much he had grown to love and need Liall. He swore if he ever got the chance, he would tell Liall so.

Then Cestimir was shaking him and he opened his eyes to see the dim outline of a squat, stone fortress against a background of those pale ghost-trees. Vladei was not in the carriage with them.

"Cestimir... where are we?"

"He... Vladei has not taken us home," Cestimir said, looking out the window. "We are at the temple ruins."

"We're in trouble."

"I'm afraid so. Very much."

Scarlet looked at the prince, wondering if he was frightened. He didn't seem so. "He won't dare to harm you."

"You do not know Vladei, Scarlet," Cestimir said, giving him his right name for the first time. "You crossed the sea from Byzantur to Rshan, yes? That is the measure of difference between Nazheradei and Vladei." He closed his eyes for a brief moment, as if he were summoning courage. "I'm so sorry I talked you into this."

The carriage door was thrown open and a hand reached for Cestimir. The prince flung it off and growled in Sinha. The figure, dimly-seen, backed off, and Cestimir dismounted the carriage with dignity.

"Ser Keriss," he called.

Scarlet clambered out after him. His eyes, far more suited to the dark than Cestimir's, adjusted immediately, and in the blue twilight he saw that they were surrounded by armed guards clad in red and gold. They were Vladei's men, and had a look of villainy that he had not seen on any Rshani's face since leaving the Ostre Sul. He realized that he liked a good many Rshani, now. Tesk, Nenos, Jochi, Cestimir, even the queen.

The guards stood a bit apart from Cestimir and Scarlet and eyed them with hostility, and it was not lost on Scarlet that not one of the armed men bowed to Cestimir.

Looming above them and sheltering them from the wind was a low, crumbling keep of stone, partially caved in on the north side. The ragged spike of a shattered tower jutted up into the star-pocked darkness above, and Scarlet could see that the place was a ruin older than memory. How many centuries had it brooded here, wasting away into the frozen mountain? It looked an angry place, and Scarlet quailed from the thought of going in there.

The guards stood a little apart from them, watching them. The nap had given Scarlet new energy, and he cast a longing look at the gray sketches of the woods nearby. He was sure the guards could barely make them out, but to him they were plain as day. Cestimir saw and shook his head.

"Don't," Cestimir mouthed, barely moving his lips.

"You Rshani may have long legs, but you can't run worth a damn," Scarlet answered back, voice low. "If I make it, I'll tell them where you are."

"You will not make it. If the cold does not kill you, the bears will."

"Are they going to kill us inside?"

It was a hard question to ask a boy, but Cestimir stared back at him fearlessly, if sad. "I don't know. Probably."

"Nothing to lose then."

"I promised you an adventure, Scarlet. I am sorry."

"Fine. You owe me one." Scarlet glanced at the woods. "Care to give me a send-off?"

One white eyebrow arched up, but Cestimir turned and strode peremptorily up to one of the red guards and thrust his face close to the man's. "How dare you treat me in this fashion!" Cestimir struck the guard a blow across the face, not a glancing one, either, and tried to shove his way past into the ruins.

Scarlet gave it a moment more before the shouting began, then bolted for the forest, quick as a hare. It was several moments before one of guards caught sight of him heading into the snow, and by the time the shouting had started, Scarlet was plunged into the blackness of the woods.

He hadn't expected thorns. There was a thick of them just beyond the stand of trees that lined the mountain road. Scarlet crashed into the frozen, leafless brush full-tilt, getting stabbed by the sharp points, stumbling and running, only to find that there was nothing beyond the stand, no ground to cross. The land dropped away from the path into a long, steep slope, down to the bottom of a hill. Running up on it blind, Scarlet lost his balance and began to fall.

A hand seized his arm, dragging him back from the edge. Scarlet found himself caught against a frame as big as a snow bear, strong and warm. Hands, neither soft nor cruel, swept him along over the patch of thorns and set him on his feet on the edge of the ravine.

Scarlet stared in shock. It was Melev, looking down at him with his milk-pale eyes. "Ser," he stammered, out of breath. He pointed in the direction of the ruins. "They're holding the prince prisoner!"

"I know." Melev's great hand clamped around Scarlet's wrist like an iron vise, and the dark blue sky turned over as he was picked up as if he weighed nothing.

"I have waited centuries for one of you to cross the great sea," Melev said, his deep voice rumbling through his chest and directly into Scarlet's skin. "And now you are here. The circle will close, the curse will end, and all will be as it once was."

It was babble to Scarlet. Mad talk. "Please. They're going to hurt Cestimir!"

"Yes."

Melev hauled him effortlessly up the side of the ravine, back to the ruins. Scarlet fought him, but it was like trying to push a mountain over.

Vladei waited for them in front of Cestimir and a squad of red guards, his arms folded and a wry smile on his face. Melev dumped Scarlet at Vladei's feet in the snow and one of the red guards grabbed Scarlet by the neck and shook him.

"Are you content, Melev?" Vladei asked, his hands perched on his hips, as if he knew Scarlet would be caught all along.

"I have the price of my assistance, as promised."

"Melev," Cestimir intoned, as if breathing the name of a god. "How could you do this?"

"It is worth one man's life to return Rshan's magic to her, to restore the glory of the Shining Ones."

"What magic? What nonsense is this?"

"The Anlyribeth stole the magic of the Nauhin, the Shining Ones. They took their revenge because we kept them in slavery. They were our curse, and never since has there been a slave in Rshan. This one," Melev clamped his hand on Scarlet's wrist again and dragged him closer. "Will restore the balance, and give back what was taken."

"Fairy tales!" Cestimir shouted. "This is madness, he's only a pedlar. An illiterate, peasant pedlar from Byzantur!"

"So it would seem, to all eyes but mine." Melev began to drag Scarlet towards the temple ruins.

"Leave him be!" Cestimir started after them and Vladei stunned the young Prince with a fist to the back of his head. Cestimir fell to his knees, moaning.

The guards brought both of the prisoners into the gray, barren fortress, and Scarlet saw what awaited them there: the hooded man, the shining sword, and the wooden platform. Scarlet felt sick and terrified at once. To die fighting was one thing, but to be led calmly to slaughter was far, far worse.

The executioner straddled the steps of the short wooden platform, his face hidden by a dark hood.

"They're going to kill us," he said needlessly to Cestimir.

"Not us," Cestimir got out, stumbling as Vladei shoved him in the back.

A red guard pushed Scarlet along again and he tried to tear his hand out of Melev's grasp to help Cestimir.

"Cesta!" Scarlet rounded on Vladei. "He's your brother!"

Cestimir had reached the steps and turned to speak to Scarlet calmly. "This happens here all the time, ser Keriss. It is nothing new." He gave Scarlet a small, nervous smile as the hooded man stepped down to bind the prince's hands behind his back. "At least, I will not be a prisoner in a throne room all my life. This way, I am free forever."

They tried to pull Cestimir up the steps, away from Scarlet. Scarlet reached out, clawing at Melev's arm to pry him off. "You can't do this, he's only a boy! Let him go!"

Vladei stepped forward and slapped Scarlet across the face. "He is a prince of Druz, meeting his death with dignity. Cease your wailing."

"Bastard!" Scarlet would have thrown himself on Vladei, but Melev picked Scarlet up effortlessly and turned towards a dark corridor that led into to the depths of the ruins. They led Cestimir up the steps, and the last look Scarlet had of Cestimir was the young Prince kneeling carefully on the wooden platform, as if afraid he could not do it with grace. Cestimir lifted his chin and turned his head to catch Scarlet's eye a last time. Astonishingly, there was pity in the prince's eyes. Not for himself, but for Scarlet.

"*Cesta!*" Scarlet howled, his voice ringing and bouncing off the stone walls.

Melev dragged him away, ignoring his cries. He even begged him. "Please, please, save him. You can't just let him die like that, please!"

Melev did not strike Scarlet to silence him. It was worse than that. Scarlet did not even seem to exist to the Ancient as he was pulled along the dark, cold corridors with their broken walls and crumbling arches, across shattered floors and through pitch-black passages, until at last they came to a large, round chamber already lit by many torches. This place was not like the rest of the ruins. There was evidence of recent repair in the wooden frame buttressing the arch, and the cracked floor had been swept free of pebbles and debris.

There was a sunken pit in the center of the chamber, round like the room. Melev tossed Scarlet into it and he fell, rolling. Melev stepped in after him, swifter than any man his size had a right to be, and grabbed Scarlet's wrist. Scarlet heard a clink of metal and felt a cold circle clamp on his wrist as Melev chained one of his hands to a round iron ring set into the sunken floor. Scarlet kicked and tried to pry him off before he could chain the other one, and failed.

Helpless, Scarlet crouched on his knees with his head down, breathing hard, waiting for whatever came next. Little flakes of snow drifted from the cracked ceiling as Melev watched him for a long moment, and then sat down cross-legged a few feet away from Scarlet. Melev rested his monstrous hands on his legs and seemed to drop into a pose of waiting.

Scarlet thought Melev was staring at him, but when Scarlet spit and thrashed in his chains, Melev did not seem to notice. Scarlet saw that his mouth was moving and a thin thread of sound came from his lips. Melev was chanting.

The words were strange, but not totally unfamiliar to Scarlet. It sounded almost like the cantos to Deva that his father had taught him, and as Melev's voice rose in volume, he realized he could definitely pick out words here and there.

"Farnorl esi, Danaae Deva er su Nauhin..."

Melev's pale, milky eyes unnerved him, and the chanting began to make his head ache right in the place between his eyebrows.

"Shut up!" Scarlet shouted, wanting Melev to do something, anything, rather than sit there and look at him like he was a bug with those sounds coming from the ancient's mouth. Yet, when Melev suddenly moved, Scarlet wished he had kept quiet.

Melev uncrossed his legs and rose with an eerie grace for one so large. His hand went into the sleeve of his thin robe and produced a small glass vial, rather like the perfume bottles Scarlet used to sell back home. Melev stood over him, impossibly tall, and reached down. Scarlet flinched, but Melev seized his chin in his hand and flicked the cap off the bottle, setting the cool ring of glass against his lips.

"Drink."

"Like hell!" Scarlet tried to twist away, pursing his mouth closed. Melev's thumb jabbed into the tender spot below his ear, and a spike of pain went through his head and neck. Still, he tried to keep his mouth closed. Melev pinched Scarlet's nose shut and cold liquid washed against his tongue. He swallowed reflexively, expecting some awful taste, but it was only some kind of pungent herb. Melev took his hands away and Scarlet coughed, spitting drops of milky liquid onto the stone. Before he could rage at Melev, his tongue started to go numb, and the last coherent thought he had before his vision melted into scenes of nightmare colors and shapes all bleeding into one another, was that Melev had fed him poison.

Blood streamed from Jochi's hand, spattering the ground with a steaming trail of red. His left shoulder was drawn down like a hunchback and the arm hung there useless, the muscles of that shoulder severed by a sword cut. A long red line ran from his temple to his jaw, and blood welled from his nose. Liall bent in the snow to look at him, and held his hand over the ragged wound to stop the bleeding.

Vladei's guards had slammed the temple's stone doors shut as soon as they heard the horses. Liall had led his men to the temple ruins, where they found it occupied by Vladei's surviving defenders of Magur. The red guards had barricaded themselves in with fallen stones and spears and their bodies. Outside, in the snowy twilight, the blue and silver-garbed soldiers of the queen gave a rallying shout and a loud crash shook the temple ruins. Jarek and Alexyin and several of the queen's soldiers were using a battering ram made out of a felled tree. A second crash and the doors cracked. Rock dust and snow trickled from the jagged battlements. Liall caught Jochi's arm just as his sword dropped from his fingers and he toppled like a felled tree. Jochi's weight pulled Liall down with him and Liall crouched on his knees, wiping some of the blood from Jochi's face. They had not known the number of red guards surviving the routing of Magur. There were more than they expected.

Jarek spun about on her heel and her blade clashed with a red guard who leaped over the outer wall. The red guard's dark face was bared, and he snarled, his mouth dripping with froth. Liall had seen enough battles to recognize killing-lust. It was a strange and fey lunacy in the Rshani blood, the berserker rage, a thing beyond their control. Jarek ended the madness quickly, parrying the strike and dipping to her knees. She slashed once with the curved edge of her sword and brought the hilt back in the return motion to jab the barbed pommel up into the red guard's abdomen, thrusting once and then twisting. Jarek jerked the barb out and the red guard staggered down, entrails spilling into his lap. Jarek kicked the corpse away, and then the queen's soldiers gave a rallying shout as they made one final stroke. The doors of the temple shivered, cracked, and crashed inward. Men screamed, high and excited, in dying or in lust to kill, and a stream of Jarek's soldiers poured through the breached opening.

Jochi pushed him away. "Go!"

Liall shook his head, but he was already picking up his

sword. Scarlet was in there. Scarlet needed him.

"Save them," Jochi murmured, breathing with difficulty.

Liall gripped his shoulder one last time, hefted up his sword, and joined Jarek's charge.

There was knot of fighting just inside the broken doors, the combatants stumbling over stones or slipping in blood. A red came at Liall and he cut the man down, his sword slicing the neck cleanly. Blades flashed in the torchlight, mingled with the screams of dying men, and the smell of fresh gore and smoke was sickening.

Alexyin put his back to Liall's, and the next several minutes seemed like hours. For Liall, it was all too familiar. First there was the fear and the fear of pain and death, then came the sudden, frantic struggle for life, pitting strength and will against steel. Swords flashed, cutting the air with an angry hum like hornets. Every clang of metal meant a blow stopped, and every cry was outlined in blood.

Finally, Liall stood beside Jarek, breathing hard and leaning on his sword. There were red guards on the floor. They were a deeper red now, their chosen color becoming their shroud. Alexyin was finishing off a red guard who was screaming in agony.

Jarek pointed. Liall spat to clear his mouth, and he saw that her soldiers had Vladei pinned against a wall. Torchlight threw weird shadows over the shoulders of the blue guards, flickering yellow, as they dodged and feinted blows with him, trying to take Vladei alive.

"Stop!"

The soldiers backed away. Vladei's sword was still in his hand, but it was broken about a foot from the haft. Vladei batted away one last blade and stood looking at Liall, his chest heaving, head lowered like he was a bull and would soon charge.

Liall trod upon the fallen banner of Ramung –two gold hatchets crossed on a field of crimson– as he crossed the room and the point of his blade came up. "Drop it."

Vladei shook his head once, either too winded or too furious for speech. Liall drew nearer, intending to run him through if he did not obey. Vladei saw the look in his eyes, and his broken sword clattered down.

They faced each other. My kinsman, Liall thought bitterly. Our fathers had been half-brothers. What would they say now, those two powerful men, if they could see us like this?

Liall sheathed his sword and stood looking at Vladei, tired to the bone and wondering how to settle this without blood. He was already known as Kinslayer in Rshan.

"Where are they, Scarlet and Cestimir? I warn you, Vladei. They had best be unharmed."

A rat is most dangerous when cornered. Vladei's hand flashed to his belt, but Liall had seen that trick before. He slammed his fist into Vladei's jaw and the knife clattered across broken tiles. Liall punched the man again and Vladei spat blood at him, his face twisted out of all recognition by rage and hatred.

Liall knotted his fist in Vladei's collar and hit him again; a backhanded blow that bloodied his nose. Vladei struggled, not having the leverage to swing properly, and Liall hauled him to his feet and slung him against the wall, smashing his face into the stone.

"Snake!" Liall kneed him in the belly and Vladei went down on his knees. The man craned his neck to look up at Liall, smiling viciously, and nearly went down on his face when Liall's fist met his jaw again.

Liall went down on one knee, there on the floor with him, and grabbed his hair and jerked his head up to make Vladei look at him. "Villain!" Liall shook him like a dog shakes a mouse. "Where is Cestimir? Where is the prince?"

Vladei gave him a bloody grin. "Gone the way of all weaklings. Did I not tell you, Nazheradei? Rshan must endure. If I have to kill every single prince in Kalas Nauhin to accomplish that, I will. We once ruled the stars. I will not let my people sink into darkness and misery with the rest of cursed Nemerl."

Liall felt the blood drain from his face. "You would not have killed him," he said, though his whole body had gone cold. Vladei could have killed Liall in that instant, he was so numb. "You lie."

"What need? The thing is done. I make no apology. I did what I had to do for the strength of Rshan." Vladei gripped Liall's hand, not to throw him off, but to clasp his fingers like they were old comrades.

"Do you not see it, the corruption at the core of our monarchy? You brought one of them here, Nazheradei. Your Hilurin whore should have been killed on sight. Would have been in a saner time! But no, we have forgotten our own history and become fallen. Like Ressanda, that red boar, with his diluted blood and his coarse body. He is the keeper of our lineage, he and his red daughter? Is that what lies in store for us?" Vladei's eyes were bright, as if filled with fire from within.

"Ten thousand years have we rotted in this place; our magic stolen, our great knowledge slowly forgotten, our books of science moldering into dust." He took a deep breath. "It had to stop, brother. I had to stop it."

"You're insane."

Vladei laughed then, showing crimson teeth. "I see it is useless to argue with you. You will not see. Turn and look then, prince. Turn and see what end awaits all traitors to Rshan."

Jarek's soldiers held Vladei while Liall went to the wooden platform, where the crumpled form lay nearly hidden from sight. The platform was recently constructed: a new addition to the dead temple. Liall had a mad thought, wondering if the trees that had been felled to build this thing had any inkling what they were being killed for. Unfortunate trees, destined to be planed slabs soaking in the red blood of Rshan's rightful king.

Cestimir's bright hair was untouched. His features were tight and closed, denying, as if at the very last instant he had decided he was tired of playing a foolish game, and went away in his own mind to some fairer dream. The young body below was unmarred, only a single, neat cut in the area of his heart where the sword had gone in. A swath of blood, like a broad line of paint, blossomed from the cut and flowed to his knees, ending there to mark the moment his heart ceased pumping.

It was a tidy death. However Vladei had detested Cestimir in life, he had given him a king's execution.

Liall knelt and touched Cestimir's face, finding his skin still warm. They had not been late by much.

There was a sound beside him, and Liall looked up, too stunned for tears, to see Alexyin standing over him.

"I trained him from birth to be a king," Alexyin intoned, his face haggard. His white braid was spattered in red and hung over his shoulder, snarled and matted. "He was the last, great promise of the monarchy," he told Liall. "But he slipped away from me, clever lad. He never wanted it. Two deaths in one day, two princes taken from Rshan."

Alexyin stood over the ashes of his life's work, and chose. Later, as Liall pondered on the matter, he realized that it was doubtful that he would have stopped Alexyin, even if he had known what the man meant to do.

Alexyin leapt off the scaffold and crossed the chamber in the four great strides, to where the soldiers held Vladei. Even as Vladei opened his mouth to gloat, Alexyin cut him down.

Vladei's hate seemed to take all the color out of his face when it fled. Alexyin's sword opened Vladei from belly to shoulder, and he looked down, staring, at the red stripe across his clothing before it became a red banner, and the great wound opened like a mouth, spilling him, steaming, onto the frozen dirt and broken rock.

The soldiers leapt back in shock and dismay, letting Vladei slump into a messy heap. No one strikes a prince of Rshan, and Alexyin was a Setna, one of the Brotherhood. They cast looks Liall's way, seeking direction. Jarek pushed her soldiers aside to stand before her men, her stern face upturned to Liall, awaiting orders as a khatai should.

Liall came down wearily from the platform and encompassed the whole of the temple with one swing of his arm.

"Search it. Find ser Keriss. Move!"

They scattered. Alexyin stood rock-still as if in shock. He kept shaking his head, though the day was far past denial. "You must kill me now," he said.

That was the law, Liall supposed. The cold had seemed to leech into his bones, and he moved as if in a dream, putting one foot in front of the other until he was near enough that only Alexyin could hear him speak. "You will not die. You will help me find Scarlet."

Melev's heavy hand was over Scarlet's heart. The Ancient was kneeling close to Scarlet, so close, and then he seemed to breathe the words into him:

"My power to you."

Scarlet gasped as Melev's fingers seemed to dig inside him, up under his ribs, as if Melev were digging through cartilage and muscle to burrow into his heart.

"My will, my heart... your eyes. *See.*"

Melev's hypnotic voice compelled Scarlet, and he tried to focus on the Ancient's face, only to have his broad features slither away into a folding, dancing ribbon of light. Scarlet tried to speak and nothing came out. His hands were chained weights.

"See," Melev commanded. "Let your mind break free of the world, and tell me where the Anlyribeth have taken it."

Melev pulled him closer, and it felt like Melev's hand was gripping his bones, ripping him apart. Scarlet mourned the loss of his voice. A scream might have lessened the pain. Melev was ruthless, pushing Scarlet further into an agony so intense it seemed impossible he was still alive. As Scarlet writhed to be away from him, Melev burrowed closer, so for a moment it seemed as if they were grappling, joined as if in sex, fused as one body and writhing in completion.

The world spun around. Light bloomed in the darkness, faces like pale flowers, and Scarlet saw the Hilurin spirits he had once glimpsed in a bare stand of junipers back on the Nerit, that night when Cadan had nearly killed him. That night when Liall saved him. Cadan's hands had been around his throat, then, cutting off his life. Now Melev was digging his heart out with his fingers.

"Tell me," Melev intoned. "The instrument of making. The magic. Where has it been hidden?"

Scarlet struggled wildly to answer, to scream that he knew of no such thing, but the pain grayed out his vision and suddenly he was simply not there any longer. He believed he had passed out. He seemed to float in a warm void, those shifting, colored lights all around him.

He blinked, or thought he did, looking up at the myriad shapes all in motion.

A young Hilurin man, no older than he, surely, took more solid form in the shifting lights and came forward. "Deva, he means," the boy said in a gentle voice. "She was the great ship of iron that brought the Shining Ones here, and then failed them. They were marooned on this continent of ice, stranded far from their homes."

The boy was First Tribe, but unlike anyone Scarlet had ever seen: features sculptured like white marble, jet black eyes, fringed so thickly with ebony lashes that they looked like bruises high on his cheeks. His brows were black ribbons of silk across his unlined forehead, and the beauty of youth was upon him like a crown. His smile was infinitely gentle. Scarlet had never seen such a smile, except perhaps from Scaja in his earliest memories.

Yeva Bilan, Scarlet called, thinking he must be the Flower Prince. Surely this man was the beloved of a goddess.

Visions flashed by his sight: his old friend Kozi, who disappeared one year; Cestimir, who smiled at him unafraid and held his hand over his heart with blood seeping through his fingers; Scaja and Linhona holding hands under a rain of ash. He suddenly saw Jochi's face and recalled the history lesson Jochi had given him, only now it seemed as if he were reliving it himself, and he could see the ocean rise and the land drowned, and the earth shaking down the great towers of lost Rshan.

Melev pressed him then, and Scarlet opened his mouth in a soundless scream. Melev's will pushed and battered his mind to ask something of the beautiful Hilurin prince, but no sound would come out. Pain dragged him under, threatening to drown all sanity, and he sent a helpless plea to the prince instead.

Help me.

The prince stretched out his hand, and Scarlet heard him send the command to Melev: *These are mine. My people. Let him go.*

Melev recoiled, and for once, Scarlet saw emotion on his face: fear.

Scaja smiled at Scarlet across a universe of stars, and the sky broke in half before the sun caught fire and burned him alive in it, drowning him in cold, blue seas.

He dreamed.

Scarlet saw a flutter of colors, and a swarm of small people, no higher than his own chin, appeared. He could see they were Hilurin, all black-haired and ebony-eyed, so that for a moment, he felt a rush of homesickness.

Channels, said a disembodied voice. The face of the gentle prince swam into view. *Symbiosis*, the prince said, smiling. *A true joining of races. None dreamed it could ever be broken, until the ship failed and the miles of ice defeated us.*

Scarlet saw the Anlyribeth and the Shining Ones working together to repair the great beast of iron that rode the black sky between the stars; saw the misery on their faces when they failed time and time again. Decades passed like blown leaves, and a great many of the Shining Ones died.

Denied their weightless life inside the belly of Deva, the sentient ship, the tall Shining Ones could not adjust to land living. Many walked like old men, hunched over from the weight of their spines and great shoulders, their bare feet dragging in the snow. The prince smiled sadly at Scarlet.

Over time, they began to notice that we Anlyribeth did not suffer like them. Our bodies were smaller, better able to adapt, better able to exist on scarce food, whereas the Shining Ones needed great amounts of food to sustain their internal heat. Just breathing the thin air was an effort.

They had no energy left over to find sustenance. We were industrious and clever. We thrived and took care of our own, but paid little heed to the starved Shining Ones, who had never needed our help in such base matters before.

At last, the unthinkable happened. Anlyribeth were once trusted helpers and allies, gentle companions and kindred spirits of the mind. Now, they were potential food. The reaction was utter shock and horror. The offending Shining One was quickly slain by his own fellows, but the damage was done.

We tried to flee. We were not vengeful. We did not wish the Shining Ones ill. All we wanted was our freedom. When we left, we took nothing from the iron vessels. We did not touch the Instruments of Making, knowing the Rshani would need them to survive.

They had not reckoned, however, that several thousand millennia of mental co-existence would give the Shining Ones an even greater weapon against them. Even if they had been told, they would not have believed it. Scarlet watched as the Shining Ones herded the Anlyribeth back to them with the force of their minds alone, and watched as they sorrowfully put collars on their small necks and silver bracelets on their arms, forcing their new slaves to serve and sustain the race of the Shining Ones.

It might have ended there. Might have, but did not. We could have served the Shining Ones forever, and eventually forgotten who we were, but the habit of exploration would not leave the minds of the Shining Ones. They must always have something new to conquer, some new path that has not been traveled. They decided to rebuild their homeworld, to make of it a replica of Danae, but they could not do it alone.

The Instruments of Making were taken from the ship and the old ones sought out their Channels –the Anlyribeth who their minds were bonded to– once more.

Some Anlyribeth had to be compelled to reunite their links with their old companions, now their masters. Many others had died, but there were enough Channels to forge a link, enough to create power and build castles, walls, battlements; a city. A great fortress rose in the shallow bowl of the mountains now called Fanorl, and eventually a civilization where the elder race ruled and the younger Anlyribeth toiled and were made mental thralls to serve the power of the Shining Ones.

Long centuries we lived like that, locked inside our own minds, our power bound to theirs, mind-blinded, useful only as physical slaves to service their wants and as tools to focus their power. They used us in other ways, too, our women mostly, but even our handsome youths were not safe. This world had made their lusts grow strong. Now they each sought for themselves power, beauty, and sex to fill their appetites. Some of us, however, were loved.

The prince smiled again but pain edged every word. *I was Txaxa, t'aishka to Sadyn, who was high in their esteem, a leader of many. Sadyn treated me well, better than any Rshani. Rshani is the name they took for themselves after they used the Instruments of Making and the genetic material of the snow bears to forge a child race able to sustain themselves on this frozen continent. But Sadyn could not see what it did to me to live with what my kin endured under his people. I tried to tell him, but he, like all Rshani, was blind to it. By this time there were few true Shining Ones from that first landing left. They all vanished into the heart of the mountains called Fanorl, and were never heard from again, save in the Ancients who wandered out many, many years later, and who were themselves also changed from their original form.*

It was I, the trusted one, who finally crept into the stone temple they had erected around the ruins of the metal ship and stole the Creatrix, the Instrument of

Making with which the Rshani had forged their city, using only the power of their minds linked through their mortal Channels, the little Anlyribeth. I took it and set free Deva, the powerful sentient force housed inside the ship that drove it through the vast, black abyss of stars. I also freed my kin, and we together created a great Channel to open the boundaries of the world and hurl our physical bodies into the void beyond. We did not know what, or if anything, awaited us there, only that it was our last chance.

What they found was Byzantur, with its mountain of magnetic iron meteorite that repelled the sensitive aliens of Danaee, but which left the Anlyribeth unaffected.

"But," Scarlet fumbled for words, his voice suddenly unlocked. "This... Creatrix. What happened to it? We Hilurin have no legends of it."

The prince's fingers pressed Scarlet's four-fingered hand, and when he withdrew, a red flower was etched into the skin of Scarlet's wrist like a tattoo, which faded as quickly as it had appeared.

"I think you know, do you not? Listen, my descendant..."

Liall heard a shout echoing down the dark corridors of the deserted ruins. It was not a Rshani voice, but higher and lighter. He grabbed a smoking torch and ran with Alexyin, shoving the burning brand into every doorway down the long maze of corridors, but they were lost.

Alexyin grabbed Liall's arm and made him stop. "Listen!" he hissed.

The torch sputtered in the dark. Wind howled thinly

from a hundred cracks in the walls, and below that, faintly, he heard the sound of chanting.

The maze confused them. Sounds seemed to come first from one direction and then another, tricking the ear. At last, he heard another sound, a shimmering metal noise like chains sliding over rock, and it gave them a direction to follow.

Liall prayed as he went, or tried to. He had no tongue for it, but Scarlet believed. Surely his goddess would save him, even if she wouldn't listen to Liall. They stumbled over a broken step in the corridor and saw that it led to a higher level, and from there, through a bricked archway, they saw a faint glimmer of yellow light.

"Scarlet!"

The light grew much brighter, and when Alexyin and he burst through the last doorway into the round chamber, they found it filled with torches.

Incredibly, Melev was there, toppled over like a fallen tree in the center of the sunken floor, his bare legs sprawled out. Liall had little thought to marvel at his presence, because he saw Scarlet across from Melev, crouching with his small wrists chained to the floor. Scarlet's body was bent double with his forehead resting on his knees, and he was silent and deathly still.

Like Cestimir, Scarlet did not move as Liall approached him. Liall knelt. "Please," Liall whispered, reaching out to touch his hair. He slipped his hand under Scarlet's chin and lifted Scarlet's face to see if he still lived.

Scarlet gave a gulping sigh and coughed on the thick smoke. His eyes opened a crack. "Liall?"

Liall groaned and embraced him, chains and all, too grateful to form any thoughts except *thank you, thank you, oh thank you for this!*

Alexyin knelt beside Melev and rolled him over, and Liall heard Alexyin gasp. He looked over to see Alexyin backing away from Melev's body in horror, and he saw the twin black holes scorched into Melev's face. The great lamps of Melev's luminous eyes had burned out.

11.

Mourning Call

Liall was there when Scarlet woke, sitting on the edge of the great bed and holding his hand. Scarlet looked around, seeing the now-familiar outlines of their bedroom, blinking. He tried to sit upright and found that he could. Someone had dressed him in a plain sleeping tunic and the pain was gone. "Melev..." he began.

"Is dead," Liall said gently. The prince was wearing something odd. It looked like a virca, but was very plain with no buttons or ornament. The fabric was all in muted shades of gray and violet mingled together, so that when Liall moved, it resembled a brooding cloud in a thunderstorm.

Mourning clothes, Scarlet thought. He closed his eyes. "And Cestimir?"

Liall took a shaking breath. "Him, as well."

"Oh, Deva... Liall, I'm sorry. So sorry. If we hadn't gone—"

Liall cut him off. "Do not. This was no one's fault except Vladei's." He stroked Scarlet's dark hair away from his face. "What happened in the ruins, when you were alone with Melev?"

Scarlet lay back down and closed his eyes. "I saw dead ones in the stone circle, Liall. My parents, people I'd known, my old friend Kozi. Many spirits."

"It was a dream, t'aishka."

"No," Scarlet said, knowing better. "It was real.

And.... Liall? I think I was the one who killed Melev. My Gift isn't the same as it was in Byzantur. It's changed. It's so much stronger now." He looked at Liall with dawning comprehension. *Channels*, he thought. "It's changed because of you, because of us."

"Hush, you must rest," Liall soothed. Clearly, he thought Scarlet to be babbling.

"It was real," Scarlet insisted, but how to explain? He barely understood it himself.

"Real or not," Liall choked out, seeming grieved beyond words, "the man who put you there is dead, and Vladei is dead, too."

"Vladei," Scarlet echoed, hating him and not sorry at all. "But.... are there any are more like Melev?"

"Not here."

"Oh," Scarlet said, disappointed. Scarlet sensed that it was hugely important for him to find one like Melev, but the why of it was beyond him.

Liall frowned. "What is it?"

"The spirits were Anlyribeth, those who were Hilurin before we took a new name. We used to live here, Liall. Thousands of us," he rushed on, aware that his voice was unsteady and he sounded like a madman. "I saw so many things... the crash, the Rshani enslaving the Anlyribeth, then the earth shook and cracked and the Anlyribeth left. Melev said we took something from the Shining Ones when we left here, a great instrument called the Creatrix. He wanted it back and I tried to tell him we didn't have it, but he didn't believe me. We *don't* have it, Liall, but I know where it is!"

Liall looked almost frightened. "Scarlet!" Liall snapped, silencing him. He took a deep breath and reached for Scarlet. "These are forbidden things, my t'aishka. You must never mention them outside of this room, to anyone else. Do you promise?"

Scarlet sensed how right Liall was. No one must ever know what he had discovered in the temple ruins. Who could be trusted with such knowledge? "I promise," he said.

"Good." Liall pushed Scarlet's black hair out of his eyes. "How do you feel?"

"Well enough, now." Scarlet spared him the knowledge of how Melev had pressed him and tortured him in that odd no-space between worlds. He looked miserable enough. "Oh, Liall, I'm so very sorry I lied to you about the withy magic. I shouldn't have. I should have trusted you."

Liall pulled him close. "No. I am the one who should apologize. The truths I withheld from you are far worse. No more. I will never keep anything from you again."

Scarlet clung to him. *Deception,* he thought, suddenly remembering the cryptic, ruddy-haired Fate Dealer in Ankar, and the cards the Fate had read for him: *Be on your guard. You will be told a lie or you will fall in love with one, and you will follow it to the ends of the earth.*

Well, he was at the end of the earth, no doubt, and if Liall had told him he was an exiled prince when they first met on the Nerit, Scarlet would have laughed at him. If Scarlet had shown Liall the withy magic when they barely knew each other, Liall would have left him entirely alone, and Annaya might be dead. Perhaps not all lies were an evil, or else they'd both be damned by now.

"I don't want to keep anything from you either. Liall... I saw Cestimir in that place," Scarlet said haltingly. "The stone circle."

Liall drew back and looked as if he might weep. "You did?"

"In the Overworld, I think. That must have been what it was. He looked happy."

Liall covered his face with his hands and sat for several

moments like that before his hands dropped in a useless gesture. "I wanted so much to save him," Liall said. "Like Nadei. But I failed both times." He drew Scarlet to him again, hugging him fiercely. "All this time I have been trying to shield you so much. I failed to see you did not need protecting. I have been a fool."

Scarlet was too heartsick over Cestimir to be glad that Liall was finally seeing things right. It was only a tiny glow against the heavy pall of sorrow over his heart. "It doesn't matter now." And truly, it didn't. Liall's secrets had been needlessly withheld from him so long that they had lost their importance. He hoped Liall felt the same way about his magic. Scarlet wanted to end that difficult part of their lives together with no more words, like closing the pages of a book. Story over. Tell me another one, mum, this one's played out.

Carefully, he pulled away from Liall. "I've got something else to tell you," Scarlet said, and watched how Liall's face went still and cold in that way he had, the old walls rising up between them.

Liall's mouth trembled and he bowed his head. "T'aishka, please do not leave me." He drew in a shuddering breath. "I will beg if you like."

"It wouldn't do any good, you fool," Scarlet said impatiently, "for I'm not going anywhere."

That took a moment to sink in. "Oh," Liall said thinly. "Forgive me. There is still a part of me that believes I do not deserve your love or your loyalty. It is very easy for me to believe that you would wish to depart."

"Well, I don't," Scarlet scolded. "Now stop that, you want-wit, before I clout you one."

Liall smiled a little. "Speak on, then, my lord."

"I just wanted to tell you that I've been wrong. I was out of my element here, and instead of turning to you, I got angry. I was angry that I had to depend on you. It made me feel weak and it made me take risks to prove myself, when there was no need. You'd never asked it of me. This place is... so foreign. I can't learn it all in a day. You'll have to teach me, Liall. Please?"

Liall leaned forward and cupped Scarlet's cheek, drawing him in for a brief and loving kiss. "I will. And I want to tell you the truth about Nadei," he said, his voice very soft. "I want you to know why I lied to you, why I tried so very hard to deceive you and keep you ignorant of my past."

Scarlet blinked.

"You were not expecting me to say it in that way," Liall murmured. "Have I never admitted fault to you before? I want to tell you everything now."

"Now?"

"Yes."

Scarlet nodded slowly, greatly troubled. "All right. If you're sure. I want to get out of this bed, though."

Liall helped Scarlet into a heavy robe, and they moved out of the bedroom and into the den, sitting side by side on the large couch.

Liall sat stiffly, not looking at Scarlet. It was harder than he thought to begin. Where to start? *How do I say to him the things I cannot admit even to myself?*

Liall formed several sentences in his mind, discarded them all, and finally looked to Scarlet helplessly. "It is difficult for me to talk about him," he admitted. "I know that no one believes it, but I did love Nadei very much."

"*I* believe it."

There was an ache in Liall's hands, and he looked

down and saw that they were clasped together so tightly that he had bruised his knuckles. "You remind me of him a little," Liall said softly. "Of his good qualities. You are cocksure and you are stubborn and you are proud to a fault. Those were the things I loved about him."

Liall took a heavy breath before continuing, steeling himself. "He was my brother," he blurted. "My elder brother, but only by two years. By the time we were youths, our age difference was invisible. I believe that is when it began. Someone mistook me for the elder once, because I was a little taller than Nadei, and I think someone must have whispered something to him later, that perhaps I was getting too big in other ways as well, that perhaps I had begun thinking of myself as more suited to the kingship than he. Royal courts are full of gossips and mischief makers."

Scarlet nodded solemnly at that.

How well he knows, Liall thought. I hope that one day he forgives me for bringing him here.

"It was never any one thing," Liall tried to explain, frustrated that he did not have a clear-cut scenario to present. "Like most family stories, ours is messy and incomplete. As boys, we were very close. He was the elder, but I protected him. I covered for him when he made mistakes, and I sheltered him from criticism and harm. We never had a true falling-out, and nothing was ever said, but in those few years before we became men, when bonds between brothers are so important and so fragile, we developed a rift. Nadei wanted fiercely to be king, and I never wanted it at all. I saw what power had done to my mother and I wanted no part of it, but none of that mattered, because Nadei believed I wanted what was his. It changed him."

Liall fell silent for a moment, gazing into the past, until he felt Scarlet's hand on his.

"What happened?"

Liall shrugged as if it were a light matter, when it was anything but. "He ceased to be my friend. We rarely spoke. He cultivated his own circle of followers who found favor with him by denigrating me in small ways. Not that I was not equal to their games, but... I did not wish to play. They bored me with their intrigues and their gossip. I was even thinking about leaving Rshan, like the journeyman princes in the old days, when my mother betrothed me to Shikhoza."

Scarlet stiffened a little. Liall could not blame him. Shikhoza had gone out of her way to make Scarlet feel like the illiterate country lad he was, someone who would be better occupied tidying royal beds than sleeping in them.

Liall gripped his hand. "I know she has behaved terribly towards you, but I want you to remember that she was not always like that. She was enough to make me give up my plans to leave Rshan, at least for a while. But then... well, I suppose she recalled who she was, and all the things she would never have as the wife of a lesser prince. Nadei was not very kind to her either, and then there was Vladei, who had sued very hard for Shikhoza's father to let them marry, but the old man never thought Vladei would be worthy of her. Once Vladei realized he could not win Shikhoza back, he turned on her. He made her life a hell inside the Nauhinir, and she, in her turn, decided to make mine one."

"What did she do?" Scarlet whispered.

Liall smiled a little, only because if he did not, he would weep. "She became Nadei's mistress behind my back, though she hated him in her heart. I thought at first it was because she hoped he would marry her and make her queen, but I should have known she was subtler than that. No. She knew I loved her, so she slept with Nadei to make me hate him. She did want to be queen, you see, but not to Nadei. To me. Perhaps she did have some feeling for me after all, or maybe she just knew that Nadei was too susceptible to what others thought of him. He was easily swayed by opinion and gossip. In a king, that is a fatal weakness. She wanted me to take the road so many princes take to power: the quiet assassination of a rival."

Scarlet seemed to have stopped breathing. "Did you do that?" he quavered. "Liall, please tell me you didn't."

Liall nearly became angry then. "No. What do you think of me? I laughed at her plots. I would never hurt Nadei." Then he realized what he had said. "I mean," he stammered. "I would never have... it was not intentional. There was," he had to stop and take another deep breath, "there was a bear hunt. Nadei and I rode for the silver and blue, as always, and we killed the beast together, but there was some dispute over whose spear had actually ended the snow bear's life. To this day, I swear I saw my own spear strike the bear in the throat and Nadei's bounce off its flank and skitter up under its ribs. A severe blow, but not the killing shot. Credit for the kill, the blood honor, went to me, but Nadei loudly disputed it all the way back to the palace. When we were home and in the hall, he was still angry, still crying foul and saying I had cheated and lied to get the blood honor, that I had bribed men to say it was my spear that felled the bear, and that I had dishonored the hunt forever. I tried to laugh at him and make light of it, like I had been doing for years but... damn it all." He ground his fist into his palm, not seeing how Scarlet shrank from him.

"Suddenly, I was just so damned *tired* of him. He wasn't a man ready to be king, he was a boy who imagined slights everywhere. I shouted at him and told him so before witnesses in the hall, when I could stand his insults no more. My mother was there and heard everything, and

I think by then even she knew that we needed to have it out between us, so she did not interfere or send guards to pull us apart."

It was the next part that made Liall's voice stopper in his throat. He tried to speak past it and could not, then Scarlet's arms were around him, and suddenly he could say it:

"We fought. I had been with the army in the Tribelands. I was a younger prince, not the heir, and could bear the risk of battle if I wished. Unlike Nadei, who was never allowed to be put into harm's way. I was a trained soldier, so I was better with my fists. I won and he took it badly. He came at me with a knife," Liall said into Scarlet's shoulder. "I am battle-trained. He came at me and I turned the blade on him and drove it into his side, but... but too high. It pierced his organs and he died within a few minutes, right there on the crown dais, with my mother screaming his name."

Scarlet's arms tightened around Liall. "I'm sorry."

"I did not mean to do it," Liall vowed. "I swear I did not mean to. It happened so fast, I..."

"Quiet. I know. I should have known."

Scarlet held him for a long time while Liall inhaled the scent of Scarlet's skin and listened to the sounds outside the room: a clink in the dining nook, the soft fall of footsteps echoing on stone, wind on the casements, servants going about their duties, Nenos giving orders in his gentle voice. These were sounds that he had grown up with and thought never to hear again. Like Scarlet's trust, they were gifts he had been given back, and now he must take care to guard them.

"Liall, what's going to happen now?"

"I honestly do not know." Liall kissed him and got up heavily. "I have to speak to Alexyin, find out what he plans to do. He was the queen's advisor and—"

Liall turned sharply when he heard Scarlet gasp. Scarlet had turned to look at the large casement that dominated the room, and now he rose and moved toward it, gripping the edges of heavy drapery in each hand. The storm had broken and the sky cleared to show a black dome glittering with stars, and Scarlet stood gazing out, his head tilted back as he stared in stunned awe. His chest rose and fell slowly, as if he scarcely dared to breathe.

"Is this magic?" Scarlet asked at last, his voice daunted and overcome with wonder. He had been told countless times that there was no magic in Rshan.

They will call this an omen, Liall thought, and moved to stand with Scarlet, tilting his head back to watch with Scarlet as the opalescent streams of light chased each other across the indigo canvas of sky.

Scarlet watched, wide-eyed and awed into silence, and Liall smiled to see his admiration. Colors, colors, colors. One after the other in a vast cascade sparkling above the land, like a shimmering silken veil that descends and descends but never seems to touch the ground. The *ostre sul,* the lights in the darkness, which Liall had seen it more times than he could remember, but never like this, never with such a man beside him, who artlessly accepted a flawed world as the price of living, and committed his whole heart to love while still reserving his selfdom. Unlike Liall, Scarlet had always known who he was. Liall had been the one who was lost and needed convincing that he wanted to be found at all.

Who was the man Scarlet loved? Was he a displaced prince or a bandit Kasiri? Or, as Scarlet had once accused, was he like Cadan, a dark soul only needing the right set of downfalls to turn him into a brigand and murderer? Liall realized then that he had tried so hard not to be Prince Nazheradei that he had misplaced himself. Some part of him had been fast asleep since his exile from Rshan, perhaps only waiting for the right catalyst to rouse it or the right soul to share a life with. He no longer had to fear his own dreams.

In some dark and frightful corner of Liall's mind, a bit of sun grayed the deep night, and he saw Nadei with the knife in his hand before his brother lowered the blade and closed the door between them forever. Liall had finally faced the true and naked memory of him, without denial, without excuse, and so the price of the past was paid.

Scarlet craned his neck to look at Liall, the question bright in his dark eyes.

"Yes." Liall cupped Scarlet's cheek as the lights painted glimmering ribbons of silver in his black hair, smiling to hide the staggering sense of relief as Nadei's face grew dimmer and dimmer in the grayness. "That is what it is, t'aishka. Magic."

"What does that mean?" Scarlet begged, suddenly earnest. "T'aishka."

Liall bent to kiss him, long and possessively. "Forever beloved," he answered at last. "One who I would love from life to life, in whatever existence awaits us beyond the Overworld. One I believe I have known before, many times."

Scarlet looked up at Liall searchingly for a long moment before he poked Liall in the arm. "Romantic."

"Entirely guilty, I fear," Liall grinned, and then became serious again. "We should plan on a journey," he murmured, his fingers stroking Scarlet's face. "After a new heir is named and the kingdom settled." Excitement and new hope touched Liall's voice. "A fresh start for us."

"North?"

"We're as far north as one can get in this world, my love. I was thinking south."

Scarlet gave Liall a narrow look, but his mouth

quirked. "Sailing there, are we?"

"Months and months, yes."

"What's south of Byzantur?"

Liall's blue eyes twinkled. "I had a notion to explore the Southern Kingdoms. Artinia and the like."

"Artinia," Scarlet breathed.

Liall nodded, gently tucking a lock of Scarlet's dark hair behind his ear. "Artinia. That is little more than a fragment of a tale among Hilurin, is it not? Like a line dropped from a fable, the barest bit of story some tale-spinner thinks can be cut without incident."

"Is it real?"

"So the mariners say," Liall smiled, teasing. "Of course it is real. Have you not learned by now that all fairytales have some measure of truth in them?"

"And we're going?"

"We go together, or not at all. I have found that the company of a certain redbird is all I need to make life worth living again."

Scarlet seemed to think about it for several moments. "Masdren is going to be cross with me."

"For?" Anxiety tinged his tone.

"For breaking my promise to settle down and become a proper Hilurin. That's twice now. He'll be very cross indeed this time."

Liall threw his arms around Scarlet with a growl and lifted him off his feet. "So you like to frighten your lover, do you? I thought you were reconsidering."

"Never. You won't be rid of me that easily," Scarlet chuckled. "We can send word to him, can't we? And to my sister in Nantua. Oh, Annaya will never believe it all!"

"We can send word and a barrel of gold to go with it, if that's your pleasure, my t'aishka," Liall answered, laughing. Liall buried his face in Scarlet's neck and inhaled his apple-sweet scent. "Oh, my dear one..."

There was a knock at the door, and outside in the hall rose the sound of many voices.

Scarlet sighed as Liall set him down reluctantly. "Do you want me to see what they want?"

"No." Liall walked to the door, frowning. "I will send them away." He entered the common room and called for Nenos, but the servant was in the outer foyer, and when Liall opened that door he found Nenos overwhelmed by a great crowd of men and women who packed the wide hall outside the apartments. Ressanda was in the forefront, standing beside Alexyin and Khatai Jarek. Golden-eyed Jochi was there, too, pale and bandaged with his arm in a tight sling, but on his feet. Liall stood staring at them, and they all fell silent as one. Ressanda was first. He went to one knee and bowed his head.

"Hail Nazheradei, King of Rshan na Ostre."

To run from something your entire life, to think you have escaped it utterly, and then to have it overtake you in the space of an instant. For one long moment, Liall literally could not breathe.

"No," Liall whispered, stricken. "Not me, Ressanda. Never." He held out his hands beseechingly to his old teacher. "Alexyin, please. I cannot..."

"There is no other," Alexyin said, also falling to his knees. Liall had never seen him look so old. "It is you, or our kingdom dies now. The barons cannot agree on another, and there will be war."

Jochi caught Liall's eye and nodded, a gentle expression of understanding on his features. "It must be," he said. He leaned heavily on Alexyin's shoulder to kneel as well. Jarek bowed shortly, as a soldier should to her ruler, and knelt heavily on the polished floor, her armor creaking.

Liall scanned the faces behind Alexyin and Jochi, barons and nobles all, and saw they were right. There were many expressions: hope, dislike, excitement, greed, outright hate. Everything hinged on his answer. If he declined in favor of Ressanda or some other worthy noble, the frail truce with Eleferi would be broken. New allies would become new enemies. Even Shikhoza would turn on her recent display of alliance and become a mortal enemy if she sighted the possibility of the crown again. The realm would be torn apart.

"The council of Barons has convened and decided," Ressanda intoned like a prayer, his head bowed. "We are in agreement. You are our king."

Ressanda's daughter, Ressilka, elegantly knelt at her father's side and made a humble obeisance to Liall. The crown of her red-gold hair shone in the lamp light: Ressilka of the royal blood, who had been destined to marry a prince, and someday must, if the line of Camira-Druz was not to die out entirely.

Slowly, Shikhoza's hand rose and settled on Eleferi's shoulder, and they knelt as one. "Hail, King Nazheradei," Shikhoza proclaimed in a cool voice. Her gaze was shrewd. She knew that Liall had little choice, or none at all.

Eleferi's head was bowed with Shikhoza's, obeisant and humble, but Liall knew their hearts were not turned, only their public policy, and for a moment he utterly despaired, feeling trapped and breathless, until he felt the warm touch of a smaller hand in his. Liall looked down to see Scarlet at his side. Relief and gratitude flooded him.

"I'm here," Scarlet said simply. His grin was a pedlar's grin, endlessly confident and proud and honest. "I'll always be here, Liall."

Liall gripped Scarlet's fingers tight in promise. "And I will always be yours," he vowed. "I swear it." Liall turned to the watchers. His thumb brushed the back of Scarlet's hand in a private caress. "It is the old way," he announced in a ringing voice that carried down the halls.

"My t'aishka is Hilurin, and he has the magic of the Anlyribeth. If any man objects to this, I will answer him with my sword."

None spoke a whisper, and Liall drew himself up taller, though inwardly he felt as if the very earth had rattled under his feet. "And this is not the end of the changes to come. As king, my brother Cestimir would have led us —not forward into a new world that our people fear so much— but back to the old one, where we welcomed many nations to Rshan and feared none, and we were known and respected by all. It is time we remembered who we are."

"Hail, King!" Ressanda called out in his deep voice, raising a fist to the air as if daring anyone to silence him.

"Hail, King!"

Other voices took up the call inside the palace, echoing far down the stone corridors and in towers and salons and chambers. The sound rose like a wave, falling like a choir or a patter of rain: Rshan's ancient plea at the death of monarchs, the sunrise after shadow, triumph after defeat, the mourning call of a kingdom pleading for a king.

Author's Bio

Kirby Crow worked as an entertainment editor and ghostwriter for several years before happily giving it up to bake more brownies, read more yaoi, play more video games, and write her own novels.

Changing weather patterns, watering bans, and pesticides have unhappily forced her to give up growing roses, alas.

Her published novels are **Prisoner of the Raven** (historical romance, Torquere Press, 2005), **Scarlet and the White Wolf: The Pedlar and the Bandit King** (fantasy romance, Torquere Press, 2006), **Mariner's Luck** (fantasy romance, Torquere Press, 2007), and **The Land of Night** (fantasy romance, Torquere Press, 2007). They are available from Torquere Books, most online book retailers, and Amazon.

Kirby is a Spectrum Book Awards nominee, and is hard at work on two more fantasy novels and one horror novel, to be announced on her website. http://kirbycrow.com

Land of Night